His gaze softened. "You said that your heart is filled with temptation."

"But I didn't say for whom," she reminded him quickly. Perhaps if she didn't voice the source of her sinful thoughts alound, then her transgressions would not be so grave.

Bringing her fingertips to his mouth, he pressed his lips against the back of her hand, gazing deeply into her eyes. "There is no need for you to speak a name. I know of whom you speak."

The touch of his mouth on her skin was electrifying. Closing her eyes, she allowed herself the iniquitous indulgences of the blissful moment. If a kiss on the back of her hand could have such a devastating effect on her, she was reasonably sure he would spare her no mercy were they alone, in bed. . . .

Also by Lori Copeland
*Published by Fawcett Books:*

PROMISE ME TODAY

# PROMISE ME TOMORROW

## Lori Copeland

FAWCETT GOLD MEDAL · NEW YORK

A Fawcett Gold Medal Book
Published by Ballantine Books
Copyright © 1993 by Lori Copeland

Library of Congress Catalog Card Number: 93-90197

ISBN 0-449-14752-5

Manufactured in the United States of America

First Edition: September 1993

# Author's Note

The McDougal sisters are a pain. I could pinpoint the concise area of pain, but you get the drift. Abigail, Anne-Marie, and Amelia are smart and pretty enough to turn any man's head, but they choose to abandon the opposite sex—to stick together through thick or thin. Trouble is, the thin times are coming faster than the thick times. They know better than to do the things they do: they just prefer to be a pain in the . . . well, you get the drift. The sisters, who run the mission in Mercy Flats, Texas, do the best they can with the three orphaned girls, but the Lord forgives, He doesn't make perfect.

In *Promise Me Today* we saw how Abigail had Barrett Drake scratching his head with bewilderment.

Well, sit back and hold tight as Anne-Marie tries to tame Creed Walker, a man who has no intentions of being tamed. . . .

# Prologue

**Five miles from Nacogdoches, Texas: March, 1865**

Some people said they had it coming; others said it
was a shame they hadn't gotten it sooner.

A March wind savagely whipped the jail wagon along
the dusty road as three young women dressed in nuns'
habits clung desperately to the bars, eyes clamped shut,
praying for deliverance.

The driver, slumped over the front of the wagon,
could do little to console the screaming women, considering he had a Comanche arrow sticking through his
back.

War whoops filled the air as four young braves chased
the wagon, their black hair whipping wildly about their
bronzed faces as they rode hard to overtake their prey.

"What do they want?" Amelia shouted, her voice
nearly drowned out by the sound of thundering hooves.

Anne-Marie, eyes closed, gripped the beads of her
rosary until her knuckles were white. "Hail, Mary, full
of grace," she murmured, "the Lord is with thee—"

"They want the horses!" Abigail's heart pounded like

1

the heathens' own war drums as the savages continued to gain on them.

"Tell them they can have them!"

"I hardly think they're listening, Amelia!"

"Holy Mary, Mother of God, pray for us sinners now and at the hour of our death—"

*Oh this is so typical,* Abigail thought cynically. Anne-Marie prays while Amelia falls apart at the slightest sign of adversity. Of course, this could turn out to be more than a slight bit of misfortune, she conceded as her eyes darted back to the braves. But she wasn't worried. Lady Luck had always seen the McDougal sisters through the worst of times, and she wasn't likely to fail them now.

"If you'd listened to me and let Amy handle it"— Anne-Marie put the blame where it belonged—"we wouldn't be in this pickle! I told you we shouldn't have tried to trick Ramsey McQuade!"

"How was I to know he had us figured out?" Abby shouted. "He was ripe for the kill. Posing as a wealthy Negress had been brilliant—Amy could *never* have pulled it off!"

Amelia's eyebrows shot up. "And *you* did? Ramsey knew exactly what you were up to. Just because you think all men are stupid doesn't mean all of them are. If you ask me—"

"No one did, Amelia!"

"Ramsey McQuade looked *brilliant* standing by the sheriff on the outskirts of town when we rode out with his money," Amelia went on, determined to make her point.

Abby shot her a scathing look as the wagon lurched

over a rut, pitching the vehicle into the air and Amelia to the floor.

Clasping her hands over her face, Amelia began crying and wouldn't stop, even when Anne-Marie shot her a warning look.

When the visual reprimand had no effect, Anne-Marie diverted her litany long enough to give her a swift kick with the toe of her boot.

"Good Lord, Amelia, control yourself!" Abigail snapped when Amelia bawled harder. You'd think she was the only one about to be scalped. Besides, nobody was going to be scalped. As far as Abigail was concerned, the braves could have the horses *and* the wagon, but if they laid one hand on her or her sisters, she'd personally see that they'd rue the day they were born!

As the jail wagon careened wildly along the road, three men, sitting on top of three separate hilltops, watched the scene playing out below them.

To the west, a dapper little man riding a dark sorrel sawed back on the bridle reins as he caught sight of the spectacle.

He sat for a moment, absently removing his spectacles to wipe away the thick layer of dust coating the lenses.

The sight of four young braves in hot pursuit of a wagon was of little concern to Hershall Earl Digman. Hershall didn't go borrowing trouble, thank you. He had quite enough of his own.

And it wasn't unusual for Comanches to be stirring up trouble. With the attraction of Mexican horses drawing them south, they were raiding deeper and deeper into Texas.

Since the wagon was of no value, the young bucks were obviously in pursuit of the horses, and there was little Hershall could do or planned to do about it.

Flexing his sore shoulder muscles, he lifted his face to the sun, momentarily dawdling as he soaked up the warm rays.

To the east, Morgan Kane slowed his horse to a walk. His first instinct when he spotted the wagon was to ride to the women's aid. Even from this distance, he could see the wagon driver was dead or gravely injured. The women were at the Indians' mercy, and Morgan knew that with Comanches, there would be none.

As much as he would have liked to help, Morgan felt his sense of duty outweighing his instinct. Weather had already delayed him by several days; he didn't need another interruption.

But as the women's cries shattered the peaceful countryside, Morgan shifted uneasily in his saddle. A gentleman by nature, he wasn't happy about the situation. The wagon was whipping down the road, the horses completely out of control now.

*Whores on their way to jail,* he argued when an inner voice nagged at him.

*No one deserves a death like those women are about to face,* the voice argued back.

*Damn Comanches!* Between the Comanche and the Kiowa, a man wasn't safe to travel the main roads.

Lifting his arm to wipe the sweat off his face, Morgan fixed his eyes on the braves as they drew closer to the wagon.

\* \* \*

To the north, an Indian riding a large chestnut stallion topped the rise.

Tall and notably handsome, he had piercing black eyes, straight brows, high cheekbones, and a prominent nose that bespoke his Crow heritage.

The wind whipped his jet-black hair as his dark eyes studied the scene below him.

*Comanches.*

Kneeing his horse forward, he rode closer, his eyes focused on the runaway wagon.


The jail wagon bounced along, tossing the McDougal sisters around like rag dolls. The Indians were so close now that Abigail could see their dark eyes and youthful grins through the trailing dust. The boys couldn't be more than fifteen or sixteen, she thought.

Averting her gaze, she tried to block out the sound of thundering hooves. She had heard stories of women being captured by Indians and taken to live as their wives. Never in her wildest dreams could she, Abigail Margaret McDougal, imagine being a sixteen-year-old boy's *squaw*. She couldn't imagine being any man's squaw, and she'd fight until there wasn't a breath left in her if one of those heathens tried to make her one!

Her face puckered with resentment. She'd *die* before she'd let that happen. If they caught her, she would fight, and fight dirty. She would pinch and spit and hit and bite, and if that didn't work, she'd kick, and she knew *where* to kick because she had heard two men talking one day about getting kicked there, and presumably it wasn't where a man longed to get kicked.

And if that didn't work, Anne-Marie would think of

something to save them—Abigail's eyes darted back to the Indian drawing even with the wagon. She had to!

Jumping astride the lead horse, the brave tried to slow the team. The animals, wild-eyed from the chase, ran harder.

Hershall sat up straighter, watching as the ruckus neared a rowdy climax. By *Jove*, he suddenly realized, those weren't women; those were *nuns* in that jail wagon!

Amelia's throat was hoarse from screaming, but they couldn't stop her. The sounds of the Indians whooping and hollering as victory drew closer would terrify a saint!

Glancing frantically over her shoulder, Abigail groaned when she saw a bend coming up in the road. That's all they needed! They would be killed for certain now!

The horses galloped around the turn, and the wagon tilted sideways. Clutching the bars, Abby bit her lip until she tasted blood as the wagon tipped up to roll precariously on two wheels.

"Pray!" Anne-Marie demanded. "Pray!"

Morgan Kane edged his horse closer to the edge of the knoll. Either his eyes were playing tricks on him or those were *nuns* in that wagon, he thought. Damn. *Nuns*.

The wheels hit another pothole, and the wagon went airborne again as the horses thundered around a second bend in the road. The women screamed as they heard the right front wheel snap. Lurching to its side, the wagon skidded across the road toward a briar-infested ravine.

The Indians sent up a shout of victory as Hershall spurred his horse into action. Holding on to his hat with his hand, he plunged his horse down the ravine.

Morgan Kane was already riding down the hillside as the Crow kneed his horse and sprang forward.

The wagon rolled end over end down the incline, violently tossing the McDougal sisters around inside the small cage.

When the wagon finally came to rest on its side at the bottom of the ravine, two braves were already working to free the horses. Blades glinted in the sunlight as the leather harness was slashed, then with another victorious shout, the youths mounted the two horses and rode them back up the steep incline.

Morgan Kane was riding hard as he approached, but the Indians whipped the horses into a hasty retreat. Yelping with triumph, the braves galloped off to rejoin the remainder of their raiding party, who by now were waiting a safe distance down the road.

The braves cut their ponies across the open plains, their jubilant cries ringing over the hillsides.

Dropping off his horse, Morgan ran to peer down the steep slope, certain the women had been killed.

A trail of dust marked the wagon's lightning descent, but the vehicle was nowhere in sight.

Morgan whirled, reaching for his gun at the sound of approaching hoofbeats. An Indian riding a large chestnut stallion was moving in fast.

Morgan took aim, but stopped short when the Indian lifted his hand in a gesture of peace. As the horse came to a halt the Indian slid off the animal's back and hurried to look over the side into the gulch.

A moment later both men spun at the sound of Hershall's horse thundering toward them.

When Morgan saw that the approaching rider was having difficulty controlling his horse, he shouted at the Indian and they both jumped out of the way as Hershall shot into the clearing.

Sawing back on the reins, the little red-faced shoe salesman managed to stop his horse just short of plunging headlong over the ravine.

As the dust settled Hershall calmly settled his bowler back on his head, then climbed awkwardly off his horse. Shrugging his shoulders uncomfortably in the too-small jacket of his striped seersucker suit, he tipped his hat at the two men cordially.

"Afternoon, gentlemen."

Morgan nodded, slowly holstering his gun.

"My, my, my, my!" Hershall, round-eyed now, scurried to gape over the rim of the gulch. Fishing a large handkerchief from his pocket, he mopped anxiously at his perspiring forehead. "A most *frightful* turn of events," he fretted. "Are the women . . . ?" Hershall just couldn't bring himself to voice his fears. The thought of three sisters meeting such an untimely death was simply deplorable.

The men edged closer to the ravine, their eyes trying to locate the wagon.

"Guess there's only one way to find out." Morgan glanced over his shoulder to make sure the braves hadn't decided to come back for their horses. "We'd better make it quick."

"Oh, my, my, my, my!" The thought of those savages returning just made Hershall sick. "Why ever do you suppose nuns would be riding in a jail wagon?"

Morgan shook his head. "I couldn't say."

The Indian was already making his way down the ravine. His moccasin-covered feet slid in the rocks and loose dirt as he moved along the incline.

Hershall cupped his hand to the side of his mouth and whispered, "Does the savage speak English?"

"I don't think so." Morgan started down the ravine, following behind the Indian.

Glancing anxiously at his carpetbag full of shoe samples, Hershall reluctantly joined the two men, who were already halfway down the slope.

By the time the three men reached the bottom, they could see the jail wagon lying on its side. The backdoor was broken open, and the nuns lay inside in a broken heap.

*Wonderful,* Hershall thought, setting his hat more firmly on his head. *Now I've got to bury three nuns.*

Morgan solemnly made the sign of the cross, then strode to the wreckage. "We better get them buried."

"Oh, my, my, my, my." Hershall thought he might faint. "I'm developing a simply pounding headache from it all."

Shoving the broken door aside, the Indian ran his dark eyes over the crumpled heap of women. His fingers touched the side of Anne-Marie's wrist, feeling for a pulse.

Stirring, Anne-Marie opened her eyelids to encounter a pair of coal-black eyes.

Bolting upright, she screamed, and the Indian, Morgan, and Hershall jumped as if they'd been shot.

Realizing that the good sister thought that the Crow

was part of the band who had been chasing the wagon, Morgan attempted to calm her. "It's all right, Sister. You're safe now."

Anne-Marie stared back at the assortment of strange men, bewildered. She couldn't recall ever seeing such a mixed bag of masculinity.

She looked from the tall man with incredibly broad shoulders, to the dandy in a puckered seersucker suit, whose main concern at the moment seemed to be preventing his hat from blowing off, to the splendid-looking savage, whose dark eyes caused her to have the giddiest feeling when he centered his gaze upon her.

Amelia and Abigail were slowly coming around. Groaning, Abby tried to untangle her limbs from Amelia. "Sweet Mother of God, every bone in my body's broken!"

"*Sister* Abigail."

Abby winced at the sound of Anne-Marie's voice, groaning again.

"Your habit, Sister. It's askew."

Abby quelled the urge to shout back that her *bowels* were askew, let alone her habit! Pushing herself upright, she shook Amy, gradually becoming aware of the three men staring through the bars at her.

*Great day in the morning!* Hershall was nearly felled by the nuns' beauty. He had never seen three more beautiful women!

"Oh, dear Lord," Amy muttered, rolling to her back, glassy-eyed.

"Sister." Abby punched her warningly. "Are you hurt?"

"Are you crazy—I just had the shi—"

Abigail swiftly elbowed her again, quelling Amelia's obscene retort.

Amelia looked up. Upon seeing the men gaping at her, she pasted a serene smile on her lips and hastily made the sign of the cross. "Why, yes, Sister. I believe I've survived the fall quite nicely."

"God has smiled again," Anne-Marie said. "We must thank Him for His graciousness."

"Are you ladies all right?" Morgan asked, still finding it hard to believe that they had survived the fall with few serious injuries.

Amy grunted, trying to sort her arms and legs from Abby's. Both women groaned as pain shot through their lower limbs.

"Sister, would you kindly get *off* me?"

"Certainly, Sister, if you will kindly get your *foot* out of my *pocket*."

"Well, nothing seems to be amiss," Anne-Marie assured the men brightly as she hastily straightened her veil.

Hershall bolted forward to assist Sister Abigail from the wagon. Removing his bowler, he placed the hat over his heart, bowing from the waist down. "Hershall E. Digman, at your service, ma'am."

Eyeing him sourly, Abby slid out of the wagon before he could assist her. But Hershall insisted on helping her to the nearest rock. Sitting her down, he wrung his hands with despair when he noticed the beginnings of a dark bruise forming on her temple.

"You are most fortunate," he said, fussing, "*most* fortunate, my dear lady, that you weren't killed."

Pushing back the sleeve of her habit, Abby examined her skinned elbow. Was he serious? Fortunate? She didn't feel "fortunate." She had just eaten ten pounds of dust and nearly been scalped. If she got much luckier, she wouldn't live to tell about it.

Anne-Marie swayed with sudden light-headedness, and the Indian quietly stepped forward to assist her.

"Thank you," she managed. She got out of the wagon, her hand resting lightly on his bronzed forearm, an arm of such impressive width that it made her hand appear tiny.

His somber gaze met hers, and Anne-Marie felt the oddest quirk in the pit of her stomach.

Shaken, she quickly severed the electrifying contact and stepped aside as Morgan reached to help Amelia down.

As Amy reached for Morgan's hand she caught the look in Anne-Marie's eyes, silently urging her to maintain her best veneer of "sisterly" decorum. Well, Anne-Marie didn't have to worry about that! Amy knew how to act her part as well or better than her sisters.

Lifting her chin, she reached for Morgan's hand, but *drat it* the heel of her shoe caught in the hem of her habit and she pitched face-first out of the wagon.

Averting her eyes, Anne-Marie listened to the confusion as Amy stumbled out of the wagon, knocking Morgan to the ground, then landing squarely on top of him.

"Oh, my!" Amelia gasped, attempting to regain what little composure she could under the circumstances. Scrambling to her feet, she tried to help Morgan up. "I'm ever so sorry, Mister . . . ?"

"Morgan Kane," Morgan supplied, momentarily dazed by the impact.

The Indian suddenly lifted his hand to command silence. As he nodded toward the road his eyes mutely warned of impending trouble.

Panic seized the small group as they listened to the sound of approaching horses.

"The remainder of the raiding party," Morgan guessed.

"Oh, my, my, my!"

"We'd better be on our way, gentlemen."

"Oh, yes, I think that would be most prudent of us," Hershall agreed. "Most prudent."

Pushing his glasses up on the bridge of his nose, Hershall extended the crook of his arm to Abigail.

Surveying it glumly, Abby knew she had little choice but to let the simpleton help her.

Morgan took Amelia's hand and began pulling her toward the incline. "We don't have much time. If you can't make it up the hill, I'll carry you."

"I can make it," Amelia assured him, still so humiliated by her clumsiness that she could *die*.

"Wait," Anne-Marie murmured, closing her eyes as dizziness nearly overcame her again. The Indian paused, supporting her weight until the light-headedness passed.

Morgan and Amelia were already scrambling up the hillside. Amelia's feet slid in the loose dirt, but Morgan's hands boosted her onward. She turned, offering him an affronted glare. "Sorry, Sister—we have to keep moving." He meant no disrespect to the sister, but he wasn't thrilled about the prospect of his hair hanging from a Comanche's lodgepole tomorrow morning, either.

The Indian and Anne-Marie systematically made their way up the incline. When she occasionally lost her footing, the Crow's hand was there to steady her.

Hershall attempted to take Abby's hand, but she repeatedly pushed his efforts aside. If she'd ever seen a worthless man, this was it. A dapper dandy for sure, with his hair slicked down and his spectacles sliding down the bridge of his nose.

Scrambling up the incline, she glanced over her shoulder, concerned about Amelia, who seemed disoriented. Of course, she conceded, with Amy, one could never be certain. Amy was in a daze most of the time.

Abby felt her feet slipping in the loose rocks, but Hershall's hand chivalrously shot out to support her backside. She irritably swatted it aside and muttered, "Pervert."

*Pervert? Well!* Jerking his waistcoat back into place, Hershall made up his mind right then and there that it would be a cold day in Hades before he'd offer her *his* assistance again!

As the six scrambled over the gully they spotted the dust of the returning Comanche raiding party.

"They're moving in fast," Morgan warned.

"We're going to have to make a run for it," Hershall shouted.

Whirling, he raced for his horse, leaving Sister Abigail standing, hands on her hips, glaring after him.

The Indian bolted onto the stallion, pulling Anne-Marie on behind him.

Morgan caught Amy around the waist and lifted her into the saddle. Springing up behind her, he turned to the others. "We're going to have to split up!"

The Indian nodded, trying to control his prancing stallion.

Hershall's horse was sidestepping nervously as he attempted to mount. Abby glanced anxiously at the approaching cloud of dust, then back to Hershall's bumbling attempts to get on the horse.

When it became clear that they were going to be scalped if he didn't get his foot in the stirrup soon, she smothered a curse and irritably marched over and hoisted him into the saddle with her shoulder.

"Why, thank you, my dear—"

"Just shut up, Hershall!"

Planting her foot atop his, she gathered her skirt around her thighs, grasped the tail of his coat, and hefted herself up behind him, forcing Hershall to grab frantically for the saddle horn to keep them both from being hurtled to the ground.

Giving the horse a sound whack across the rump, Abby sent it bolting into a full gallop as Hershall held tightly to his hat.

"Abigail! Amelia! Remember Church Rock!" Anne-Marie shouted as the Indian turned his chestnut stallion and rode off in a southerly direction.

Amelia and Abigail were too busy hanging on to their horses to answer.

*Why?* Anne-Marie thought anxiously as she lifted her face to appeal to a higher source. Why, with three choices, did she have to get stuck with a sausage!

# Chapter 1

The big chestnut stallion raced headlong across the dusty plains, carrying two riders pressing low against its sides. Man and beast had ridden hard for over an hour and the animal was heavily lathered, its flanks heaving from exertion.

Anne-Marie McDougal locked her hands around her benefactor's waist and held on tightly, praying she would survive this newest catastrophe in her life.

Glancing over her shoulder, she was relieved to see no sign of the band of youthful braves who had been chasing them for over an hour.

The Comanches, the sudden flight from the jail wagon, and now galloping across the countryside with a savage was like an awful dream; but Anne-Marie knew it wasn't a dream, it was really happening.

Tightening her grip around the Indian's waist, she wondered about this uncivilized creature who had literally swooped down from the heavens to save her from a fate worse than death.

And who were the two men who had snatched her

sisters, Amelia and Abigail, to safety, and then sprinted
their horses in opposite directions?

A new, more disturbing thought assailed her. What
if the three Samaritans had not come upon them? Anne-
Marie shuddered to think where she would be now.

She held on as the Indian cut the chestnut off the trail
and pushed the animal up a steep ravine. If only she
had thought the last scam through more carefully. She
had warned Amelia and Abigail it would be risky to
make a fool of Ramsey McQuade. He was an intelligent
man, and she had known he couldn't be fooled as easily
as the others.

She struggled to fight back the panic welling up inside her. She had never been apart from Abigail and
Amelia, and the thought was frightening. She and her
sisters had faced life together, afraid of nothing, fearful
of no one. If anything happened to Abigail or Amelia,
Anne-Marie couldn't bring herself to go on. But she
couldn't allow herself to think such thoughts. Optimism
was her strength, she couldn't lose it now. She had escaped, unharmed, hadn't she? And the two men who
had rescued Abigail and Amelia were white men, not a
red savage like her protector.

The Indian's stoic silence was beginning to grate on
her. Obviously he neither understood nor spoke a word
of English; however, they would have to communicate
soon. She had to make him understand that the Mc-
Dougal sisters' ill-fated abduction and grievous arrests
were a mistake. She and her sisters had been in the jail
wagon because of a simple misunderstanding. The Indian must help her find the nearest stage or rail station
so she could return to Mercy Flats, Texas, immediately.

There, by the grace of God, she and her sisters would

be reunited—provided her sisters' rescuers had been as cunning in eluding the Comanches as the savage.

No, she assured herself, Abigail and Amelia were fine. At this very moment they were probably as confused and frightened as she was, but they would be back together soon, very soon. And they would continue providing funds for the orphanage in Mercy Flats, just as they always had.

Leaning closer against the Crow's back, she shouted above the racing wind. "It's getting colder. Can we stop soon—is there a town nearby?"

When the Crow showed no signs of responding, she sighed, realizing that communication was impossible. He didn't understand a word she said, but it didn't matter. She would forgo small talk if only he was skilled enough to get her to the nearest town with her scalp intact.

She was limply clinging to the man's waist by the time he finally angled the horse down a ravine and through a deep thicket. She tensed, wondering what he planned to do now. This was the moment she had been dreading since being snatched from the jail wagon.

Half turning, the Crow grunted, pointing toward the ground.

When Anne-Marie was slow to comprehend, he grasped her by the arm and eased her off the back of the horse. She had been astride the animal for so long that her legs threatened to give out. As she stumbled the savage's hand reached out to steady her.

Motioning her to a nearby log, he slid off the horse and set to work. In a surprisingly short time he had a fire going, its warmth gratifying in the deepening twilight. The day had begun warm and balmy, but during the afternoon clouds had formed overhead and now the biting wind carried a hint of snow.

Anne-Marie tried to ignore the grumbling in her stomach. She hadn't eaten since sometime early this morning, and she had no idea where her next meal would come from. The Indian appeared to have little provisions for travel: a canteen was all she could see. His tribe could be nearby. Yet if that were true, she thought, considering the worsening weather, why hadn't he elected to seek shelter there?

"I'm hungry," she said, patting her stomach to convey her misery. "I'm hungry!" she repeated, using the same insistent gesture, hoping he would comprehend her need.

Giving her a brief, vacant stare, the savage moved closer to the fire.

In the light he looked wild and uncivilized. He was lean, and he smelled as if he hadn't washed in months. His thick black hair was shaggy and unkempt. Nut-brown skin stretched tightly over high, hollow cheekbones, making him seem, in the deepening shadows, even more ominous.

Her eyes traveled the length of his ragged filthy buckskins. He was from an impoverished tribe, she decided. Even the leather moccasins he wore were old and threadbare.

Pity momentarily flooded her before she reminded herself that he was, after all, an uncivilized creature. Her compassion deepened when she saw that he was trembling from the cold.

Drawing a deep breath, she glanced about the campsite, wondering if either one of them would make it through the night. She didn't see how. They had nothing, virtually nothing, to protect them from the elements.

"Do you have a blanket? A *blannnket*?" she enunciated.

The savage refused to meet her eyes. His gaze fixed on the shower of sparks shooting up from the dry timber.

"Perhaps we should huddle together!" she shouted. "We'll have to do something or we'll both die!"

The man remained stoically silent.

She thought for a moment, then tried again. Pointing at the fire, she lifted her brows questionably. Food? Surely he could understand that! They had ridden for hours. He had to be as hungry as she was.

Didn't his kind run down rabbits on foot or catch fish with their bare hands? As she glanced around the campsite her heart sank when she spied a stream that was little more than a trickle of water. There would be no fish in there to ease their hunger.

She rose to begin a frustrated pace around the campfire as she tried to think of a way out of this. If she had to be stuck with a man, why couldn't it be one who understood simple English?

Positioning herself on a rock, she listened to the sounds coming from the bushes. She wasn't squeamish; it took more than rustling sounds in the thicket to spook her; but she had never been out much alone at night.

And she had never depended on a man for anything.

Silently she cursed the fact that she was dependent, for a time at least, upon this particular man.

Glancing around, she bit her lower lip. If it wasn't so dark, she'd scare up her own supper. Her eyes returned to the dense thicket. But it *was* extremely dark.

In another few minutes she would barely be able to see her hand in front of her face; and, she continued rationally, she didn't even have a gun.

Shivering, she burrowed deeper into her woolen habit. The shrieking wind reminded her of how little protection the garment would be in a full-blown blizzard. Her gaze returned to the Indian. At least her habit was warmer than what he was wearing.

The Crow stirred, adding wood to the fire, seemingly oblivious to her presence.

Miniature snowflakes began to form in the air as two forlorn figures huddled close to the fire.

When an hour of silence had passed, Ann-Marie decided to take matters into her own hands. She was so hungry she couldn't sleep, even if she wanted to, which was impossible in such deplorable conditions. She had no idea what she would find beyond the rustling bushes, but she—

She stiffened as the corner of her eye caught sight of something slithering across the ground. A lizard, seeking the warmth of the fire.

As she reluctantly lowered her eyes to the toe of her boot, her throat constricted so tightly with fear that she couldn't make a sound.

A pair of reptilian eyes stared up at her.

There were few things in life Anne-Marie feared, but a lizard was counted as one of them. As a child, she had slipped into an abandoned well and spent the next five hours in a bed of various species of lizards before Father Luis and Sister Agnes had been able, with the help of a long rope, to pull her out.

For years afterward Anne-Marie couldn't close her eyes without reliving the horror of that old well and the slithering reptiles that had mercilessly crawled over her body while she lay motionless with terror.

Cold yellow-green eyes stared back at her as Anne-Marie attempted to find her voice. She squeaked, then squeaked again, trying to gain the Indian's attention.

Unaware of Anne-Marie's dilemma, the Indian calmly piled more wood on the fire.

By willing her vocal cords to move, Anne-Marie succeeded in making a small, barely perceptible noise pass her lips as her eyes riveted on the intruder reclining on the top of her left boot.

Glancing up, the Crow caught the sister's anguished stare. He got slowly to his feet, his eyes silently warning her not to move. Anne-Marie struggled to keep from fainting as she saw the glint of a knife appear in his hand.

With catlike stealth, he advanced on the lizard. The knife blade, reflecting off the fire's dancing flames, looked more sinister than any gun. The Crow's black eyes glittered as he concentrated on his prey.

Anne-Marie's gaze beseeched him to move faster, but he showed no signs of understanding. Instead he crept closer, each step methodically calculated.

While still twenty feet away, he took aim and let the knife find its mark. In the blink of an eye, the lizard's severed head embedded itself in the soft earth. As the reptile's body thrashed wildly about in the throes of death, Anne-Marie lost her fight to hold on to consciousness.

Her eyes rolled back in her head, and with a soft whimper she slumped to the ground in a wilted heap.

\* \* \*

Snow was falling heavily as the Indian knelt beside the sister to check her pulse. She had been unconscious for some time, and concern clouded his features.

As he laid his fingers on the base of her throat, his eyes softened when he detected a strong heartbeat. *For so small a sparrow, the sister has much spirit,* he reflected as he gazed at her delicate features.

Bending forward, he gently picked her up and moved her closer to the fire.

His dark eyes lingered on her beauty as he slowly straightened his lithe body. Snow was gathering on her dark lashes, and in the flickering firelight her face radiated a childlike innocence.

Kneeling again, he tucked the skirt of her habit around her tightly, making sure the wind could not penetrate her small frame.

As he stood, his eyes moved regretfully to the bushes where he had thrown the lizard carcass. Too bad she was so afraid of the creature; it would have made an adequate meal.

His eyes once again returned to the sister. Such a beautiful woman to have chosen to live her life out in a convent. He briefly speculated as to why.

A moment later, carrying his knife, he disappeared into the heavy thicket.


When Anne-Marie opened her eyes, large, cottony white balls were coming down, settling like feather down on the crests of her cheeks. For the longest moment she couldn't remember where she was.

Looking up, she saw a layer of white coating the tops of the trees, their branches decked out in glistening winter finery. Icicles dripped from the boughs of cedar trees, making them sparkle like ornaments on a Christmas tree. She lay drinking in the magnificent sight. The night was so silent she could hear smoke drifting from the fire.

As her memory rushed back she suddenly bolted upright, wondering where the Indian was. The campfire blazed brightly, but the Crow was nowhere in sight. Panic seized her, and she called out, her voice hollow in the icy stillness.

She sat for a moment, trying to collect her thoughts. What if he had left her? What if he had just taken the horse and ridden off, leaving her to fend for herself? A groan escaped her when she remembered the lizard and the speed with which the Indian's knife had severed its head.

A sound drew her attention, and she glanced up, wilting with relief when she saw the man returning, carrying something in his right hand.

"There you are!" she called out. "I was afraid you'd left me here—all alone."

Her eyes focused on the meat he was carrying, and her stomach rumbled with hunger. "Thank goodness you found something to eat." What, she wasn't sure, but by now it didn't matter. She'd settle for anything to appease her empty stomach.

Moving to the fire, the Indian deftly skewered the meat and hung it over the hot flame.

"What is it?" she asked, not really expecting a response, but just to hear a voice breaking the unnerving silence. "Well, no matter, it looks delicious," she added a moment later.

They sat in silence, surrounded by falling snow and the occasional sound of fat dripping into the fire.

When the meat was nearly black, the Indian removed it from the spit and laid it aside to cool.

After a while he tore the meat into chunks and handed her a portion. She couldn't hide the trembling in her hands as she took it from him.

His eyes darted to hers briefly, and she smiled back in gratitude. "Thank you. It smells wonderful."

Picking up the crusted meat, she told herself to be grateful for the kindness he had shown her. Maybe they couldn't communicate, but at least he had treated her with respect, and she should consider herself fortunate.

The Crow paused as if waiting for something.

When she returned his gaze vacantly, his eyes fell away, and he began eating.

When he had tossed the last bone aside, he settled near the fire and closed his eyes.

Anne-Marie watched, wondering who he was and if there was a woman somewhere tonight concerned about his welfare. He was a handsome man—or he could be with the proper care.

"Maybe we should sleep close together." The suggestion came out louder than she'd intended. She didn't mean anything by the suggestion. She didn't know him, and yet she instinctively felt that he didn't plan to do her harm. If they combined their body heat, they might survive the night.

In the distance coyotes—or perhaps something worse—howled. She wasn't sure, and she wasn't going to dwell on that fact for fear that panic would set in again.

"With the weather the way it is—the good Lord would not hold us accountable for trying to survive the elements,'' she continued, more to herself than to him, because it didn't appear that he was listening.

The wind howled through the bare tree branches as she lay on her side and stared at him across the fire. Good heavens. What if he did understand, and he was thinking that she was inviting him . . . ?

Recoiling from the thought, she huddled deeper into her habit. She was only trying to be charitable; she didn't want him or her to freeze to death. At the moment he was her only hope of reaching a town alive, and the thought of *anything* warm, no matter how unkempt and smelly, appealed to her survival instincts.

''Well . . . you can let me know if you should change your mind,'' she finished lamely. Maybe he did understand, she mused, but he was married, and his wife wouldn't.

Rolling to his side, the Crow presented his back to her.

Sighing, she closed her eyes, the weight of the world suddenly heavy on her shoulders.

She didn't know about him, but she had to stay alive. The McDougal sisters were the only support the Mercy Flats mission had.

Morning dawned, and the Indian doused the fire long before daybreak. The snow had tapered off to occasional blowing flakes, but the air was still bitterly cold. Only the golden sunrise filtering through the trees promised a pleasant day for traveling. The orange ball of sun, now beginning to top the trees, brought a smile to Anne-Marie's face and a renewed optimism as she accepted the Indian's hand and he pulled her up behind him.

It was late morning when the stallion carrying a nun and an Indian topped a rise.

Peering anxiously around the Crow's shoulder, Anne-Marie couldn't hold back the shout that bubbled to her throat when she spotted the small community spread out below them. *"Hot damn!"* They'd made it! They'd beaten the elements, and she was going to live!

The Indian glanced over his shoulder at her, and for the first time since they'd met, Anne-Marie thought she detected shock on his perpetually stoic features.

Catching herself, she added a perfunctory *"Praise the Lord,"* and hurriedly crossed herself.

Nudging the stallion forward, the Indian rode into town.

# Chapter 2

Streeter, Texas, was the typical border town. Anne-Marie could hear the clang of the blacksmith hammer as they passed the livery; the mercantile sat next to the café, and the hotel was facing west so it wouldn't bake in the late afternoon.

The saloon, the Gilded Dove, was just beginning to come to life as the Indian and nun rode through the center of town.

An occasional head turned when the couple rode by, but for the most part folks in Streeter were accustomed to strangers. The train ran right through town every Tuesday and Friday morning, regular as clockwork, so the comings and goings of outsiders never caused much of a stir.

Though, admittedly, a nun riding horseback with an Indian wasn't a common sight.

Reining the horse in front of a hitching post, the Indian climbed down and then lifted a hand to help the sister.

Adjusting her rumpled skirts, Anne-Marie glanced up and down the street, relieved to see they weren't attracting the curiosity she'd feared they might. "I want to secure a room at the hotel right away," she murmured.

Looping the reins around the hitching post, the Indian pointed to the train depot.

Anne-Marie located the hotel near the large water tower sitting next to the wooden train platform and nodded. "Oh, yes—thank you so much for all your trouble . . ."

Her words dribbled off when she realized she was talking to his retreating back. She watched as he disappeared into the mercantile, closing the door behind him.

Straightening her habit, she turned with quick, determined steps and headed for the hotel. She would secure a room, order a hot bath and a hot meal, and then lie down in a soft bed and sleep for hours. She wasn't ready to presume that Lady Luck was on her side again and that the train hadn't come through yet today; but she wasn't worried. Although she was rumpled and penniless, she was still wearing her disguise, and any God-fearing man or woman would be eager to provide a woman of the cloth with food and comfortable quarters while she waited.

Another day or two delay was minor considering all she'd endured, she told herself brightly.

She opened the door and allowed the delicious warmth of the hotel lobby to wash over her.

A moment later the front door opened again, and Anne-Marie stepped out, drawing a deep breath as she straightened her veil.

*So much for God-fearing, charitable souls.* "May they all rot in hell," she muttered as she crossed the street.

Turning to her right, she headed for the mercantile where the Indian had disappeared earlier.

As the bell over the door sounded the proprietor turned from where he'd been stacking boxes on his shelves, his automatic greeting momentarily halted when he saw the nun. Climbing slowly off the ladder, he wiped his hands on his apron as he walked toward her, smiling. "Afternoon, Sister."

"Good afternoon." Anne-Marie looked around the room, trying to locate the Indian. He was standing near the back, looking at a display of knives in a glass case. As he glanced up and recognized the new arrival, he quickly stepped away from the counter and disappeared behind a tall stack of dry goods.

The kindly-looking clerk viewed the nun's rumpled habit, still smiling pleasantly. "Something I can help you with today?"

Anne-Marie leaned over the counter, trying to see around the stacks of woolens and linens. Was it her imagination or was the Indian actually trying to avoid her? "Nothing in particular, I'm just browsing, thank you."

"If you see anything you want, I'll be happy to get it for you."

"Thank you, I'll let you know."

Moseying toward the bolts of colorful ribbons and lace, Anne-Marie kept an eye on the Crow, who—no, it wasn't her imagination—was making himself conspicuously absent. Apparently he understood enough to think his part in the rescue was over, but since he *had* rescued her, and she now found herself without a cent to her name and no one charitable enough in this lousy town to lend her their help, he was, most certainly, still responsible for her.

Turning accusing eyes on him, she was annoyed to see he was returning her silent reprimand with a sur-

prisingly astute one of his own, one that clearly inti-
mated he considered his part done.

Finished.

Over.

Stepping to the counter, the Crow pointed to an
expensive-looking rifle.

Climbing off the ladder again, the clerk said, "You
want to see the Sharps carbine?"

The Crow gave a brief nod.

"You got enough wampum to purchase it?"

The Crow nodded curtly.

"All righty." The clerk took the rifle off the shelf
and handed it to him.

After a cursory inspection the Indian nodded, indicating
his approval.

"Guess you'll be needin' shells? A box do you?"

The Crow nodded.

Anne-Marie watched the exchange with growing interest. The Indian seemed to have no trouble understanding the clerk. No trouble at all, yet he'd pretended
he hadn't understood a word she'd said for the past
twenty-four hours.

Laying the cartridges on the counter, the clerk totaled
up the purchase. "Looks like you owe me a hundred
and twenty-five dollars."

Anne-Marie's lips parted indignantly as she saw the
Crow produce a small leather pouch attached to his
breeches and calmly remove several gold coins. Judg-
ing from the lumps in the pouch, there was more where
they came from, maybe a lot more.

Why, the man had enough money to burn a wet mule!
Anne-Marie fumed. What was he doing with that kind of
money? He didn't have a penny an hour ago—or did he?

The proprietor tossed a few coins of change onto the counter while glancing at Anne-Marie. "Find everything you need, Sister?"

"Thank you, I'll just be looking today. Does the stage come through here?"

Picking up his purchases, the Indian turned and walked out the door. Anne-Marie's teeth worried her lower lip as she watched him leave.

"The stage? Sure does, every month, just like clockwork."

"Every *month*?"

"Yes, ma'am, came through last week. Be back in another three. Used to come through once a week, but with the train and all, it wasn't gettin' many passengers."

"How often does the train come through?"

"Twice a week, regular as clockwork."

The man seemed to have a fixation on clocks, she thought. "On what days?"

"Tuesdays and Fridays."

Her frown deepened as she watched the Indian cross the street. "Today is Saturday, isn't it?"

"That it is, Sister. Saturday."

*Two* whole days stuck in town without a penny. She smiled, bowing her head subserviently. "Thank you, you have been most kind."

Plucking an apple from a barrel, the proprietor polished it on the sleeve of his shirt then handed it to her. "An apple a day will keep the doctor away," he offered with a twinkling eye.

Nodding, Anne-Marie jammed the apple into her mouth as she stepped out of the store.

*Now what?* she thought as she stood looking up and

down the unfamiliar street. Her eyes located the Indian, who was walking in the direction of the sheriff's office.

Where did he think he was going with his pouch full of coins and a new, expensive rifle? Her eyes followed him as he strolled past a saloon.

Since he had taken it upon himself to be her protector, the very least he could do was see that she was properly protected, she thought, seething.

What was she to do about the price of a train ticket or, for that matter, where was she supposed to stay until the blasted thing got here? Men. No matter what color skin, they were all alike.

Taking another bite of the tart apple, she made a face as she stepped off the planked sidewalk and hurriedly crossed the street, falling into step behind the Crow. If he had understood that clerk, then he was going to be made to understand in no uncertain terms that he wasn't going to desert her now.

"I would like a word with you, Mr. Indian!" she barked.

When his footsteps didn't falter, she articulated more loudly. "I know you have money, and obviously I don't, so don't you think that since *you* appointed yourself my rescuer, it's only fair that *you* see to my well-being until the train arrives on Tuesday?"

He walked on.

Anne-Marie's temper flared. "I *know* you can understand what I'm saying—you understood the clerk at the mercantile perfectly!"

Snatching the apple out of her mouth, she hurled the uneaten portion at him, thumping him soundly between the very impressive width of his shoulders.

"ANSWER ME! DO YOU HEAR ME? I *SAID*, ANSWER ME BEFORE I KNOCK YOUR HEAD OFF!"

The door to the sheriff's office opened, and a deputy cautiously stuck his head out to see who was causing all the racket.

At the sight of the lawman, the muscles in Anne-Marie's stomach tightened. For a moment she had forgotten her disguise. Nuns didn't fling apples at Indians' backs and threaten to knock their heads off at the top of their lungs.

"Afternoon, Sister," the deputy called lamely as she passed him.

Nodding severely to the deputy, she marched past the jailhouse door, still dogging the Indian's steps.

Anne-Marie told herself she was being silly when the deputy continued to stare after her. Neither she nor her sisters had ever been in Streeter, Texas, before, so no one could possibly recognize her as part of the three women who had been operating con games in the area.

"Oh, Sister?"

Anne-Marie froze, not particularly liking the tone of a second man's voice who had suddenly joined the conversation.

"Oh, Sisterrrr?" repeated the mocking voice.

The Crow's footsteps picked up as he walked faster.

Anne-Marie was close on his heel when the voice sang out again, "Oh, Sisterrrr!"

Turning around slowly, Anne-Marie swallowed as she saw a large man with a silver star on his chest striding toward her. A man in a brown suit spiritedly followed on his heel.

"Sister, I wonder if I might have a word with you?" the sheriff inquired pleasantly.

*Darn!* Anne-Marie agonized. Darn! Darn! Darn! A. J. Barthlomew, the man she and her sisters had scammed just a few short weeks ago, was standing beside the sheriff, his swarthy features molten with anger.

Whirling, Anne-Marie started to make a run for it when she suddenly felt the cold barrel of a .32-caliber Colt resting lightly between her shoulder blades. "Now, now, what's your hurry, little lady?"

"Sir, how dare you—"

"Is this the woman, A.J.?"

"That's her, all right. I'd know those lying green eyes anywhere!"

"Now, Sheriff," Anne-Marie began, then immediately piped down when she saw that the deputy had cornered the Indian and was herding him back, at rifle point, in her direction.

"Now, see here, how dare you treat a woman of the cloth—"

"Save your breath, lady." A.J. sneered. "We've got you dead to rights. *No* woman sells me a herd of stolen beef and lives to brag about it!"

The sheriff ushered the Indian and the nun down the sidewalk over Anne-Marie's loud and spirited objections.

Entering the jail, the deputy grabbed a ring of keys from a hook on the wall while the sheriff herded Anne-Marie and the Crow into a cell.

"I demand you release me this instant! You just can't grab innocent people—" She glared accusingly at A.J. Barthlomew. *"Innocent nun,"* she amended as she turned pleading eyes to the sheriff, "off the street and treat them like common riffraff just because some wild man is making ludicrous accusations."

"There's two more of 'em around somewhere," A.J. warned the sheriff.

"We'll find them, A.J. They couldn't have gone far."

The Indian balked as the butt of the sheriff's gun pushed him into the cell.

"Git on in there, boy."

Glaring at the Crow, Anne-Marie warned him silently that if he could speak, he better darn well be doing it.

The Indian refused to meet her eyes.

Slamming the cell door shut, the sheriff smiled reassuringly as he slipped the key into the lock. "Now, don't you be worrying your pretty head, ma'am, you and the Injun will have yourselves a fair trial. I guarantee you that."

"I demand proper legal representation! Get me an attorney!" Anne-Marie shouted as she clasped the bars with both hands.

"Why, certainly, ma'am." He turned to A.J., smiling. "I believe the lady would like a word with you, A.J."

Anne-Marie's face visibly paled. "*He's* our lawyer?" she asked lamely.

The sheriff nodded. "Yes, ma'am, but don't worry your pretty little head none. Not only is A.J. the town's finest attorney, but he's the onliest."

Anne-Marie's heart sank. "Onliest what?"

"Onliest attorney." The sheriff's smile widened. "He'll be speaking on you and your friend's behalf."

# Chapter 3

"I don't know *how* he recognized me."

Anne-Marie sank down on the cot opposite the Indian, frustrated. It had been over a month since they'd sold Barthlomew that herd of stolen cattle, and she'd have sworn she'd seen the last of that fool.

Springing back to her feet, she started talking under her breath as she paced the small cell. "Just don't—how—the man—Amelia—then Abigail said—rotten luck—"

The front door opened, and the sheriff came in with A.J. trailing behind. Hooking his hat on a peg, Ferris Goodman walked over to the wood stove and poured two cups of steaming black coffee.

"Sheriff," Anne-Marie called, "can I have a word with you?"

"No, ma'am."

Handing A.J. a cup of coffee, the sheriff sat down behind his desk. "Now, A.J., tell me again what happened."

A.J. pointed an accusing finger at Anne-Marie. "That

woman and two others dressed just like her sold me a herd of stolen beef.''

"You're certain it was this woman."

"As sure as hair grows on a pig's back!''

"And the Injun?''

"I don't know nothing about the savage, but the way I figure it, he was with her when they rode into town, so they must be in cahoots with each other.''

"Well, your word's good enough for me.'' The sheriff got up and walked to the cell where Anne-Marie stood, gripping the bars. "Don't suppose you plan on telling me where your sisters are?''

"I don't *know* where they are!''

"Then by the authority vested in me by the great state of Texas, I hereby sentence you and your friend here to hang at sunrise.''

Anne-Marie's mouth dropped opened. "Now just a minute! What happened to my *fair* trial?''

The sheriff met her eyes with an unwavering gaze. "You just had it.''

"Just had it?'' Apparently they'd *had* it, all right, but good.

Returning to his chair, Ferris took a swig of coffee, peering over the rim of the cup at A.J. as he tried to talk above Anne-Marie's vehement protests. "You know, A.J., I'd still like to know how you let yourself get swindled by a woman. Don't rightly seem like you.''

A.J. hated to admit it, but the woman had taken him slicker than glass.

"She told me the cattle had been a gift and they had to sell them because the mission couldn't afford to keep them. Some orphanage they ran needed money, not cattle, she said. Well, hell, Ferris, who's going to question a nun, much less three of 'em?''

"Well, now, I might have questioned getting a top head of cattle for hundreds of dollars below market price," Ferris argued.

It wasn't for Ferris to say, but falling for that old swindle was down right stupid, if anyone was to ask him.

"No, you would have fell for it just as slick as I did," A.J. grumbled. "It sounded on the up-and-up, so I marched myself right over to the bank and got the money real quick like before the sisters could change their minds."

"Guess you wish you'd marched a little slower?" Ferris was having a hard time hiding a grin behind the rim of his cup.

"I was there to buy cattle, and the price was right," A.J. said sullenly.

Ferris couldn't keep from laughing now, even if he'd tried. "And you never *once* suspected them women was pullin' a fast one on you?''

"Do I look like an idiot, Ferris? Of *course* I didn't know I was bein' played for a fool! Why, that one over there even wrote me out a bill of sale, right there in the saloon, big as all get out." He snorted with disgust. "I should've known something was wrong when they high-tailed it out of town as soon as they had the money in hand. No one's seen hide nor hair of 'em since—not until I saw that one ridin' into town with the Indian, the both of them as brazen as a two-bit whore."

Ferris looked up as the Crow suddenly got to his feet and walked to the front of the cell.

"Gentlemen, twenty-four hours ago I didn't know this woman existed."

The Crow's eyes pinpointed Anne-Marie.

Anne-Marie's mouth dropped open as she stared back at him. "What?" Had he *said* what she thought he'd said?

"I said"—the Crow's eyes locked with hers as he repeated in perfect English—"I am *not* with this woman."

She knew it! He had been deliberately making her think that he couldn't understand English, and now he not only understood it, but he was speaking it!

Chairs scraping against the floor, Ferris and A.J. came to their feet.

"You were sure enough with her in the mercantile a little while ago," A.J. reminded him.

"True, but it appears that Mr. Barthlomew and I have met with the same misfortune, that of being unsuspectingly taken in by a wolf in sheep's clothing—or"—his eyes returned to Anne-Marie—"as is the more applicable case, a thief in nun's clothing."

"Care to say how she took you?" the sheriff inquired, surprised by the sudden turn of events.

The muscle in the Crow's jaw visibly tightened. "I rescued her from a jail wagon."

"Rescued her from a jail wagon, huh?" Goodman and Barthlomew exchanged amused looks.

"The wagon was being pursued by Comanches. When I saw what I assumed to be three nuns in danger, I rode to their aid."

"And the other two nuns?" Ferris smirked. "Where might they be?"

"I don't know. Two other men rode to assist the women at the same time I did."

"My, my, was that a stroke of luck on them women's part or what, A.J.? Three men, all ridin' in to help them nuns at the exact same time?"

"More than a stroke of luck, Ferris. I'd say it was a miracle." A.J. crowed.

"I'm telling you, that's exactly the way it happened," the Crow insisted, but he could see the sheriff wasn't buying a word of it.

"Well, Injun, you speak real educated like, but the fact is you rode in the company of a cattle thief, and right now, since I've got no way of knowing if you're telling me the truth about all this jail-wagon and band-of-Comanches stuff, I'm bound by the law to let my decision stand."

"You are making a mistake," the Indian warned.

"Could be, but if I was you, I'd just sit back and keep quiet." Ferris glanced at A.J. and winked. "You and the little lady got yourselves a big day ahead of you tomorrow."

"Well, if that doesn't beat all!" Anne-Marie whirled to confront the Crow as the sheriff and A.J. walked out the door. "How *dare* you make me think that you didn't understand a word I was saying—"

"How dare you pose as a *nun*?" he returned dispassionately.

"What *difference* does it make who I am?"

"The difference is that I wouldn't have given *you* or your friends a second thought if I hadn't believed three *sisters* were about to be scalped."

"But I *was* about to be scalped!"

"But *you're* not a *sister*."

"Oh! You're impossible!" Ripping aside her veil, Anne-Marie freed her long hair to tumble loosely over her shoulders. Her usual way of worming out of tight situations wasn't working, so it looked like she was forced to resort to drastic measures. No man, no matter how infuriating, could resist a helpless, simpering female.

Covering her lovely face with her hands and dropping her chin, she began to sob. After a few moments of this display, Anne-Marie spread her fingers, peering out to witness the Indian's reaction. Then she saw that he was ignoring her. Totally *ignoring* her!

Discarding the theatrics, she switched to her wounded look, a tactic absolutely no man could survive, no matter how unsympathetic.

"Some protector you are," she accused with her lower lip trembling pitifully.

Walking back to the cot, he sat down. "Why should I protect you?"

"Because *you* appointed yourself my protector when you rescued me from the jail wagon yesterday!"

"Today I unappoint myself your protector."

"You can't do that."

"I just did."

"Fine." She sat down on the cot, crossing her arms and giving him a cold stare, another surefire tactic to bring a man to his knees, no matter how mean and hateful he was; and this man was the meanest one she'd ever had the misfortune to meet, that was for sure.

"Fine," he said, and stared back at her just as coldly.

They sat in stony silence, staring contemptuously at each other.

Finally Anne-Marie heaved a sigh of aggravation as

she loosened the collar of her confining habit. Reaching into the large pocket sewn into the front of her habit, she pulled out a piece of ribbon and tied her hair back out of her face. With her face fully exposed, she was truly a beautiful woman. It would have been a shame, the Indian decided, if she really were a nun, for this woman was made for a man's pleasure.

"Who are you and why did you pretend not to understand English."

His gaze slid over her impersonally. "Why would you choose this disguise?" he asked.

"Why not?" she answered breezily.

His eyes darkened to a dangerous hue. "Only godly women wear the habit. It is a sign of their devotion to the Lord's work; it is not worn as a ruse to steal from unsuspecting men."

"I have no idea what that A.J. person was talking about," she contended. "I haven't duped anyone out of anything and I didn't sell any cattle. It's all a mistake, I tell you. A big mistake."

"Do I look gullible enough to believe that?"

"Well, you should talk. No, you don't look gullible enough to believe that," she mimicked, "but then I'd bet my last dollar you're no more an Indian than I am a sister!"

"Then you would lose your last dollar." He settled back on the cot, leaning against the wall.

He did, for the world, look like a full-blooded Indian, but he sure wasn't acting like one.

"You're not a normal Indian," she scoffed, "and if you are, you're not uncivilized and ignorant like you want everyone to believe."

He laughed, a cold mirthless sound in the small cell.

Combing her fingers through her hair, she glared at him. "What's so funny?"

"If what I've gotten myself into couldn't be deemed ignorant, I don't know what would. I'm sitting here in jail, with a con artist, waiting to be hung at sunrise."

"They'll never hang us," she said dismissively. "By morning they'll realize their mistake . . ." Her voice died away as the sound of hammering reached them.

Running to the windows, she looked out, her heart springing to her throat when she saw the large platform being erected in front of the jail. "Well, will you look at that. What do you suppose they're building?"

"A gallows."

Her face drained of color. "You're kidding?"

"Do I look like I'm attempting to amuse you?"

She turned to glance over her shoulder at his solemn features. He didn't look like he was kidding; he looked dead serious.

Shuffling back to the cot, she sat down again, sighing. Although he might look like an Indian, his speech was obviously that of an educated man. She had always been smart, too smart for her own good, so if the two of them put their heads together, they could think of a way out of this.

"Tell me who you are, honestly."

"It is not important that you know."

"It is, too. Tell me your name." If she was going to die with him, she'd at least like to know his name.

"Creed Walker."

"That isn't an Indian name."

"I didn't say it was."

"What is your Indian name?"

His eyes fixed straight ahead. "A Crow does not speak his own name."

"Well, for heaven's sake, why not?"

"Has anyone ever told you you talk too much?"

"No."

"Consider yourself told."

"I know you *look* like an Indian, but you don't sound like one," she said, undaunted by his observation. After all, he was just a man.

"Let's assume I've not been living among my people for many years."

"Why did you pretend not to understand me when I talked to you?"

"Because it suited my purposes not to."

"Well, Mr. Walker, does it suit your purpose to get us out of here?"

His brows drew together autocratically. "I don't know what I can do. In case you haven't noticed, I'm behind bars, too."

"We have to do something," she said tremulously. "We can't just sit here and let them hang us." She looked terrible in hemp!

He looked at her, shaking his head with disbelief. "Hasn't it sunk in yet? We're not getting out of here. The jail is too tight, the sheriff is too crooked, and we are going to hang."

"Pooh! Something will happen—it always does." She refused to believe her luck had run out.

They glanced up as the front door opened again, and the deputy entered this time, followed by a black man. He was the most fancy duded-up black man Anne-Marie had ever seen. By his clothing he appeared to be a gambler. From the top of his black derby to the equally black patent-leather shoes, he reeked success. The dark broadcloth suit fit his physique like a second skin. There was a slight bulge beneath the red satin vest, and Anne-Marie surmised that the man was heavily armed. His flawless white shirt was accentuated by an impeccably tied brown cravat that matched the color of his glittering eyes to perfection.

The Negro's teeth glistened like cotton as, grinning, he spotted Anne-Marie and the Indian huddled together on the dirty bunk.

"Yessir, dat's her all right, Mr. Deputee. Dat's de woman who done stole my grandmammy's brooch, den took off like a scalded cat. Yessir, dat's de one all right!"

Striding over to the cell, the black man pointed his be-jeweled finger at Anne-Marie reproachfully. "Thought you'd git away with it, did you, Sister? Well, I can promise you dis, I's not a-gonna let you, you hear me? Now, give it back, right now!"

Wide-eyed, Anne-Marie backed deeper into the cell. She'd never seen this man before in her life much less swindled him out of a brooch. "I . . . don't have your mammy's brooch—"

"She's a-lyin', she's a-lyin'! Sheriff, I *insist* you open dat cell door and conduct a search of a personal nature of this thievin' wench! She done stole my grandmammy's brooch, and she not a-gonna git away with it. I have my papers; I's a free man and I refuse to be treated dis way!"

The deputy clearly didn't know what to do. "Now, Mister—what'd you say your name was?"

"John Quincy Adams, sir!"

The deputy studied the dandified man sourly. "John Quincy Adams?"

"Dat right, me mammy named me after de president. Now, dere I is, showing de nice sister my dear ol' grandmammy's brooch—she dead now, God rest her sainted soul—de *very* brooch her dear ol' sainted mammy had given her, when de sister, she says, 'Oh, it's so lovely, may I share its unusual boodie with Sister Louise, who's dis minute buying flour and molasses in the mercantile?' " Quincy Adams looked right down put out with himself. "Well, likes the fool I is, I lets her talk me into giving her my grandmammy's brooch and I says, 'You and Sister take yore time a-lookin' at the fine piece of jewelry whiles I jest go over here and sit down under a tree and wait, and I wait and I wait for her to git back, but she never gits back! She done up and disappears. Gone, vamoosed!"

"I don't know what this man is talking about! I haven't stolen any brooch!" Anne-Marie contended heatedly.

John Quincy Adams had said all he was going to say on the subject. "Open de cell door, Mr. Deputee, and we'll jest see who's lyin'."

"Well, I don't know, Sheriff Goodman is across the street—"

"Won't take one minute to git dis here matter done cleaned up. Alls I want is my brooch back, that's alls I want."

"Well." The deputy glanced out the window, but he didn't see Ferris Goodman anywhere. "Don't guess it could hurt nothing to search her—but you'll have to stand back and let me do it."

Adams nodded genially. "Dat be fine with me, alls I want is my brooch back."

"I don't have his ol' brooch!" Anne-Marie protested as the deputy slipped the key in the lock and opened the door.

She gasped as she heard a sound thump, and the deputy slumped to the floor, unconscious.

"Now, you just have yoreself a nice little snooze, Mr. Deputee," Quincy invited cordially.

"What in the hell took you so long?" Creed snapped as Adams handed him a pearl-handled pistol.

"What took me so long? I've been trailing you from the minute you got involved with this woman—which, I might point out, was pretty stupid—and then when I saw you were in this fine mess, I had to go rustle up some clothes and come up with a plan to get you out."

"We don't have time to discuss the merits of my wisdom," Creed interrupted.

Striding to the window, he looked out, relieved to see that Ferris Goodman along with A. J. Barthlomew and three other men were busy hammering nails into the scaffolding. "We've got to get out of here."

Anne-Marie listened to the men's exchange, her bewilderment growing. "Do you two *know* each other? *What* is going on here?"

The men ignored her.

"We'll have to make a break for it," Quincy said in a low voice, and it suddenly occurred to Anne-Marie that his speech was as educated as the Indian's.

Why, those low-down, conniving—these men were worse than she was when it came to deceit.

"If we're quick, the sheriff won't notice a thing," Quincy predicted. "With all that banging and sawing, we should be able to get out of here without causing a stir. Let's go.''

Creed stepped out of the cell and the two men headed for the door.

Anne-Marie watched, dumbfounded that they were going to leave her.

"Wait a minute! Are you just going to walk out of here and leave me?''

When they didn't answer, she scrambled to her feet. "Oh, no you don't. I'm coming with you!''

Racing out of the cell, she pressed tightly against Creed's backside as he opened the front door a crack and looked out.

"There's a buckboard sitting in front of the bank.''

Adams rolled his eyes. It sounded risky to him. "Let's separate and make a run for three horses.''

Creed studied the nearly deserted street. It was too early after the afternoon siesta for most people to be up and about. "Not a chance. We'll have to take the wagon.''

They all shoved their way through the door at once.

"Uh-oh,'' Anne-Marie shouted, panic raising her voice several octaves as she saw the sheriff look up and spot them as they raced toward the wagon. "The *sher-rrrif saw ussss!*''

Ferris Goodman couldn't believe his eyes. That Indian and nun had escaped—and they had a black man with them now! Dropping his hammer, he shouted, "Hey! Where do you think you're going?''

Anne-Marie held her skirts high as she ran toward the wagon, fighting to keep her footing in the rutted street. If she fell, she didn't fool herself into thinking Creed Walker would rescue her a second time.

The three dashed for a lone buckboard where a team of horses sat dozing.

Scrambling aboard, Creed reached out and grabbed Anne-Marie's hand. With a mighty push, she heaved herself up between the two men and all three scrambled for a position on the small board seat.

"Hold on!" Creed shouted as he swung the horses into the street. Anne-Marie felt a hard jab in the ribs as Quincy reached for a shotgun lying on the wagon floor.

"Hee-ya!" Creed yelled as the buckboard raced past the newly constructed platform, scattering lumber, nails, and men in its wake.

A burst of gunfire rained over the careening wagon as it rolled out of town.

Clinging to the wooden seat, Anne-Marie shut her eyes tightly. The buckboard bumped and banged along the rutted road as Creed cracked a whip over the horses' heads, urging them on to even greater speed.

Quincy attempted to hang on to the shotgun as the wagon lurched crazily across the countryside.

Glancing over her shoulder, Anne-Marie felt her heart pounding as she saw riders in the distance rapidly approaching, hot on their trail.

"Faster, faster, they're gaining on us!"

Creed swung the whip harder, snapping it smartly over the ears of the team.

As the buckboard raced along, a tarp covering two wooden boxes in the bed of the wagon came loose and began flapping in the wind. Before Quincy could secure the rope holding the tarp, it ripped free of the wagon bed.

Anne-Marie's eyes widened as she spotted the two

strongboxes with WELLS FARGO emblazoned on the sides.

Seeing the look on her face, Quincy glanced over his shoulder and yelled, "Holy moley!"

"What's wrong?" Creed shouted.

Quincy shook his head, his eyes frozen on the two strongboxes. The buckboard hit a deep rut and bounced awkwardly on its side as Quincy and Anne-Marie held on for dear life.

As the wagon hit another rut the gun suddenly flew out of Quincy's hand.

Anne-Marie made a grab for it, and the gun discharged, the explosion propelling the shotgun to the floor of the buckboard.

The Indian swore, grabbing for his thigh as the reins fell to the floor. The smell of burning gunpowder filled Anne-Marie's nostrils as she scrambled to retrieve them.

Climbing back on the seat, she gasped when she saw the crimson patch of blood soaking above the knee of Creed Walker's breeches.

"Holy—*now* what'd you do?" Quincy yelled as he grabbed the reins from Anne-Marie's hands.

Before she could deny that she'd done anything, the buckboard bounced again, pitching Creed off the seat and out of the wagon.

As she whirled to look back Anne-Marie's heart sank at the sight of the Crow's lifeless form sprawled in the middle of the road.

*Brother*, this just wasn't her day!

# Chapter 4

Quincy scrambled over Anne-Marie as the buckboard bumped and crashed its way through the heavy underbrush. Half standing, he hauled on the reins and pulled back with all his might.

Gripping the sides of the wagon, Anne-Marie held on as Adams gained control of the team. Gradually he angled the buckboard back around until he got the team on the road again.

Creed was lying on his side groaning as Quincy brought the wagon to a halt beside him. Jumping down from the seat, Anne-Marie ran to kneel beside him.

"Are you all right?"

"No, I'm not all right! You've nearly blown my leg off!" He lay back, agony and fury fighting for dominance on his usually stoic features.

"Oh, my goodness." She reached toward the gaping wound, then quickly drew back her hand. "What do you want me to do?"

"Take one of the horses and ride as hard as you can in the opposite direction."

He groaned, struggling to sit up.

"It would be my pleasure," she snapped, glancing over her shoulder to see how close the posse was, for there would surely be one after them by now. "But you'll just have to put up with me awhile longer, because if we don't get out of here, fast, none of us will live long enough to argue about it."

Creed collapsed back to the ground, moaning in agony.

"Riders are moving in fast," Quincy warned as he tried to get Creed back on his feet. "Come on, brother, we've got to get you back into the buckboard."

"Go on without me," Creed panted, clenching his jaw against another spasm of pain.

"I can't do that," both Quincy and Anne-Marie said in unison. After all, Anne-Marie acknowledged silently, he had saved her from certain death, not once, but twice in the past twenty-four hours, and if the sheriff and his men caught up with him, Creed was sure to hang.

Creed lay for a moment, his hand gripping his blood-soaked thigh. Anne-Marie stared at the crimson pool, knowing he had to have help soon, or he would bleed to death. Biting her lower lip, she tried to think.

"Creed?"

He opened his eyes and glared at her.

"Nothing, I just wanted to be sure you hadn't died on me."

"Don't even think of leaving me alone with this woman," Quincy warned him.

Rolling to his side, Creed tried to sit up.

"Here, let me help," Anne-Marie offered.

He drew back, his black eyes glittering precariously. "I can manage on my own."

Stepping forward, Quincy gently grasped his friend beneath his arms and lifted him to his feet. "Lean on me until I can get you back to the buckboard."

They could hear the sound of riders approaching at a fast gallop.

Quincy supported Creed's weight as he helped him back to the wagon. Creed was barely lucid now, his features contorted by pain. He lost his fight for consciousness as Quincy reached the bed of the wagon. Realizing that he would need some sort of covering, Anne-Marie quickly retraced the wagon tracks to look for the canvas that had blown off the strongboxes. She finally located the crumpled tarp several yards away, then raced back to the wagon and tucked the canvas tightly around Creed's limp body.

Knowing they had to move quickly, she motioned for Quincy to drive the team as she jumped aboard the wagon.

With a shrill whistle, John Quincy Adams flicked the whip over the horses' heads, and they were off again, the posse hot on their trail.

"What do you mean you *no sabe* what happened? It's your job to *sabe* what happened!"

Malpas was red-faced as he tried to explain to the boss what had just taken place. Even he didn't believe it!

"I say to you, Señor Streeter, I do *know* what happened. One minute the buckboard is loaded and waiting, the next minute it is—how do you say?—vamoosed." He shrugged entreatingly.

"Gone?" Loyal Streeter asked in disbelief. "A hundred thousand dollars of gold, just *gone*?"

Malpas's swarthy features heated with color. "Sí, señor, vamoosed! An *indio*, a *negro*, and a *sor*, came running out of the jail. Before Malpas realize what is happening, they grab the *carro* and ride out of the pueblo!"

Loyal swore heatedly. "Where was Ollie when all this was taking place?"

Malpas shamefully avoided his boss's piercing gaze. "He run after the *carro, señor!*"

At the disturbing news, Ferris Goodman, who had been silent for most of the conversation, quietly reached for his hat and rifle.

"You put every man you got on this, Ferris," Loyal ordered as Goodman opened the door. "Whoever took that gold couldn't have gotten far."

As the door closed behind the sheriff's back Loyal walked back to his desk. "Damn bunch of incompetent fools," he muttered. "A hundred thousand dollars worth of gold, *gone*."

Malpas kept his eyes on the scuffed toes of his boots. *"Sí, señor."*

Loyal's scowl was even blacker when he looked up and saw Malpas still standing there. "Shouldn't you be out there looking for that wagon instead of standing here, *sí, señoring* me, dammit!"

Malpas was already running toward the door. "Do not worry, Señor Streeter, as you say, they no can get far. When we find the hombres, we string them up by their heels and return the gold to you, pronto!"

Streeter's features flexed with fury. "You have that gold back here by sundown. You understand?"

*"Sí,* sundown, *señor."*

\* \* \*

"Do you have the slightest idea where we're going, ma'am?" Quincy had been pushing the team hard for over two hours, and he still didn't know where he was headed.

"No, but I'm thinking." Anne-Marie turned to check on Creed again. The wound looked terrible, but she didn't know what to do for him. If she could just get him to Old Eulalie, she would know what to do. *Eulalie.* Why hadn't she thought of Eulalie sooner?

"Mr. Adams, do you know approximately what vicinity we're in?"

"Yes, ma'am, I was raised in these parts."

"Are we anywhere near Addison's Corner?"

"Yes, ma'am. Addison's Corner is nigh onto fifteen miles down the road. Why? You know they'll have someone checking out all the small settlements around here." Quincy gradually slackened the horses' pace to a ground-covering trot. There'd been no sign of riders for over an hour now, but that didn't mean they could relax their vigilance.

"Have you ever heard of a woman called Eulalie?"

Quincy visibly paled. "You mean that old witch woman who lives with all them cats and dogs?"

"Oh," Anne-Marie scoffed, "Eulalie isn't a witch; she's just eccentric."

Quincy kept his eyes fixed on the road. "Yes, ma'am, whatever you say."

"Do you think you could find Eulalie's cabin?"

"The witch woman's house?" Quincy's eyes grew round as teacups. "No, ma'am, don't you go expecting Quincy Adams to go within ten miles of that woman!"

"Oh, shame on you, Quincy Adams! Eulalie isn't a witch, and if you think anything of your friend at all, you'll help me find her house before he bleeds to death. Old Eulalie's the only chance we have of helping him through this crisis."

"How do you know the old witch woman?" His eyes rounded again at the thought of the old woman. She was downright scary. "You're not one of her kind, are you?"

Anne-Marie sighed as she fondly remembered Eulalie. "No, I'm not a *witch*. Eulalie and I go back a long way."

The woman known as Old Eulalie was something of a mystery and a legend in this remote region of Texas. The valley where she lived was well known to the locals, but neither the Indians nor the whites bothered her. Even though she never considered herself as one, Eulalie was regarded as a witch instead of a healer, which was her true calling. The only visitors she received were those who needed her medical powers.

Anne-Marie was well acquainted with the magical healing powers of the old woman. She had first met Eulalie when Abigail had somehow contracted a strange illness. The doctor in Mercy Flats had told Anne-Marie that her sister was going to die, but Anne-Marie refused to believe it.

Then, one night while Anne-Marie sat at Abigail's bedside, she looked up to see one of the Spanish orphans entering the room. In a quiet and reverent voice, he told of a strange woman who lived alone and performed miracles like God.

With the somewhat dubious help of Father Luis, Anne-Marie was allowed to use the boy's services in order to find the old woman's house.

Anne-Marie affectionately remembered the way Eulalie had miraculously saved her sister from certain death. When Anne-Marie and Abigail returned to Mercy Flats, they had a new respect for the healing art and had made a lifelong friend. And now, as Anne-Marie gazed at the pale face of her protector, she felt that if anyone could save him, Old Eulalie could.

She turned and continued, "Anytime we pass through the area we visit with her, but"—Anne-Marie looked around—"nothing looks familiar to me."

"That's because we're coming in the back way to the old witch's cabin—"

"She's *not* a witch, quit saying that."

"Yes, ma'am."

Anne-Marie laid her hand on Quincy's arm. "We have to find Eulalie, Mr. Adams, we don't have any other choice."

"Oh Lord," Quincy groaned, "I don't know how I get myself in these messes," but Anne-Marie noticed he was turning the buckboard around and heading toward a break in the terrain she had not noticed before.

It was over an hour before they spotted the gnarled cedar that marked the entrance to the small valley where Old Eulalie lived. As snow began to fall Anne-Marie frowned, glancing at the darkening sky. With everything that had happened, the threat of another spring storm was all they needed.

As Adams guided the team down the furrowed path, Anne-Marie glanced over her shoulder to find Creed already covered with a light powdering of snow.

As the buckboard rattled to a halt the door to the shanty opened and the barrel of a shotgun appeared.

"Who's there?" a gravelly voice demanded.

"Anne-Marie, Eulalie. I need help!"

The barrel of the gun disappeared, and the door immediately swung open.

"One of the McDougal young'uns? Well, land sakes—haven't seen you in a coon's age." The old woman shuffled out onto the porch and began to make her way down the rickety steps.

Jumping down from the wagon, Anne-Marie ran to the back of the buckboard, jerking the tarp off the still-unconscious Creed.

"What brings you out this way, child?"

Eulalie pulled a worn shawl tighter around her stooped shoulders as she approached the buckboard. "Land sakes! You're going to freeze to death out here!"

Her eyes lit on the black man, nervously holding the reins of the exhausted team.

"Git on in by the fire, and I'll fix something to warm your innards."

Quincy glanced at Anne-Marie, shaking his head.

Anne-Marie shot him a silent reprimand, much as a mother would do to a child misbehaving in public.

"Mr. Adams, Eulalie has graciously invited us to share the warmth of her fire. Now *get down* off that wagon seat and help me get Mr. Walker into the house."

"Oh Lordy." Quincy mentally crossed himself before he set the brake, then climbed reluctantly off the wagon to help.

Though Eulalie moved with a shuffling gait, she appeared ageless. Her toothless grin was topped by eyes twinkling with intelligence. She'd never said why she'd chosen to hide herself in a hovel built from pieces of lumber and tin she'd found by the wayside, and Anne-Marie had never asked. Eulalie survived by trading her healing herbs with locals, but for the most part, people thought her to be a witch and left her alone.

Quincy pulled Creed's body out of the wagon, giving Eulalie a wide berth as he carried the Crow's unconscious body up the rickety steps.

Eulalie moved aside, her eyes twinkling with mischief as the black man crept by her. Leaning forward, she hissed, "Gonna git you, boy!" and startled Quincy so badly he almost dropped the Indian.

"Eulalie," Anne-Marie admonished. "Mr. Adams already thinks you're a witch, so please don't complicate the matter any more than necessary."

Entering the cabin, Anne-Marie was reminded that Eulalie wasn't the tidiest of housekeepers. She would gather up anything and everything that she found or traded for, so the furnishings inside the cabin were as much a hodgepodge as the structure itself.

"Who is he?" Eulalie said, pointing a gnarled finger at Quincy.

"He's with him." Anne-Marie pointed to Creed.

Her sharp old eyes surveyed the Crow's limp body. "Who's he?"

"An acquaintance. I accidently shot him."

"Shot him?"

"Yes, it was an accident, Eulalie, but he's lost a lot of blood."

Eulalie looked deeply into Anne-Marie's eyes. Anne-Marie hated admitting it, but she wouldn't lie to Old Eulalie.

"We were trying to outrun the law," she murmured.

Eulalie cackled. "Outrun the law, you say?" She glanced at the black man. "Well, get him in the house, and I'll take a look at him."

Anne-Marie hurried up the steps behind Quincy as he carried Creed into the shack.

"Shoo! Get out of here! Shoo!" Eulalie waved her hands at the dozen or so cats that converged on the door to greet them. "Drop him on the table so I can have a look at that wound."

The cabin reeked of foul cooking odors, stale cigar smoke, and pungent animal excrement. Quincy deposited Creed on the kitchen table, then stood to the side, trying not to look at the gory injury.

The leg was abnormally large, as if all the blood from Creed's body had pooled in one place. Eulalie's gnarled fingers probed the torn flesh and Creed moaned.

"It don't look too bad."

The smells, combined with the sight of the withered crone poking her dirty fingers into the wound, were too much for Quincy.

Eulalie and Anne-Marie both turned when they heard a soft thud as Quincy passed out cold on the dirt floor.

"Well, I guess he'll need something stronger than tea when he comes to," Eulalie surmised. Drawing Anne-Marie aside, she murmured, "Get me some hot water, and some rags from the shelf."

The fire felt heavenly, but at that moment Anne-Marie was too concerned about Creed to enjoy its warmth. A scratching in the corner of the room momentarily drew her attention to a small raccoon who had taken up residence; he peered back at her with alarmingly resourceful eyes.

A mother cat and four kittens rested on a rug in a corner nearer the fireplace. As usual, Eulalie had a collection of critters that believed the cabin to be their own.

Pouring a pan full of hot water, Anne-Marie carried it and the clean rags to the table, stepping over Quincy in the process.

Using Creed's knife, Eulalie slit the Indian's breeches from waist to ankle and peeled them aside. Her eyes stopped momentarily on his manly endowments. Anne-Marie flushed as she heard the woman's murmured, "My, my, my, you got yourself quite a man here, young'un."

Anne-Marie's cheeks burned at the implication, but she had to agree with Eulalie. Creed was quite a man. His body was long, lean, well muscled, and— She turned her head, rattled by her thoughts.

"That buckshot's got to come out." Eulalie motioned for Anne-Marie to move closer. "Hold the lantern higher."

"Where am I?" Creed mumbled, momentarily stirring as the lantern light seared his eyes.

Anne-Marie leaned over him anxiously. "Don't be alarmed, we're at a friend's cabin."

"Where's Quincy?" he mumbled.

Anne-Marie pointed to the crumpled heap lying at the foot of the table.

"Never could stand the sight of blood," he murmured. His eyes closed, then opened briefly to stare at the old crone hovering above him. "What's going— who?"

Grasping his hand, Anne-Marie held it tightly. "You're going to be fine."

Creed wouldn't bet on it. His thigh felt like it was on fire, and the old woman who bent over him smelled like she'd been pickled in hundred-fifty-proof whiskey. The sound of mewing cats came to him, and when one began licking his bloody fingers, he jerked his hand aside.

"Shoo. Get away from here," Eulalie scolded, nudging two of the felines out of the way with a booted foot. Turning back to the wound, she talked as she worked. "Where's your sisters, Amelia and Abigail?"

Sighing, Anne-Marie said wearily, "Eulalie, you wouldn't believe what's happened." As Eulalie dug the buckshot out of Creed's leg, Anne-Marie filled her in on the events of the past few days.

"You think Abigail and Amelia are safe?" Anne-Marie asked, once the tale was unfolded.

"Can't say," Eulalie admitted, "but you girls have always been good at taking care of yourselves."

Anne-Marie swayed with exhaustion as she held the lamp closer to the bleeding wound. "I hope so, Eulalie. Abigail and Amelia are all I have."

An hour later Eulalie had carefully picked out three large pieces of shrapnel, each one plinking loudly in the enameled pan lying beside the table. As she probed the torn flesh Creed moaned, his teeth clenching as the point of the knife discovered yet another fragment. Each one that clinked into the pan made Anne-Marie feel more guilty as she watched the Crow's face turn pale as a ghost's. She was almost grateful when he dropped into unconsciousness again.

"Will he be all right?"

"For sure he's a might stronger than his friend there." Eulalie motioned to the black man stretched out cold beside the table.

As Eulalie bandaged Creed's thigh Anne-Marie tried to avoid looking at his exposed body.

Noting her guarded look, Eulalie chuckled, wickedly

amused by Anne-Marie's innocence. "I guess that look of yours tells me he really ain't your man."

"No, he was just kind enough to help me, and look at what I've done to repay him."

"He'll live; all he needs is a few days to mend. And from the looks of you, a rest wouldn't hurt you any, either. Let's get him into bed, then you try to get some sleep."

As Anne-Marie tried to move Creed he came to again, weakly pushing her away. "I can get to the bed on my own."

At the sound of a stranger's voice, the curious cats advanced on the table and stretched full length to get a look at the wounded man.

"Get away from him, you pesky critters," Eulalie grumbled. Clamping the short stub of a cigar between her lips, she lit it with a taper from the fireplace.

Between Eulalie and Anne-Marie, they got Creed off the table and dragged his body the few steps necessary to get him into the small cot in the corner of the cabin.

No sooner had they gotten him settled than they heard a moan coming from the man on the floor.

Quincy sat up, grasping his head with both hands. "What happened?"

"You fainted," Anne-Marie told him.

"Fainted?" Quincy hurriedly got to his feet. "No, ma'am, I didn't faint—I must've tripped over one of those cats, or something."

"That was probably it." Anne-Marie and Eulalie exchanged amused looks.

Quincy spotted Creed lying on the cot. "Is he going to be all right?"

"Eulalie says he'll be as good as new in a few days."

"That's good." He reached up gingerly to probe a knot the size of a goose egg forming on the side of his head. The blasted thing was throbbing like a sore tooth!

"It wouldn't hurt any of us to get some sleep," Eulalie said.

Quincy edged toward the front door. "Well, I'll just be going on out to the lean-to. If you need anything, I'll be close by."

Eulalie met his eyes, understanding passing between them. "It's not necessary for you to sleep with the horses. Plenty of room for all of us in here, where it's warm."

"Thank you, ma'am, but I'd be more comfortable sleeping in the lean-to." And he was certain it would smell better.

"Suit yourself, just wanted you to know you're welcome." Shuffling to the stove, Eulalie took the lid off a pot and inhaled the steamy contents. "Better have a bite to eat before you go. Mornin's a long way off."

Quincy's stomach rolled at the mental picture of Eulalie's gnarled old fingers probing Creed's bloody wound. "Thank you, ma'am, but if it's all the same to you, I'll be going now." Giving Anne-Marie a cursory nod, he strode quickly out the door, latching it behind him.

The shanty settled down for the night. Anne-Marie made herself a pallet beside the bed as Eulalie moved to the fire and lowered herself into her rocker with a jug of homemade brew tucked under her arm.

Anne-Marie had tasted some of the potent brew once. One swallow had nearly taken the top of her head off. Stretching out on the pallet, Anne-Marie closed her eyes, conscious of hunger pangs, but too tired to do anything about them.

Fatigue swiftly took her, and she drifted off with the smell of Eulalie's cigar surrounding her.

# Chapter 5

The sound of a rooster's crow shattered the cabin's sleepy silence. The boisterous cock-a-doodle-do was accompanied by a weak ray of sunlight struggling to penetrate the dirty windowpane.

Rolling to her side, Anne-Marie came awake slowly. Creed was sleeping now, having tossed and turned the better part of the night.

Eulalie was standing at the stove dishing out portions of cornmeal mush for the cats. The customary cigar dangled precariously from the right corner of her mouth as she stirred the bubbling mixture with a heavy wooden ladle.

"You must be hungrier than a polecat," she called when she saw Anne-Marie's eyes were opened.

"I am! Whatever you're cooking smells wonderful."

"Nothin' fancy, just plain old mush, but it'll keep starvation off your doorstep."

Getting up, Anne-Marie had to step over and around several cats and the raccoon as she crossed the room. The animals were scattered around, their heads buried in various bowls of food.

A tap sounded at the front door and Anne-Marie called out, "Come in, Quincy!"

Quincy appeared in the doorway, his coat dusted with light snow. "Morning, ladies."

"Mornin'," Anne-Marie and Eulalie called back.

"Snow about over?" Anne-Marie asked brightly.

"Yes, ma'am, seems to be tapering off." His dark eyes quickly moved to the cot in the corner. "How's he doing this morning?"

"He's quieter now." Eulalie motioned Quincy to have a seat at the rickety table. "Hope you like mush."

"Yes, ma'am, I do." Quincy sat down, and shortly thereafter Anne-Marie set a steaming cup of chicory in front of him.

"I hope you were warm enough in the lean-to."

"I slept just fine, ma'am."

Eulalie and Anne-Marie sat down, and the three ate in silence for a moment.

Spreading butter on her bread, Anne-Marie hesitantly broached the subject that worried her most right now. "What do you think we should do about those strong-boxes, Quincy?"

Keeping his eyes on his plate, Quincy said quietly, "I think we have to keep them, ma'am."

"You don't have to be so formal; you can call me Anne-Marie."

"Thank you, ma'am."

"You really think we should keep the strongboxes?" Anne-Marie took a bit of bread, chewing thoughtfully. "Wouldn't that make us thieves, though we took them by accident?"

"I suppose it would, but I don't see we have much choice but to keep them."

"How so?"

Quincy looked up, his dark eyes respectful. "Doesn't it seem coincidental to you that those two strongboxes were in that wagon?"

"No. The boxes could be the railroad payroll, and it was just being delivered to the bank."

"Could be, but I don't think so."

Anne-Marie sat up straighter, her eyes filled with interest. "Are you suggesting something funny is going on—like someone might have been transferring those boxes to their own wagon instead of delivering them?"

He shrugged, his tone remaining neutral. "I guess most anything's possible."

Anne-Marie looked at him, skepticism forming in her eyes. "Exactly why are you and Creed traveling together?"

The combination of an educated black man and Indian keeping company suddenly seemed suspect to her, unless there was an underlying motive, one the men had failed to mention.

Accepting another hunk of bread from Eulalie, Quincy busied himself buttering it.

"What were you and Creed doing when Creed rescued me?" she repeated.

"I think Creed should explain that, ma'am."

She studied him, trying to decide why he was being so evasive. "Friends, maybe?"

"Yes, ma'am." He glanced up, smiling. "We're that all right."

Her gaze narrowed on him again shrewdly. "Is it possible that you know something about that gold you're not telling me?"

Was that why he was choosing his answers so painstakingly?

"Ma'am, I guess when it comes right down to it, I don't know much of anything," he conceded humbly.

"Well." Anne-Marie sighed, biting into her bread. It was plain to see she wasn't going to get anything out of him. "I suppose Creed will know what to do about the strongboxes once he wakes up."

Quincy kept his eyes on his plate. "Yes, ma'am, I expect he will."

Anne-Marie watched as he ate the meager fare with appreciation. She was convinced he was hiding something from her. Turning back to Eulalie, she asked quietly. "Is it okay if we stay a few days—long enough for Creed to get back on his feet?"

"Stay as long as you want. Be happy to have the company."

Turning to Quincy, Anne-Marie tried to gauge his reaction to her suggestion. "Is that okay with you, Quincy? You don't have to be anywhere at any particular time?"

Now she had him. If he was up to something, he'd have to tell her or he wouldn't be able to finish whatever he was up to on time.

"That's fine with me, ma'am."

*Oh, he was smart,* she thought, he was smart, all right. If he and Creed were up to something, she'd never hear it from John Quincy Adams.

The morning seemed to be one of waiting. Eulalie waited on her baking, while Anne-Marie and Quincy waited on Creed's return to consciousness. Eulalie wondered if she'd baked enough bread for everyone and had put enough cinnamon in her apple pie; Anne-Marie wondered if Creed was really going to be all right and if Quincy was deliberately lying to her; and Quincy wondered what he and Creed were going to tell Anne-Marie when his friend finally did wake up.

It seemed the whole world waited on Creed Walker.

But Creed was locked in a world of his own, drifting between awareness and unconsciousness. In lucid moments he recognized the smell of cinnamon and baked apples, but that wasn't what Anne-Marie and the old woman were trying to force down his throat. As he obediently tried to swallow the bitter concoction, he was vaguely reminded of the time he became sick with the white man's fever and the medicine man had forced something equally vile through his parched lips.

Occasionally he could hear Anne-Marie voice aloud his own concerns.

"He seems so weak."

"He's as strong as an ox," a gravelly voice answered somewhere above him. He felt Anne-Marie's cool hand touch his face as the noxious brew was once again raised to his mouth.

"But will he live?"

Creed wanted to assure her that he would, but somehow he couldn't force the words from his throat.

"He'll make it," Eulalie confirmed as she lit yet another cigar, then took a healthy swig from the whiskey jug that was always near at hand.

If only the old crone would give him some of her whiskey. Creed's musings circled that thought and eventually came to rest upon Quincy. He could hear pounding in the background and could only surmise that Quincy was trying to repay the old woman for her generous hospitality.

Mercifully he once again passed into unconsciousness, his last thoughts being of beautiful emerald eyes.

By late afternoon Anne-Marie was tired of waiting. She decided the patient needed a good washing, if not for himself, then in respect for those around him. Although Eulalie wasn't enthusiastic about the idea—she couldn't remember when she herself had last had a bath—she agreed to help.

Armed with soap and hot water, the angels of mercy scrubbed, lathered, scoured, and powdered until they had the Indian, in Quincy's opinion, smelling like a girl. Quincy stood by helplessly, hoping to spare Creed this appalling exhibition of maternal clucking, but powerless to prevent it.

Afraid they might try to do the same to him, he quickly excused himself after supper and escaped to the shed.

As Eulalie settled down in the rocking chair Anne-Marie decided to read a book of poems by the popular poet Walt Whitman. She loved poetry; she'd even written one or two poems herself. When she asked Eulalie how she happened to have the volume *Leaves of Grass*, Eulalie said she couldn't remember where it'd come from, but Anne-Marie was welcome to read it if she liked.

As a gust of wind rattled the old shanty, Anne-Marie lost herself in Whitman's magic. The sound of a strangled snort would momentarily distract her, and she'd glanced up to see Eulalie's head starting to nod. Frowning, she noticed that the cigar in the corner of the old woman's mouth was bobbling, then tilting precariously in the corner until it was barely hanging by a spit thread.

Shaking her head, Anne-Marie returned to "Song of

Myself'' as the clock on the mantel methodically ticked away.

*Smoke.* Creed opened his eyes as the smell of smoke filled his nostrils. Coughing, he struggled to sit up.

Angry red-hot tendrils were licking a trail from floor to ceiling, hungrily devouring the dry timber. Heat, as intense as the bowels of hell, suffocated him as he blindly groped for the edge of the bed.

He tried to think. Where was he?

Rolling off the bed, he gritted his teeth as a white-hot pain shot up his leg. Through a blanket of smoke he dimly saw the old crone's lifeless form slumped forward in her chair, the roaring flames, like a pack of wild animals, greedily consuming her dress and hair.

He threw his arm up to shield his face from the scorching heat while his eyes searched the room. The flames were spreading, leaping across the dry timber, destroying everything that stood in their way.

"Quincy! Are you in here?" he shouted. His lungs burned, and his eyes blurred as he tried to make his way across the room.

"Over here." Anne-Marie's barely perceptible voice came to him over the sound of the roaring inferno.

"Where are you?"

"Over here, near the kitchen table."

"Get on the floor and crawl to me!"

Gasping for breath, Anne-Marie slid off her pallet and began to crawl on her hands and knees across the floor.

"Where are you?" Creed insisted.

"Where are you? I can't find you!" Panic tore at her as she unsteadily crawled her way across the room.

"Over here—here, take my hand!"

Anne-Marie struck blindly through the thick smoke, relieved when she felt a large hand latch onto hers in the reddish darkness.

"Where's Quincy?" Creed yelled.

"Outside—lean-to!"

Struggling across the floor, he half dragged, half pulled Anne-Marie along behind him.

The fire raged out of control. Like flaming arrows of destruction, rafters rained down on their heads as Creed and Anne-Marie tried to make their way outside.

"Eulalie!" Anne-Marie cried out. She struggled to break away to search for the old woman. "Where's Eulalie?"

Holding tight to her hand, Creed blindly felt his way across the room. When he finally located the door, he realized he didn't have the strength to reach the latch.

Rolling to his side, he kicked the door with his foot, and the panel gave way with a splintering sound. The flames gained new life as fresh air was sucked into the room.

Grabbing Anne-Marie around the waist, Creed rolled out onto the porch and down the steps onto the snow-covered ground.

Drawing in deep drafts of fresh air, together they staggered to their feet and began to scramble away, nearly falling over half a dozen cats in the process as they sought protection under a nearby tree.

Collapsing beneath the cedar, they fought for breath as they saw Quincy burst out of the lean-to, leading the frightened team of horses.

Moments later the roof of the cabin caved in, and the shanty was engulfed in a ball of fire.

"Eu-Eulalie," Anne-Marie sobbed.

"She's gone." Bracing his hands on his hips, Creed leaned forward as a spasm of coughing overcame him.

Anne-Marie stared at the cabin, which was rapidly being reduced to ashes and embers. "Gone?"

When the coughing spasm had passed, he leaned against the tree, trying to catch his breath. "I'm sorry, she was gone before the fire woke me up."

Anne-Marie couldn't believe Eulalie was gone.

Compassion shadowed Creed's face now. "Are you all right?"

Numb with grief, she nodded.

Reaching out, Creed briefly laid his hand on her shoulder. "Quincy needs help with the horses." He moved away, leaving her to stare at the raging inferno.

"What happened?" Quincy shouted as Creed limped toward him. Quincy's head snapped around as he took in his friend's appearance. The animals kept shying away from the fire, and he struggled to hold them while trying to keep his gaze off Creed.

"I woke up and the cabin was in flames."

Together, Quincy and Creed managed to move the team to safety.

When Creed returned, he found Anne-Marie still sitting on the ground, oblivious to the light covering of snow. She was unaware of the tiny raccoon who had taken refuge at the foot of the twisted cedar. Overhead, a hoot owl settled himself in the cedar branches, causing snow to rain down upon her.

Creed quietly knelt beside Anne-Marie, who continued to stare blindly at the fire. They watched in silence as the side walls collapsed and sent up yet another shower of sparks.

"I can't believe she's gone," Anne-Marie said softly.

"I'm sorry." If only the fire had awakened him earlier, he might have saved her; but as it was, there was nothing he could have done.

Anne-Marie turned to look at him, her eyes red from smoke and the misery she felt at her friend's death. "What happened?"

Wiping a sooty hand over his face, Creed winced when he realized blisters were beginning to form on his palms. "It's hard to say. The old woman must have had too much to drink and fallen asleep while she was smoking."

Fighting back tears, Anne-Marie wondered why she wanted to reach over and put her arms around his neck and comfort him. She'd made such a mess of things, and she knew he rued the day he had stopped to help her.

She watched as he knelt beside her, exhausted, his face and chest streaked with smoke, his hair slightly singed, his—

Suddenly a giggle bubbled in her throat, and she lost the will to smother it. Clasping both hands over her mouth, she giggled harder.

Her sudden giggles drew Creed's attention from the flaming ruins. "What in the hell are you laughing at?"

Not trusting her voice, she closed her eyes and took two deep breaths. How was she ever going to explain?

"You," she snickered.

"Me?" Creed failed to see how anyone could find anything funny about this hellish situation.

She giggled again, and once started, she couldn't stop. Leaning over, she buried her face in the smoky folds of her habit, grateful that she had decided to sleep in it.

"You!" she burst out, losing control again as her gaze swept him from head to foot.

Understanding finally dawned on his stoic features and panic seized him. With the exception of the bandage on his thigh, Creed Walker was buck naked.

Four men sat astride their horses overlooking the old crone's cabin. Scowling, Malpas clenched his *cigarillo* tightly between his yellowed teeth.

"We could be in real trouble, boss, if we don't get that buckboard of gold back," Ollie said.

Loyal Streeter didn't like it when things went wrong, and losing a hundred thousand dollars' worth of gold had put him in a real ugly mood.

Leather creaked as Malpas shifted in his saddle. "No worry. We find the *pendejos*." He squinted, his shifty eyes measuring the terrain. Malpas would find the gold; he was no fool.

Suddenly he sat up straighter.

The men's eyes followed the direction of the boss's gaze. "You got somethin', boss?"

"*Humo*, there, just over that rise."

The men could see a cloud of black smoke rising in the distance. "Ain't that Old Eulalie's shack?" someone asked.

The horses shifted, restless to be on their way.

"That *bruja loca*?" Rodrigo reverently crossed himself. "*No vamos* around *her casa*, are we, *jefe*?" There were some things he refused to do, and rummaging around a witch's house was one of them.

Malpas studied the cloud of smoke, all the time twirling the stub of his cigar around in the corner of his mouth.

"We go messin' around a witch's house and she could like as not put a curse on us." Ollie leaned over to spit a stream of tobacco juice on the ground. Straightening, he wiped his mouth with the back of his hand. "I don't much think we need a curse on us, bad as our luck's been lately," he muttered.

"I agree with Ollie," Butch said in low tones. "I don't think it'd be smart to snoop around that old woman's house. Besides, that nun and Indian wouldn't go there. What self-respectin' nun would be caught at a witch's house?"

"*SILENCIO!*" Malpas bellowed. He began kneeing his horse forward. "Are we *hombres* or are we *mujeres*? We investigate the *humo*."

Rolling his eyes, Rodrigo hurriedly made the sign of the cross, then resignedly cut his horse in behind Butch and Ollie's.

He didn't like this—not at all.

"This is the only thing we have to make you something to wear, so stop complaining." Anne-Marie spread the tarp out on the ground. "You're just lucky we were able to find your knife."

Frowning, Creed tested the honed blade against the canvas material.

"There's not much of it," Anne-Marie noted as she glanced at Quincy, trying to keep a straight face. It was obvious that Creed didn't find his situation as amusing as they did.

"I don't need much."

"If that's the case, I sure don't think I'd admit it."
Quincy chuckled.

"Mind your own business, Adams," Creed muttered, aware of his slip of the tongue.

By now Creed wasn't picky. He felt like a fool
marching around in the petticoat Anne-Marie had
laughingly loaned him. Every time she looked at him,
her face got rosy, and Quincy couldn't keep the smirk
off his face.

Dropping to her knees, Anne-Marie held the canvas
as Creed sketched out a rough pair of leggings and vest.
"You blame me for all the trouble, don't you?"

Creed didn't answer her as he worked the knife
through the canvas.

"You do, don't you?" she persisted.

"I don't blame you."

"I can't help it that your clothes were burned. Your
pants were ruined anyway when Eulalie had to cut them
away so she could pick the shot out of your thigh."

"Let's change the subject—and stop your damn
laughing, Adams. It's not funny."

Quincy winked at Anne-Marie. "He looks right
fetchin' in your petticoat, don't you think?"

"Yes—quite fetching," she agreed, then snickered
again.

Creed ignored them as he cut around the outline for
the leggings.

"As for me shooting you, it was purely accidental,"
Anne-Marie went on.

"So you say."

"It's the truth."

Creed sliced thin strips of the canvas to lace the leggings' seam together, all the while keeping his eyes on his work rather than on her earnest features.

"And I certainly didn't—"

"Enough!" Creed roared. If she said another word, he was going to cut her tongue out with the knife!

"Sorry."

"Well," Quincy announced, having had about enough of their verbal sparring. "I'm going to leave you two lovebirds alone while I see to the horses."

As he walked off, Anne-Marie settled back to watch Creed lace the canvas together. "How did you learn to do that?"

"I'm an Indian, remember?"

"Oh—are you really, now?" she countered.

There was no doubt about his heritage, but she knew there was more to Creed Walker than met the eye.

Creed looked up to study the remains of the smoldering cabin. "We'll have to bury the woman before we go."

Anne-Marie refused to look at the burning embers. It was still too painful to think that Eulalie had died in there. "I know."

Turning his back, Creed exchanged the petticoat for the breeches he had fashioned, and finished by lacing up the front and pulling the string tight. They weren't the best, but they would keep him covered and offer him some protection from the elements.

"They don't look so bad," Anne-Marie complimented as he handed her petticoat back.

"They'll do." Creed shivered as he slipped into the makeshift vest. With the dawn, the heavy layer of clouds had parted and the sun broke through. The timid rays held no warmth. A cold breeze whipped the limbs of the old cedar, a reminder that spring was not yet here.

"Quince and I will bury Eulalie. Someone's bound to have seen the smoke and eventually will come to investigate. We need to move on."

It took a few minutes for the men to locate a pick and shovel. Leaning against the base of the cedar, Creed took a deep breath, flinching as the throbbing pain in his thigh restricted his movements.

"I don't need help, I can bury her," Quincy said quietly.

The expression on Creed's face hardened as he ignored the wound. "It'll take both of us to get the job done. Anne-Marie, where do you want her buried?"

Anne-Marie had already thought about it. "There, by the stream. It was her favorite place."

The men located a soft spot and started digging the grave. Because of the wound, Creed's movements were slow and awkward. Using the remainder of the tarp, they wrapped Eulalie's body, then gently lowered it into the ground. When they were finished, Creed looked at Anne-Marie, waiting.

"What?" she asked.

"Don't you want to say something?"

Anne-Marie stared back at him. "Say something?"

"Yes, like a prayer or something."

"Oh, yes, a prayer." Taking a deep breath, she bowed her head. "Bless Eulalie. She was good, and nice—and loved animals." She glanced up. "You think that's enough?"

Creed looked at Quincy. Quincy would have preferred to quote from the book by Whitman that Anne-Marie had been reading earlier. *The mother of old, condemn'd for a witch, burnt with dry wood, her children gazing on . . .*

Clearing his throat, Quincy said brightly, "Never did like them long eulogies. I'll hitch the team." He walked off, leaving Creed and Anne-Marie alone.

"Well, now what?" Anne-Marie asked as they stared at the fresh mound of dirt.

"You're the one with all the ideas. What do you suggest?"

Anger flooded her cheeks. "I could suggest we each take a horse and go our separate ways—but we only have two horses—and the gold." The wind whipped her hair into her face and she angrily brushed it aside.

"Is that what you want?"

Anne-Marie thought about it for a moment and then decided no, that's not what she wanted. Right now Creed and Quincy were her best hope for getting back to Mercy Flats. Whether she liked Creed Walker or not, she was going to have to put up with him awhile longer.

"No, that's not what I want."

"Then don't tempt me." Pitching the shovel aside, Creed started limping toward the buckboard, where Quincy was busy hitching the team.

"Where are we going?" Anne-Marie called as she ran after him.

"Damned if I know."

She paused, shoving her hands on her hips. "Well, damned if I do, either!"

"You'd better watch your language as long as you're wearing that habit," he snapped without turning around.

"I'll talk any way I want—*damn, damn, damn*," she taunted.

He'd scalp her, but he didn't want her scalp hanging on his horse to remind him of her, he thought as he continued walking.

When he reached the wagon, he leaned against the wheel in order to shift the weight off his throbbing leg.

"What *are* we going to do?" she demanded as she caught up with him.

"With the gold?"

"For starters."

Creed and Quincy exchanged looks, and something meaningful passed between them.

"Why do you suppose two strongboxes from California, full of gold, were sitting in front of the bank with no guard?" Creed asked.

Quincy had asked her the same thing; she didn't know then, and she didn't know now. "I don't know. What do you suppose it meant?"

Creed's eyes moved back to Quincy. "The way I figure it, a gold shipment means guards, several guards. This particular shipment of gold was sitting there unguarded. Agreed, Quince?"

Quincy nodded. "That's how it looked to me."

"But the sheriff—" Anne-Marie interjected.

"—wasn't concerned about the gold," Creed interrupted. "He was working on the scaffolding."

"Well, maybe he didn't know about the gold and that's why he wasn't concerned about it."

Quincy and Creed exchanged looks again. "Maybe," Creed conceded, "but I think that's unlikely."

"Right now it doesn't make any difference if he knew about it or not," Quincy pointed out. "He thinks we stole it."

"And if they were going to hang us for stealing cattle, then they're bound to hang us for stealing gold, whether we meant to or not,'' Anne-Marie murmured with a sense of foreboding.

Creed and Quincy exchanged looks again.

''Maybe we could just explain what happened.''

''And how do you propose we do that?'' Quincy asked. ''We can't prance back into town, you in your nun's habit, Creed in his canvas trousers, and me in this dandified getup, and walk up to the sheriff and say, 'Sorry, Mr. Sheriff, we've done taken your gold by mistake.' ''

Creed checked his grin. ''That sounds like something she would do.''

Anne-Marie's eyes narrowed with resentment. ''It does not. My sisters and I have managed to pull off some pretty brilliant cons—''

''I noticed how brilliant the three of you looked screaming your pretty little heads off in that jail wagon,'' Creed noted sarcastically.

''There you go again, insinuating that if it wasn't for *me*, we wouldn't be in this—''

''I'm not insinuating anything, I'm telling you flat out, if it wasn't for you—''

''Look.'' Quincy threw up his hands, breaking up the heated exchange between them. ''Right now it doesn't mean a rat's ass who had the gold. *We've* got it now.''

''You mean we're going to keep it?'' she asked incredulously while turning to Creed for confirmation.

''Yes, we're going to keep it.''

Anne-Marie was surprised at the cold finality of his tone.

Turning on his heel, Creed slowly moved to the back of the wagon and started to hoist himself aboard.

Without thinking, Anne-Marie rushed to help him. "Here, you can't get up there alone."

"Woman, leave me alone!" he snapped.

"You are so *hateful*!"

"You make me hateful."

"I do not!"

Climbing on the wagon seat, Quincy picked up the reins. "And both of you are giving me a headache."

The buckboard had barely rolled out of sight when four riders topped the horizon. They were a scroungy quartet, two Mexicans and two *gringos*. They gazed down on the smoldering ruins of what once was Eulalie's ramshackle cabin, scowling.

"Looks like there's been a fire," Butch observed, none too brightly.

Turning slowly in his saddle, Malpas glared at him.

"Well, guess that settles it. The Injun, the nun, and the black ain't down there," Ollie said, relieved they wouldn't have to be stirring up a witch anytime soon.

Malpas turned back, his eyes focusing on the mound of fresh dirt located near the stream. "We no *sabe* for certain the *indio* hasn't been here."

Ollie, Rodrigo, and Butch passed a series of uneasy looks back and forth as they slowly rode toward the old crone's shack.

"What'd you suppose that is?" Ollie asked, pointing to the mound of dirt as they made their way to the lean-to.

"Looks like a grave to me," Butch observed.

Rodrigo crossed himself. That was exactly what he was afraid it was.

"Maybe *sí*." Malpas chewed the stub of the cigar absently. "Maybe no."

"Whose would it be? The old woman's? That'd be unlikely seeing as how she lived by herself, didn't she? She couldn't bury herself," Ollie said.

"She could have had friends," Butch said.

"That old crone? She didn't have no friends," Ollie scoffed.

Malpas stood up in the stirrups, suddenly spotting the set of wagon tracks leading away from the shanty. "Someone been here." He kneed his horse forward.

Rolling his eyes, Rodrigo made the sign of the cross once again as he reined in behind the other three men.

The riders approached the smoldering ruins with caution. Climbing off their horses, they stood for a moment, assessing the situation. The place was deader than a *cementerio*.

Malpas started toward the mound, motioning for the others to follow him. Slowly they made their way across the intervening space until they, too, gazed upon the grave.

Pointing to the freshly turned soil, Malpas grunted. "Dig."

Butch visibly paled beneath his two-day growth of beard. "I ain't got the stomach for this sort of thing, boss. Ollie'll have to do it."

Ollie stepped back like a snake had bitten him. "Uh-uh, not me. Boss, I ain't gonna mess with no grave."

The men's eyes turned on Rodrigo, who by now was trying his best to look inconspicuous.

Malpas extended the shovel he had found thrown next

to a gnarled cedar, the menacing glint in his eyes making it clear to his fellow countryman that he had just been unanimously elected for the dirty job of seeing what was buried beneath the pile of dirt.

Groaning, Rodrigo said a fast Hail Mary before accepting the shovel.

The men stood back as he lifted the first shovelful of dirt. The sound of metal hitting rock grated on Ollie's nerves as he gradually faded into the background.

The Mexican dug for over several minutes before he struck the tarp with the tip of the shovel.

Malpas's eyes lit up with excitement. *Caramba!* The gold had been covered by a tarp! Could it be the *indio* and the *monja* had buried the *oro*, planning to come back for it later? Ah, *sí*, but it would take someone smarter than an *indio* to trick Malpas!

"Faster, Rodrigo! Dig faster. *Purate!*" Malpas shouted.

Curious because of all the excitement, Ollie moved in closer. "What is it, boss? Is it the gold?" He peered inquisitively into the open grave.

"*Sí, sí.*" Malpas grinned. A man would have to get up *muy* early in the morning to outsmart a man with Malpas's intellect!

Butch hopped into the hole to help Rodrigo wrestle the piece of heavy canvas.

Malpas leaned closer, his eyes alight with greed.

"Don't feel heavy enough to be gold," Butch said as he and Rodrigo's hands eagerly tore at the canvas.

Rodrigo suddenly paused. "Do you smell something funny, *Señor* Butch?"

Butch paused, getting a good whiff of the odor Rodrigo referred to. ''Yeah, now that you mention it, I do. Smells kinda like—''

His movements slowed as he identified the stench as one of burned flesh and coagulated blood.

''Do not stop now!'' Malpas shouted. ''Uncover the *oro*!''

As Eulalie's corpse rolled out of the tarp Rodrigo jumped back, gagging.

Whirling, Butch clamped his hand over his mouth to contain the bile that suddenly sprang up in his throat.

*''CARAJO!''* Malpas quickly averted his head. The gruesome sight brought back memories of the time he had worked in a slaughterhouse in Kansas City.

Tears smarted his eyes as he hurried away, his squat legs efficiently covering the ground as he tried to block out the sounds of Rodrigo and Butch's strangled heaves coming from the gaping hole.

His dark eyes narrowed with contempt. The *indio*, the *negro*, and the *monja* would pay for making Malpas look the *estúpido*.

They would pay!

# Chapter 6

"I'm worried." Anne-Marie indeed looked worried as she turned from checking on Creed again. He had slept since they'd left Eulalie's, and she had barely been able to rouse him throughout the day. "His fever's come up."

"I'm not surprised." The buckboard rattled along the rutted road as Quincy kept a close eye out for Southern patrols.

"He needs proper food and warmth."

"I know."

Huddling deeper inside her habit, Anne-Marie watched the passing scenery. Dirty patches of snow littered the hillsides, but the sun made the temperature bearable.

A back wheel hit a pothole, roughly jostling Creed. Upon hearing his groan, Anne-Marie quickly turned around, shooting Quincy a censuring look as she did so.

"Be careful!"

"I am, ma'am, I am."

For someone who claimed not to like somebody, it

sure seemed to Quincy that she was suddenly awful protective of Creed's well-being.

Turning back around, she poked her hands up the sleeves of her habit and tried to keep warm. "It wouldn't do us any harm to have a nice meal and a warm bed, either, you know."

"No, ma'am, it wouldn't."

"You have any ideas?" They couldn't just wander the countryside like Gypsies. They had no food, no clothing, no shelter, and it would be dark before long.

"I've been thinking . . . there's an old mission about twenty miles from here. We could hole up there until Creed's leg is better."

"Twenty miles?" She frowned. "It'll be dark soon."

"Yes, ma'am, but I figure we'll take shelter in some rancher's barn tonight, then start out first thing in the morning. There's always eggs lying around for the taking. We'll be warm and fed, and then with a little luck, we'll reach the mission by late tomorrow afternoon."

Anne-Marie turned to look over her shoulder at Creed again. "I don't know, Quincy, he needs care, and soon."

"Yes, ma'am, but I don't know what else . . ." Quincy's voice faded as the buckboard rounded a bend, and they found two Indians sitting astride war ponies in the middle of the road.

"Oh Lordy," Quincy murmured. "Hello, Trouble."

Anne-Marie sat up straighter as Quincy set the brake on the wagon. The old buckboard clattered to a halt a few feet in front of the war ponies.

The Indians, dressed in war paint, looked down on them evilly, their eyes traveling slowly over the black and the nun.

"Do you suppose they understand English?" Anne-Marie whispered.

"The way our luck's been running? No, ma'am, not a word."

The four sat in the middle of the road, sizing each other up.

Finally one of the Indians broke away, kneeing his horse to the back of the wagon. Anne-Marie closed her eyes as he slowed, peering into the wagon bed.

"O Lordy, Lordy, Lordy," Quincy agonized in a low whisper. "If you got any pull with the Man upstairs, now might be a good time to use it."

Anne-Marie didn't have any pull; chances were, the Man upstairs was pretty put out with her by now.

The Indian suddenly shouted in a tense, guttural voice to the second Indian.

Surprise flickered briefly across the warrior's features. Cutting his horse around the wagon, he joined his companion. The two men gestured at Creed as they conversed in animated, hushed tones.

"What are they saying?" Anne-Marie wanted to turn around and look, but she was too scared to move a muscle.

"I don't think we want to know."

A moment later one of the Indians trotted back to the front of the wagon and leaned over to grab the horse's bridle.

"Oh, Lord have mercy," Quincy groaned as the Indian started leading the team down the road.

They weren't going to get out of this one alive.

As the buckboard was pulled into camp a crowd gathered. Anne-Marie had never seen so many Indians: men, women, children, and all peering at her curiously.

The lead warrior shouted orders, and two young braves scattered to various tents. The women crowded closer, some touching Anne-Marie's habit, their eyes bright with inquisitiveness.

Anne-Marie's heart raced when she realized that without Creed's protection, she and Quincy were at the mercy of these savages.

As the buckboard rolled to a stop Bold Eagle, war chief of the Cheyenne band, stepped from his tent to view the spectacle. Parting the crowd, he made his way to the back of the buckboard to get a better look at the cause of all the commotion. His expression went from disbelief to immediate pleasure as he recognized his blood brother Storm Rider. His eyes grew troubled when he saw the blood-soaked bandage around Creed's right thigh.

Issuing a harsh command, he motioned for help. The flap of a tepee parted to reveal a startlingly beautiful girl with doelike brown eyes. Berry Woman, which was the girl's name, walked quickly to the wagon to peer down at the man's unconscious form. Excitement flooded her features as Creed's Cheyenne name, Storm Rider, softly escaped her lips. Leaning over, she gently touched his face.

His eyes opened, and he smiled at her.

Anne-Marie watched the exchange, surprised to feel a trace of envy. As Creed gazed at the young woman Anne-Marie could almost see something akin to love reflected in his eyes before they slowly closed again.

Bold Eagle spoke, and two braves stepped forward to lift Anne-Marie from the wagon. Without ceremony, she was taken to a colorful tepee sitting in the center of the camp. She watched helplessly as Quincy was led to a tent on the opposite side of the circle.

The two warriors loaded Creed onto a travois as the young girl hovered near his side. Slowly they made their way to the medicine man's tent.

It was over an hour before anyone returned to Anne-Marie's tepee. During that time she had sat huddled around the fire, feeling no particular sense of fear. Obviously Creed was acquainted with the Cheyenne band, and if they were going to harm her, they would have already done so.

Her thoughts returned to the way Creed had looked at the young Indian maiden. She'd hated the way her stomach had cramped up when he had looked at the girl. Obviously he knew *her* well enough.

The flap on the tepee parted and Berry Woman entered, carrying a wooden bowl of stew. Although Anne-Marie was famished, she was more concerned about Creed.

"How is he?" she inquired anxiously.

The maiden's eyes met hers coolly. "You need not concern yourself with Storm Rider. I will see that he is cared for."

"You speak English?"

"If necessary." Something in her tone told Anne-Marie that they were not destined to become friends.

Berry Woman turned to leave, then apparently changed her mind. "How was Storm Rider injured?"

"I shot him . . . accidentally."

The girl's eyes grew more opaque. "You shot the man who will be my husband?"

*"Husband?"* Was there no end to the surprises concerning Creed Walker?

"We have been promised to one another."

"Since when?" Anne-Marie didn't know why she had this sudden urge to rip the woman's hair out, strand by agonizing strand, but it was all she could do to control the impulse.

"That is not important. The arrangement is sealed, so if you have intentions concerning Storm Rider, you would do well to forget them."

Anne-Marie didn't believe her. In fact, she didn't believe anything that had happened to her during the last few days. Everything that could go wrong had done so. Now she was in some Indian camp being told to keep her hands off Creed, and she wasn't sure she liked it—not that she particularly wanted her hands *on* Creed, but she didn't like having this woman tell her she couldn't.

"You . . . and Creed," she clarified, just to make sure she understood.

"Storm Rider and I. And since he is soon to be my husband, his welfare is my concern, not yours. You will content yourself with things other than my man."

"I see." Taking a deep breath, Anne-Marie resolved to control her temper. For all she knew, the girl was telling the truth—though it seemed awfully coincidental to her that she and Quincy had just happened to run into this particular tribe—or was it merely another example of her recent foul luck?

"It is wise that you do understand."

"Listen . . ." Anne-Marie searched for a name.

"I am called Berry Woman."

"Well, Berry, my only concern is Creed's well-being.

Once he's out of danger, you're welcome to him. Believe me, I have no designs on your future husband, but I do need to talk to him, if you have no objections." After all, she had her own welfare to be concerned about.

Berry Woman hesitated, considering whether or not to trust her. "Perhaps tomorrow. When his wound has been treated and he has rested."

The two measured each other warily.

"I suppose I have no other choice?"

"That is correct."

"Then I guess I'll wait."

"Yes."

"If you don't mind, I'd like my privacy," Anne-Marie flatly stated in a tone of dismissal.

Berry Woman lowered her head submissively. "As you wish."

She exited, leaving Anne-Marie to wonder where it would all end.


Malpas was furious, and getting madder by the minute. His swarthy features were molten with anger.

Pacing angrily beside his horse, he thought about the predicament he was in. He had to find that gold, and pronto. They'd been following the buckboard tracks for hours and they were getting nowhere! Either that Injun, black, and nun didn't know where they were going or they were taking the long way getting there!

"They no fly like *pájaros*! You no look *muy bueno*!"

"We have so! We've spread like bad news and covered every inch of their trail, but they is wily, Malpas, just plain wily!" Ollie said crossly.

"Weren't our fault," Butch declared sullenly. "The truth is we've just plain lost 'em."

"How the *infierno* can we lose a *negro*, a *monja, y un indio*!"

The men hung their heads and waited till the emotional front blew over. When the boss got in one of his moods, there was nothing to do but shut up and ride it out.

Malpas had met up with some stupid people in his life, but Ollie, Butch, and Rodrigo were just plain idiots. He glanced up to study the worsening weather. "They no go far, not in this *tiempo*. They are here somewhere, *yo se*."

"Maybe they found somebody to help 'em," Ollie volunteered.

Malpas's eyes narrowed. He didn't know of *anyone* who'd help an *indio*.

The men viewed each other with uncertainty.

"Well, what do we do now?"

"What we do *ahora*?" Malpas mocked. "*Madre de Dios!* We look *mas*!"

At least one of them had a brain!

"What do you suppose Walker's doing with a nun?" Butch mused. "Last I heard, he had joined up with the North."

"*Pues*, how the *infierno* am I to know what he do with a *monja*?" Climbing back in the saddle, Malpas spat his cigar on the ground. "There's a band of Cheyenne camped out *no muy lejos de aquí*, no far from here. Maybe Walker *y la mujer* is holin' up there."

Butch, for one, wasn't real crazy about the idea of snooping around a Cheyenne camp. That could be risky business. Real risky. "We could get ourselves scalped poking our noses in them Indians' business,'' he complained. They hadn't listened to him about the old witch, but they'd better listen to him now if they knew what was good for them.

"*Nadie* gonna get scalped,'' Malpas snapped. "We ride *muy inocente* over that *dirección* and wait to see who come and go. If Walker and *la mujer* is there, they got to leave sometime, no? No hole up *por siempre*.'' As he smiled his silver tooth glistened like armor in the sunlight. "And *cuando* they do, *los saludamos*, we greet them.''

"What if they don't come out?'' Butch asked.

"Yeah, what if they ain't even in there to begin with? We could lose time just sitting there waitin' like a bunch of fools,'' Ollie said.

Malpas exploded. "*Caray!* If they are there, they come out sometime!''

"If he don't, the woman will.'' Rodrigo entered the fracas when he saw Malpas was running on a short fuse. "And when she does, we grab her.''

"What about the black?''

"We no give a *comino* about the *negro*,'' Malpas snarled. "*Por supuesto* he long gone by now.''

"What about the gold?'' Ollie knew they did give a *comino* about that. "You think Walker and the woman's still got it with 'em?''

Wedging a cigar between his teeth, Malpas struck a match on his thumbnail. "*Lo tienen* all right. *El indio* wouldn't be *estúpido* enough to let it out of his sight.'' He swore again as the sulfur flared, searing his thumbnail good before he could get loose from it.

"And if they don't have the gold, we use the woman as bait to get the Indian to tell us where it is,'' Butch decided. "Once we get the gold back, we leave the nun for the buzzards."

"Well . . ." Ollie was mean, but mean enough to leave a nun for buzzard fodder? He'd have to give that some thought.

Sucking on his blistered thumb, Malpas growled. "*Silencio!* Find that *monja y indio!*"

Reining his horse hard, Malpas spurred the buckskin and galloped off in the direction of the Cheyenne camp.

Butch, Ollie, and Rodrigo looked at one another, shrugged, then rode after him.

The Cheyenne encampment was larger than Anne-Marie had first thought. Situated in a circle of tepees, it spread out in a large clearing in the center of the camp.

Her tepee was smaller than those around it. It was made from many hides. And on those hides were symbols that seemed to tell a story, but she didn't have the slightest idea what they meant.

She slept fitfully throughout that first night. Creed's image appeared in her dreams and disturbed her sleep. Who was this strange man who had entered her life and turned it virtually upside down? Was he pledged to Berry Woman, or was he, as she suspected, a man in control of his own destiny?

When morning dawned, Berry Woman returned.

"Whose tent is this?" Anne-Marie asked as the young girl entered the tepee.

"It belongs to no one. It is provided for visitors. Bold Eagle wishes you to have a bear skin and blanket to sleep on. Walks in Morning will bring your food."

"How is Creed this morning?"

"As I have said, you need not be concerned about Storm Rider."

"But I am; he saved my life—twice."

Pride showed in Berry Woman's eyes. "Storm Rider is an honorable man."

Hoping to gain the girl's confidence, Anne-Marie switched subjects. "How is it that you speak English so well?"

The young girl began to move around the tent, searching for just the right place to put Anne-Marie's bed. "Creed taught me when he and Bold Eagle became blood brothers."

"When did Creed and Bold Eagle become blood brothers?"

"When Bold Eagle was attacked by a band of marauding Apaches, my brother sought refuge in the fort where Creed was living with Father Jacob. Together, Creed and Bold Eagle rode to avenge my brother's enemies."

"Bold Eagle is your brother?"

The young woman nodded.

"How long ago was this?"

"Many moons ago. About five of your years."

So Creed had spent part of his life at a fort among white men, Anne-Marie mused silently. "How is it that Creed speaks such good English?" That question had been plaguing her from the moment he had spoken to her in flawless English.

"When he lived at Fort Walters, Father Jacob taught him English. He learned everything—reading, writing, history. There are many among the Cheyenne who are willing to learn the white man's ways." Her eyes lowered as she continued, "Though Creed and I prefer the ways of our fathers. When we are one, we will live among our own people."

When she'd finished making the bed, she straightened and turned back to face Anne-Marie. "You will rest, then we will talk again, soon."

"If I can't see Creed, I want to speak to Quincy."

"You speak of the dark-skinned one?"

"Yes, I want to see him."

"I will speak to my brother." Berry Woman reached for the pail of water sitting by the door. "Your pail is nearly empty. I will bring you fresh water from the spring."

She left, dropping the flap back into place behind her. Apparently courtesy demanded that she provide a bed and food, even to those she disliked.

As Anne-Marie turned back to the fire she heard a hushed but heated exchange break out between Berry Woman and someone else.

A moment later Walks in Morning entered the tepee carrying a steaming bowl, which she sullenly extended to Anne-Marie. Turning on her heel, she left as quickly as she'd entered.

Sitting down on the pallet, Anne-Marie began to eat. The stew was much spicier than that of the night before. It made her eyes water and her nose run, but she continued eating, aware that she had to keep her strength up. When the bowl was empty, she fanned her mouth, muttering when she realized Berry Woman had not returned with her water.

Stretching out on the pallet Berry Woman had prepared, she nestled deeper into the furry softness and slept.

It was late afternoon when she awoke. Shadows filtered through the tent top, and she could hear the sound of the hunters returning to camp. She lay for a moment, idly scratching her arm. Her mouth still tingled from the wretched stew.

Rolling to her side, she scratched at her neck, then again on her shoulder. Before she knew it, she was itching all over. Springing to her feet, she slapped at her clothes, finally realizing that something was terribly wrong.

She stripped out of the habit, her temper flaring when she saw red ants running in a wild frenzy throughout the material.

Muttering an oath, she jerked the pallet aside, confirming her worst suspicion. Berry Woman had made the pallet over an anthill, the inhabitants of which were now angrily crawling over and through both the bear skin and blanket as well as every stitch of her habit.

"Very funny, Berry Woman!" Anne-Marie muttered, angrily shaking the ants out of the soiled habit.

She pitched the bedding outside the tepee, then, not certain the ants had vacated the habit, she hung it over a knot on a tepee pole. It dawned on her that the stew she'd eaten hadn't been merely spicy; Berry Woman had laced it with hot peppers then deliberately forgotten to return her water pail!

For the first time in her life Anne-Marie realized what it was like to be truly alone.

By the time Berry Woman returned, she had had enough. "I *want* to see Creed," she demanded.

"Storm Rider is ill and cannot be disturbed."

"If I can't see Creed, then I demand that you let me leave!"

Smiling, Berry Woman lowered her head submissively. "If that is your wish."

"You will arrange for a horse and enough food and water to last me for two days."

"If that is your wish."

"That is my wish."

The girl left quickly to make the proper arrangements.

"Well, this is just dandy," Anne-Marie fumed as she dressed. Now what had she let herself in for? There was no way she was going to stay here and be mistreated by a jealous lover.

Pacing, she tried to formulate a plan. With a good horse and the proper provisions, she would be able to make it on her own. All she had to do was find a town that had a stage or a train. It couldn't be that hard, but she'd need money. The gold.

There were two strongboxes sitting on the buckboard *full* of gold. There was so much gold that one or two coins would never be missed.

But where was the buckboard? With Quincy?

Stepping to the flap of the tepee, she looked out. Activity outside the tent was slow. A squaw stood at the fire stirring a large pot while several children played rowdily around her feet.

As the children shrieked with delight Anne-Marie quickly ducked out of her tent and darted across the clearing.

Quincy looked up, his eyes enlarging as she burst into his tent. "Quick, where's the gold?" she blurted breathlessly.

Quincy sprang to his feet. "What are you doing here?"

"I haven't got time to argue, Quincy, Berry Woman is arranging a horse for me. You can do what you want, but I'm leaving, and I need money."

"Leaving? Why would Berry Woman be getting you a horse?" He tried to make sense of what she was saying, but she was talking so fast he couldn't understand a word.

"Because she hates me."

She wasn't making a lick of sense. "You can't leave here by yourself!"

"Oh, yes I can—you watch me." She stepped back to the tent flap, looking out.

"Don't be a fool, girl! You don't know this area, and what with the war going on, you could run into all kinds of trouble wandering around out there alone."

"Well, I can't stay here and sleep on ants and eat pepper stew."

"What?"

"Never mind. Where's the gold, Quincy? I need enough to get me back to Mercy Flats."

He stiffened. "You can't take *any* of that gold!"

Dropping the flap back into place, she whirled to confront him. "Why not? You're acting like it's yours when all three of us took it!"

"Well, it *is* mine—in a way!" He realized he'd said too much, and his eyes snapped back to the fire. He hoped she wouldn't press him on the subject.

"Yours?" As she walked slowly toward him her eyes menacingly pinpointed him. "What is going on, Quincy Adams—and don't tell me you don't know, because you obviously know more about that gold than you've led me to believe!"

"Oh Lord," Quincy groaned. This was a nightmare!

She continued to descend upon him ominously. "Are you going to tell me, or am I going to have to squeeze it out of you—which, I warn you, I can do—and you're going to hate every agonizing minute of it, John Quincy Adams." Pausing in front of him, she gathered his shirt collar in her hands and squeezed until the blood rushed to his face. "Start talking, Mr. Adams. I'm a real good listener."

"You're choking me," he wheezed.

"I mean to, Mr. Adams." She tightened her grip.

This woman was mean—just plain *mean*, Quincy thought.

"All right, *all right*!" He finally gave in.

Anne-Marie loosened her hold, but not much. "What is going on with that gold?"

Glancing about uneasily, he lowered his voice. "You got to promise to keep quiet about this."

"About what?"

"About what I'm about to tell you!"

"All right, I promise."

"Oh Lord—Creed and I are working for the Union Army."

"Working for the Union Army? You mean you're both mean, low-down, rotten federal *spies*?"

"No, ma'am, we're paid agents. We was on our way to intercept that shipment of gold when Creed decided to ride to your rescue."

Anne-Marie was astounded. "You and Creed *knew* about that gold?"

Quincy rubbed his tender neck. "We knew the gold was going to be used by someone in Streeter to further the Confederate cause. What we didn't *know* was that it would be on that wagon we stole."

"*Who*'s using it to further the Confederate cause?"

"That we don't know."

She jerked him by the collar again.

"Honest, I don't! Ma'am, if you don't stop this, I won't be able to speak, ever again!"

Releasing her hold, she turned and started to pace. "Then what was the gold doing on that buckboard? Was it just being delivered?"

"We don't know. Creed and I were just as surprised to see those two strongboxes on that buckboard as you were."

"Well, this is just plain crazy! Where did you get this information?"

"We have our ways, I can assure you, ma'am."

"So that's why you and Creed are so intent on keeping the gold."

"We have to keep it. It's the reason we're here in the first place."

"But where does that leave me? I don't have any loyalty to the North, but I'm risking my neck for that gold the same as you and Creed."

"Creed and I feel bad that you're involved in this, but the gold stays put."

"But I have to have money or I can't get back to Mercy Flats!"

"I'm sorry. . . . I want to help, but my hands are tied."

Her heart sank. What was she to do now?

"Anne-Marie," Quincy coaxed, "if you'll be patient, Creed will see that you're returned to your sisters, unharmed. Once he—"

"Creed doesn't care a whit about me."

"You're wrong; Creed takes his responsibilities seriously, and right now you're one of his responsibilities.''

"Yes, and that's *all* I am—a big responsibility that he doesn't want.''

Quincy looked away. "I can't let you leave. Whether you like it or not, we're in this together. Once Creed is better . . .''

His voice trailed off as Anne-Marie spun on her heel and ran out of the tent. "Ma'am, you sure do try a man's patience,'' he muttered as he watched her go. "You sure enough do.''

# Chapter 7

"It is good to see you, my brother. Many moons have passed since we spoke." Sitting down beside Storm Rider, Bold Eagle lit the sacred pipe stone. Outside, a heavy wind buffeted the sides of the tepee.

"It has been much too long, my brother. My duties with the bluecoats have kept me busy. I apologize for not visiting my brother and his family sooner."

Smoke from Bold Eagle's pipe spiraled up in soft wisps through the darkening shadows of the smoke hole. "It is said you work hard for the white man's cause."

"What is said is true."

A twig snapped, sending a shower of sparks through the blackness. "This is wise?"

"It is what I believe, or I would not risk my life for this cause."

Bold Eagle closed his eyes, savoring the taste of the kinnikinnick. "Bold Eagle does not understand why brother fights against brother."

"It is not a matter of brother fighting against brother. The issue is that of a man buying and selling another man."

"I do not understand this way. Explain it to me."

"A man has the right to freedom, no matter what color his skin. This is the cause for which I fight, to bring freedom to all men."

Bold Eagle could not comprehend Storm Rider's thoughts. The white man fought and died for the black man, but he took food, water, and land from the red man without a care.

"The woman? Where is she?" Creed suddenly inquired, his thoughts turning to Anne-Marie.

"She is well."

Creed relaxed as the numbing effects of the sweet sage smoke and potent medicinal herbs flowed through him. "And Quincy?"

"John Quincy Adams?" Bold Eagle smiled. "He, too, is well, my brother."

Creed shifted his leg and felt a stab of pain in his thigh. Although the wound was healing, it would be several weeks before it became a memory. Passing the pipe to Bold Eagle, he acknowledged, "If your warriors had not come upon Anne-Marie and Quincy when they did, I would not want to think what would have happened. I am in your debt, Bold Eagle."

"There is no debt among brothers." Smoke continued to filter up into the shadows as the wind whistled through the bare tree branches.

It was a long moment before Bold Eagle again broke the silence. "There are men, four of them, outside the camp. They arrived the same sun, shortly after you were brought here."

Closing his eyes, Creed eased his injured leg to a more comfortable position. "That would be the posse from Streeter."

"You know of these men?"

"I recognize one of them. A Mexican they call Malpas."

"These men, they are Storm Rider's enemies?"

"Yes."

Drawing on the pipe, Bold Eagle stared into the fire. He knew of such enemies. Storm Rider had once helped Bold Eagle avenge his honor; now Bold Eagle would do whatever was needed to help Storm Rider.

"The men will not enter the camp. Of this I am certain."

"The woman shouldn't leave," Creed murmured as the medicine drew him deeper into unconsciousness. "The Mexican . . . after her .. too dangerous . . ."

"Rest, my brother."

Bold Eagle sat beside Storm Rider, the smoke drifting quietly in the stillness. This woman of the black cloth—who was she, and of what importance was she to Storm Rider?

Bold Eagle did not leave his brother's side until the fire burned low and the kinnikinnick was consumed.


Malpas stamped his feet, trying to force feeling back into his frozen limbs.

Cold wind whistled down the collar of his coat as his eyes darted back and forth, trying to ferret out any movement in the Cheyenne camp. He had been standing here for hours, taking his turn on watch; however, the Injun and the nun were still nowhere in sight. But they could not fool Malpas; he knew they were in there.

His eyes filled with resentment as he studied the circle of tepees. They were in there all right. Buckboard tracks had led straight to the Injun camp, and they could not leave without Malpas seeing them.

Ollie hunched deeper into his sheep-lined parka as he approached to relieve Malpas. The wind tore at the brim of his hat, threatening to snatch it off his head. "See anything, boss?"

"No, *nadie.*"

Squinting, Ollie viewed the camp. "What you think's going on?"

"*Le digo,* I tell you what is going on. I is freezing my *cojones* off," Malpas grumbled.

"Yeah," Ollie admitted. He knew the feeling.

"We ain't jest gonna sit here all night, are we, boss?" Butch's breath made a frosty vapor in the frigid air as he knelt beside the fire, trying to keep it going in the high wind.

"*Sí,* we sit here all night," Malpas mimicked. His eyes narrowed sharply. Their enemies couldn't stay in that camp forever; they had to come out sometime.

"We could always go in after them."

Ollie and Malpas turned to look at Butch as if he'd lost his mind.

"Them's Cheyenne *warriors,* Butch," Ollie reminded, in case Butch hadn't noticed. "A man don't just go sashayin' into a Cheyenne warriors' camp without a damn good reason."

"Yeah." Butch glanced sheepishly back to the fire. "Don't guess that would be real bright."

"Only if you grow weary of your *cuero cabelludo*—how do you say it?—scalp." Malpas grunted.

The men didn't appear to take to the thought.

Ollie's eyes returned to the tepees. "You see the buckboard anywhere?"

"*Sí*, near the large *xipi* in *el centro*."

Ollie clasped his hat to his head as he strained to see around the boss's shoulder. "Is the gold still in it?"

"I do not have eyes like the *puma*!"

They turned as they heard Rodrigo jump back, swearing as a violent gust of wind shot a shower of sparks up the back of his coat. Cursing, he hopped around the campsite, blindly slapping at his back.

Butch finally stepped over to help. "Ah, you've done gone and burned a hole in your coat, *amigo*," he chided as he extinguished the smoldering embers with his gloved hand.

Rodrigo glared at him. "Mind your own business, *gringo*."

Butch threw up his hands in resigned tolerance. "All right, all right, I was just a tryin' to help."

Ordinarily Butch wouldn't let a man talk to him like that, but the Mexican still looked a might peaked around the gills from unearthing the old witch.

"*Quitese* your bickerin'," Malpas snapped. "We 'ave a long night in front of us."

Ollie threw more wood on the fire as the three men hunkered down, prepared to wait out the Indian and the nun, however long it took.

All four hoped it didn't take long.

Morning dawned, cold and dreary. Elk Woman was assisting Creed when Berry Woman entered the tent.

"How is he this morning?" she asked in Cheyenne.

"He is stronger," the old woman said.

Kneeling beside the pallet, Berry Woman gazed at the man who had stolen her heart when she had lived but twelve summers. Creed Walker had ridden into the camp beside her brother, Bold Eagle, and had remained among her people, teaching them the ways of the white man. She had fallen deeply in love with him while she waited to become a woman. He was wise and strong, and an ample provider, having killed more buffalo than all the seasoned warriors combined. Every young maiden in camp had envied Berry Woman because it was with her that Storm Rider spent his leisure hours.

When the white men went to war, Storm Rider had ridden off to fight on the side of the bluecoats. Berry Woman had never clearly understood why, but she had accepted his absence without question; for she had intuitively known, just as Heammawihio had promised, that one day she and Storm Rider would be one.

A smile softened the corners of her lips at the thought of the time when the war would be over and Storm Rider would return to claim her as his true love.

He would ride into camp, long locks flying in the breeze, a single eagle feather braided in his flowing hair; his bronze chest bare except for the necklace of eagle bones; his splendid form encased in the finest deerskin breeches; and his dark obsidian eyes would boldly search hers and claim them for his own.

Storm Rider and Bold Eagle would come to a proper agreement, and a wedding feast would be scheduled. It would be such a glorious time. . . . Berry Woman's smile grew tender when she saw that Storm Rider was trying to open his eyes.

"Hello," she said softly.

As his vision cleared Creed saw Berry Woman bending over him, her smile as soft and welcome as a summer shower. He tentatively moved his leg, relieved to find the pain was no longer sharp and penetrating. As he struggled to sit up he found himself being lowered gently back to the pallet.

"No, you must rest. It is too soon," she scolded.

"Quincy—the gold . . . need to leave . . ."

Berry Woman frowned as she always did when he spoke of leaving. "Why can you not stay the summer with our people? Why must you always leave?" She had asked the question many times since the war began, and his answer was always the same.

"When the war is over, I will stay for a while."

"But you are ill and cannot travel."

"I have many responsibilities."

Impatience flared in the young woman's eyes. "The Crow is responsible only to the Crow."

"The woman has sisters waiting her return. I must leave."

Berry Woman did not like this green-eyed woman Storm Rider had allowed into camp. He was her only concern, and she didn't want him to leave, not now, not so soon. They had had no time alone, to talk, to plan for their wedding day.

"Why cannot the black man assume the woman's care?"

"It isn't easy to explain. I unintentionally assumed responsibility for her welfare, and she expects me to see her safely reunited with her family."

Berry Woman's jaw firmed stubbornly. "I do not understand this."

"There's nothing to understand. The woman is not your concern."

"But—"

"Enough." Storm Rider spoke with the voice of authority now.

The young woman's eyes lowered submissively. "Forgive me, Storm Rider. I will speak of this matter no more."

Creed's eyes closed as he started to drift off again. "You will see that the woman is cared for?"

She looked up. "Why would you think not? Are our people not kind and courteous? Do we not care for our guests?"

"I'm surprised she isn't in here wanting to talk to me," Creed grunted. Anne-Marie's silence was odd, knowing her as he did.

Shrugging, Berry Woman adjusted the buffalo-hide covering. "The woman is curious. Perhaps she has found other things to occupy her mind."

"Tell both her and Quincy I want to talk to them." With a posse waiting outside the camp, Creed knew they would have to think of a way to get the gold out without being spotted.

Berry Woman rose to leave. "If I see the woman, I will tell her of your wish."

"Berry Woman."

She turned. "Yes?"

His tone carried a silent warning. "The white woman is to be treated well."

Berry Woman nodded. "You need not worry, Storm Rider." She smiled. "I will do whatever the woman asks."

Later on in the afternoon, the flap of the tepee opened to reveal a relieved Quincy. Creed looked up from his pallet and answered Quincy's questioning gaze.

"I'm fine. Much better thanks to Spirit Cloud's magic herbs."

"There was a time I thought you were a goner for sure," Quincy said as his eyes took in Creed's still-swollen thigh. The cleansing fires still burned hotly in the tent, making it an oven.

"Have you seen her?" Creed asked casually.

Quincy knew who Creed meant and answered truthfully. "Yes, this morning. She's getting restless to leave."

Creed winced. "I'm surprised she hasn't told me that she's ready to leave."

"That surprises me, too." She'd made no bones about telling him, Quincy thought.

"There's a posse patrolling outside the camp."

Quincy recalled the conversation between him and Anne-Marie earlier. She didn't know about the posse. Like as not, she would have ridden directly into their camp.

"What are we going to do about it?"

"I'm not sure," Creed admitted. "I do know that we will need Bold Eagle's help in order to get out of this one," he concluded.

"And the chief will help?"

"Yes." Creed briefly reminded him of the relationship between Bold Eagle and himself.

"What are we going to do about the gold and the woman?" Quincy asked.

"Which one? They're both trouble."

Quincy chuckled. The woman seemed to have his partner treed. "The gold."

"I don't know."

"And the woman?"

Creed was silent for a moment. Anne-Marie had been nothing but a millstone around his neck. However, he felt an obligation toward her, one he was powerless to define.

"The woman is my concern and I will see that she is returned to Mercy Flats. You need not worry yourself in that regard."

By the tone in Creed's voice, Quincy knew to drop the subject. He decided not to mention Anne-Marie's intention to leave. After their conversation this morning, the woman would undoubtedly think twice about leaving on her own.

"We'll talk again later," Creed said. His leg was beginning to throb, and he wanted to sleep now. "Send Anne-Marie to me."

"You sure? She's not in the best of moods this morning."

"Send her to me." Creed had dealt with his share of testy women.

"It's your funeral, brother." Quincy took his leave shortly, emerging into the brisk spring air.

Anne-Marie was rearranging her bedding when Quincy asked for permission to enter. A cold blast of air greeted her as the black man stepped through the tent opening.

"It sure is chilly out there," he began awkwardly.

"What is it you want, Mr. Adams?" Anne-Marie turned her back on him and placed more sticks on the fire. If he'd come to try to talk her out of leaving, he could save his breath.

"I just spoke with Creed."

Anne-Marie whirled around and Quincy was instantly struck by her beauty. No wonder she had Creed acting crazy. "Is he all right?"

"Yes, ma'am. He's doing fine and he told me that he

plans to leave within the next two days.'' He watched Anne-Marie for any sign of her previous plan, but she only nodded.

''Well, good for him.'' She didn't plan on waiting that long.

''He wants to see you,'' Quincy said.

''Well, he'll just have to wait. I'm busy.''

''Yes, ma'am. I can see you're real busy.'' A grin escaped him.

''What I do about Creed Walker is none of your concern.''

''Yes, ma'am,'' Quincy said, still grinning as he turned to leave. There was something strange going on between Creed and that woman.

Yes, sir, there truly was.

# Chapter 8

As the moon slid lower Anne-Marie slipped from her tent and made her way to where the ponies were tethered. As promised, a brown-and-white-spotted pony stood in the shadows waiting for its rider.

Hitching her skirt above her knee, she grasped the reins firmly and mounted. Snow drifted to a foot in places as she rode the horse to the outer edge of camp.

A lone rider moved from the shadows, and she followed behind the buckskin along a trail leading out the back of the camp.

The wind whipped her hair savagely as the horses picked their way along the rocky path. Shivering, Anne-Marie huddled deeper into the thin trader's blanket that Berry Woman had provided her for warmth.

Turning to look over her shoulder, she felt her earlier sense of rage dissolving. Maybe she shouldn't be so impulsive. Maybe she should go back to Quincy's tent and warn him that come hell or high water she was leaving.

Maybe she was acting more like Amelia now, flighty

and high-strung instead of being guided by plain old common sense.

Maybe, being under Creed Walker's protection wasn't as bad as she thought.

Maybe, she agonized as the shadowy silhouette she had been following cut away, leaving her alone in the bitter wind and blowing snow, she was being downright foolish.

Berry Woman and River Woman slowed their horses beneath the barren branches of a cottonwood tree. Snow clouds churned beneath a watery moon.

"Storm Rider will be angry," River Woman warned as she watched Anne-Marie's horse disappear into the blowing snow.

"Storm Rider will not know," Berry Woman answered.

"He will know. When he awakens and finds the woman gone, he will ask what has become of her."

"And no one will have seen her," Berry Woman countered.

"But she goes into the dark—into the snow. She should not—"

"Whatever happens is her own foolish doing," Berry Woman snapped.

River Woman looked at her friend, sad that jealousy had overridden her compassion. "It is not right, Berry Woman. It is not our people's way. The white woman does not have the skills to protect herself. She will die."

Jealousy was an ugly emotion. A smile touched the corners of Berry Woman's mouth as she answered. "I do only what the woman asks. I do only what Storm Rider has instructed me to do."

River Woman's eyes reflected her deep concern. "It is not right, Berry Woman."

"Come, it will be light soon." Reining her horse, Berry Woman turned and rode in the direction of camp.

Anne-Marie rode for over an hour before she realized that her body was numb. Her feet tingled, and she hadn't been able to feel her hands for a while.

As dawn streaked the sky she realized she was becoming confused. At one time she thought she was riding west, but now she knew she wasn't. Slowing the pony, she studied the muted rays streaking the cold morning sky.

She was no longer riding west; she was riding south. Desperation filled her, and she giggled, realizing that it didn't make any difference what direction she rode in since she didn't know where she was anyway.

The pony sidestepped, catching Anne-Marie off guard. Reacting, she jerked the bridle around and the pinto bucked, crow-hopping blindly in the snow. She struggled to hang on, but the horse's strength was greater than her own.

Pitching wildly, the horse threw her and she struck the ground hard, tumbling wildly down a steep, snow-covered incline.

By the time she reached the bottom, she welcomed the blackness that consumed her.

Smoke from the cookfires hung over the village this morning as Creed stepped outside the tent. Testing his leg, he found his strength returning. He knew if he stayed up too long, he would open the wound again, and he couldn't spare another delay.

He was flooded with memories as he inhaled the camp aromas. Though he had spent a good part of his life with Father Jacob, the Indian ways were still a part of him.

He stood for a moment watching children play as their mothers went about their daily chores and their fathers unloaded slain deer from packhorses. A hunting party had departed before dawn; they were back with a good kill. There would be fresh meat hanging over the fires tonight.

Turning away, he spotted River Woman carrying a bundle of sticks in the direction of her family's tepee.

"River Woman," he called. "Come, sit by my fire."

River Woman's pace didn't slacken as she hurried toward her tent with an armload of wood. "I cannot, I must tend the fire, Storm Rider."

Surprised by her reaction, Creed smiled and called out again, "River Woman, you work too hard. Come, sit with me and we'll talk."

Slowly dropping the wood, River Woman turned and approached him, her eyes focused on her soft moccasins. "What is it you wish, Storm Rider?"

"Have you seen the white woman? She doesn't seem to be around this morning."

River Woman's gaze stayed riveted to the ground as she murmured, "Not today."

Creed was puzzled. Although he had asked Berry Woman yesterday to send Anne-Marie to his tent, she had failed to respond. "You haven't seen her today?"

"No. I have not seen her today."

Berry Woman turned from her fire, her eyes sending River Woman a silent warning.

"I must go," River Woman murmured. "Our fire burns low."

"If you see the woman—"

"I will not see her. I must go."

As River Woman turned away Creed reached out and caught her arm. Studying her flushed face, he grew more confused. "Is something wrong?"

Glancing at Berry Woman, River Woman shook her head quickly. "No, nothing is wrong. Please, I must go."

It was a moment before Creed finally released her arm. She was acting oddly today. "Give my greetings to your mother."

Nodding, River Woman ducked quickly into her tent. Glancing at Berry Woman, Creed wondered about the significance of the look that had passed between the two women.

Meeting his gaze, Berry Woman smiled. "Storm Rider appears much stronger this day."

"Yes, I am stronger. Have you seen the white woman today?"

Berry Woman shrugged. "I have not seen her today. Perhaps she gathers wood with Elk Woman."

Creed found that possibility even more remote. "Where is Quincy?"

"In his tent." She turned back to tend the haunch of venison hanging over her fire.

When the evening meal was eaten, and Anne-Marie still failed to appear, Creed went to question River Woman.

As the tent flap parted, River Woman looked up, apprehension mirrored in her brown eyes. Storm Rider filled the doorway, his face an angry mask.

"I asked earlier if you had seen the white woman. I want the truth now," he said.

Glancing away, she refused to look at him. "I have spoken the truth. I have not seen the white woman this day."

"When did you last see her?"

River Woman's silence was damning.

"When did you last see her?"

"I cannot—"

Entering the tent, he knelt beside her, his hand gripping her shoulders tightly. He forced her to look at him. "When did you last see her?"

The young girl still hesitated and he lowered his voice persuasively. "Tell me what you know."

"I know nothing."

"Has something happened to her?"

A sob caught in River Woman's throat. "I can't— Berry Woman will be angry."

His grip tightened painfully around her forearm. "Tell me what you know."

"She . . . the white woman rode away. . . ."

Creed frowned. "Rode away? When?"

"In the time of the moon . . ."

"And you didn't tell anyone?"

River Woman shook her head, sobbing. "She rode . . . into the darkness. Berry Woman returned to camp, but I followed the woman." Her eyes lifted defensively. "Berry Woman said she was only following your instructions."

Creed swore. "Where is the woman now?"

Tears rolled down the maiden's cheeks. "I do not know—hurt, I think."

"Hurt?"

"The pony she was riding, he . . . jumped . . . and the woman fell."

Creed could not believe what he was hearing. Berry Woman would not willingly disobey him.

"I did not wish to anger Berry Woman, so I turned back. . . ." River Woman's voice fell away.

The muscle in Creed's jaw flexed tightly as he pulled the girl to her feet. "Show me where this happened."

River Woman drew back in fear. "No, I cannot."

Ignoring her defiance, Creed pulled her out of the tent and went in search of two horses.

Silence blanketed the frozen hillsides as the horses pushed their way through the layers of crusted snow. A bitter wind battered the man and woman as they rode in silence, their eyes searching the icy hillsides.

Creed and River Woman had ridden for over an hour when River Woman suddenly reined her pony to a halt.

"Here."

Sliding off his horse, Creed limped to the edge of the steep ravine. Halfway down, he could see a crumpled form lying at the bottom of the incline. A blanket of snow covered the familiar black habit.

Swearing, he turned, shouting to River Woman. "Go! Tell the chief I have found the white woman, and she needs care."

As Creed made his way down the incline River Woman turned her horse and galloped back to camp.

* * *

Anne-Marie drifted in and out of consciousness, faintly aware that she was dying.

Dying wasn't so bad. Nothing at all like she had thought it would be. There was no pain, just a nice numbness that filled her whole body.

She hadn't heard any trumpets yet, but she expected to hear them anytime. She could picture St. Peter calling his trumpeters together, and right this moment they were getting ready to blow her right up through the Pearly Gates.

No, she realized that she was confused. Blow wasn't the proper word, *herald* her through the Pearly Gates. Yes, that was it. They were getting ready to herald her arrival. At least she hoped it was St. Peter, and not the other one. She knew she hadn't been the most obedient subject, but she hadn't been the worst, either. And every misdeed she'd done, she'd done with the purest of intentions.

Yes, she'd be heralded up somewhere anytime now. After all, she had been lying in the snow for how long now? An hour? Two hours? Ten hours? It must be closer to ten hours, but then, if it was ten hours and not one hour or two hours, she would surely be wherever she was going by now, wouldn't she?

An ache, deep inside her, made her think that she was still on earth, a nice place that had nourished and sheltered her and brought her good and bad times. She suddenly had the urge to cry. Her death would bring such pain to Amelia and Abigail.

She hated to be the cause of such pain.

The McDougal sisters were all each other had, and now there would only be the two left to carry on the mission work. In one way she wanted to stay and help, but in another she longed to be where it was warm and dry—but not overly warm and dry.

Creed Walker's face floated above her, and she squinted, trying to see if he had a trumpet to his lips. Wasn't that just like him—always showing up where he wasn't wanted.

Deciding he was hornless, she lethargically reached out to lay her numb hands against his rugged features. No matter where she went lately, he was there. It was almost like fate had planted Creed Walker in her life and wouldn't let her lose the crop.

"Ohhh, you've come to save me again, but you're too late this time," she said crossly, realizing that even after all they'd been through, she was beginning to like him. Really like him, she mused, although she couldn't imagine why. He hadn't been particularly nice to her, although she had to admit that he hadn't had much of a chance. What with going to jail and then ending up with a buckboard full of gold and being shot and Eulalie's cabin burning to the ground and him running around naked as the day he was born—well, she supposed, under the circumstances, few men would have been overly gracious.

It was really too bad she was dying. Berry Woman thought Creed was going to marry her, but if she weren't dying, she just might decide to put a kink in the woman's marital plans. Why, who knows, if she wasn't in the process of passing on this very minute, she might conceivably have fallen in love with Creed Walker. She, Anne-Marie McDougal, who never even liked men, in love with an Indian?

If her lips weren't frozen stiff, she'd laugh.

She closed her eyes as the cry came over her

again. *I'm alone. I'm hurt. I can't move. And I'm scared. Not one soul cares where I am, or what happens to me—except Abigail and Amelia.* She smothered a sob that tore at her ribs and made breathing unbearable.

Where were those blasted trumpets!

"Breathe deep, Anne-Marie."

A heavy robe settled around her, and the warmth felt heavenly. The time had come: she was dead.

"Where's your trumpet?" she murmured, wishing whoever had come would hurry because she was so cold. "I didn't hear it."

"I didn't blow it."

The voice sounded close, and not at all like an angel. It was deep and masculine—oh dear. Was it the devil himself come to claim her? Her heart hammered against her ribs painfully as she tried to open her eyes, but the lids were frozen shut. "I'm sorry . . . don't take me . . . I won't do all those bad things anymore. . . ."

Creed fastened the heavy robe around her, his features drawn with concern. She was covered with snow, her lips blue white, her eyelashes icy.

"Anne-Marie, can you hear me?"

Oh, darn. It was Creed Walker's voice. What was *he* doing here and passing himself off as one of St. Peter's trumpeters!

She tried to ask him, but her lips refused to form the words. She swallowed, tried again, but the sound wouldn't come.

"I'm going to move you. We're going back to camp now. Put your arms around my neck."

"Do I have to?"

"Yes, you have to."

Wouldn't you just know he would try to boss her around—even now?

As a pair of incredibly strong arms picked her up, she sighed, laying her head on the trumpeter's shoulder as she lapsed into unconsciousness.

# Chapter 9

Pain slowly dragged Anne-Marie back to awareness. Her first thoughts were that her toes stung like fire, and she couldn't feel her face at all. She groaned, struggling to sit up.

"Drink."

She didn't recognize the voice, but a gentle hand supported her head and pushed a cup against her lips. Drinking greedily of the warm thin broth, she then dropped back to unconsciousness.

Twice more she awoke to find the same compassionate hands urging the cup back to her lips. Once, she thought she heard Creed's voice, but it seemed different somehow, restrained, concerned, and she couldn't think why.

The third time she roused, her eyes opened slowly, trying to gain her bearings.

Her surroundings were strange, unfamiliar. Then understanding slowly dawned on her; she was lying in the medicine lodge where Creed had been. She recognized the intricate drawings, the ornate shields that lined both sides of the buffalo-skin walls. And the heat. The incredible heat.

Afraid to move, she looked out of the corner of her eye and saw the aged medicine man sitting beside the fire, smoking a pipe.

A burst of cold air swept the room as the tent flap parted and Creed Walker entered. When he saw her eyes were open, he knelt beside her, taking her hand.

Swallowing thickly, she tried to speak, but only a croak escaped her parched throat.

"You have slept a long time."

Frowning, Anne-Marie lifted her hand to her throbbing temple. "What happened?"

"It appears you want to kill yourself."

"Me?" She didn't think so. It was a sin to take one's life. Sister Agnes had warned her of that often enough.

The Crow's fingers lightly brushed her cheek, and the motion brought about the nicest feeling inside her. "Are you in pain?"

"Some," she murmured. Her head hurt and her body ached everywhere that could ache.

"Wise One Above has again smiled upon you. You have some frostbite, but Spirit Cloud says you will live."

Anne-Marie wasn't sure if she heard relief or regret in his voice.

"How . . . how did you find me?" Events of the past few hours were beginning to come back now: the flight from camp, the worsening snowstorm, losing her direction, the fall from her horse into the ravine.

"River Woman led me to you."

Anne-Marie frowned. "How did she know where I was?"

Creed hesitated, choosing his words. "River Woman saw you ride out of camp. She and Berry Woman followed to make sure your escape was successful."

Sighing, Anne-Marie closed her eyes. "Berry Woman hates me."

He chuckled, a nice, rich-sounding timbre. "Berry Woman feels you are a threat."

Anne-Marie wanted to look him directly in the eyes to see if he thought Berry Woman was right, but she didn't. Why should the suggestion that he found her desirable be anything but laughable? They had only known each other a short while, and so far she had been nothing but a hindrance to him.

Admittedly she lacked experience where men were concerned, but simple logic told her that few men would be attracted to a woman who had landed him in jail and shot him, too. "I acted foolishly."

Berry Woman had eagerly provided her with a means of escape and now she knew why. The woman knew Anne-Marie could not possibly survive alone in the wilds.

Turning aside, Creed dipped a cloth in a bowl of warm water. "Bold Eagle extends his apology for your injuries. It is not the Cheyenne way to dishonor a guest."

As he talked he smoothed the cloth back and forth across her brow, his touch surprisingly gentle. Anne-Marie wasn't certain if the odd tingling he awakened inside her was the result of his compassion or merely the lingering effects of frostbite. Either way she found it pleasurable.

"Berry Woman is aware that her actions have shamed her family and her heritage," he apologized.

Drawing a ragged breath, Anne-Marie opened her eyes to meet his direct gaze. "She's in love with you, you know." The observation was too personal, she knew that, but for some reason she wanted to know if he returned her love.

He was silent for a moment, then: "I am aware of Berry Woman's devotion."

She didn't know why, but his admission was unsettling. Was Berry Woman telling the truth? Did he plan to marry the young woman once the war was over?

"She says you and she will marry someday."

He was quiet as he dipped the cloth in the pan of water, then wrung it out.

"*Are* you in love with her?"

"You ask many questions." Moving to the edge of the pallet, he settled his leg more comfortably and proceeded to change the subject. "Why did you decide to leave? Are you not treated well?"

In view of what had happened, Anne-Marie realized her reasons for leaving were inadequate if not downright scatterbrained. She hadn't the slightest idea where she would have gone had her ill-fated attempt to escape proved successful. She had no money, no provisions, and her pleas for assistance had fallen on deaf ears in Streeter.

"I admit running away wasn't the smartest thing I've ever done, but I'm worried about my sisters. I'm capable of returning to Mercy Flats on my own."

A dangerous light entered his eyes. "Alone? Are you not aware of the perils that await a woman traveling alone?"

Her chin lifted. "I'm not afraid—my sisters and I

have traveled alone many times and no harm has befallen us.''

His gaze traveled over her slowly, lingering on the rise and fall of her breasts longer than Sister Agnes would have thought proper.

"There are ways a man can hurt a woman and not physically harm her. Rude, vile ways that your innocence makes you unaware of. It would be wise for you and your sisters to reconsider your ways and change them.''

"I am a resourceful woman, Mr. Walker. You would be surprised how much I know.''

Their eyes held for a long moment.

"No, I don't believe I would be, Miss McDougal.''

Anne-Marie looked away first. "If you are engaged to another woman, you should not be looking at me this way," she chided, although his look threatened to take her very breath away.

He conceded the point with a nod. "You will forgive my temporary insanity.'' He leaned back, his dark eyes dancing with amusement as he lit a cheroot and inhaled. He looked different to her today, more white than Indian, more male than she cared to notice.

"If you had escaped, what makes you think you wouldn't have gotten yourself in deeper trouble?'' he asked.

"I'm not a child. . . .'' Resentment momentarily flared in her eyes before the numbness in her feet reminded her of last night's childish actions.

The teasing light disappeared as his features gradually sobered. "I have come to strike a bargain with you.''

She glanced up. "A bargain? With me?''

He nodded. "I have come to ask your help."

Her eyes narrowed with skepticism. "What kind of help?" Now what was he up to? He clearly had the upper hand in their situation; they were in his blood brother's camp, among his own kind. Why would he need her help?

"I want you to help Quincy and me get the gold out of camp."

"Why should I do that?" She was already more involved with John Quincy Adams and Creed Walker than she cared to be. If it weren't for that blasted gold, she would already be on her way back to Mercy Flats.

"If you will agree to help, I will see that a fourth of the gold is donated to your mission."

"A fourth," she breathed, trying to envision how much that would be. Even without prolonged calculation, she knew it would be a lot. A whole lot. "What would I have to do?"

"You must think of a way to remove the gold from camp, undetected."

"Undetected?" Her forehead creased in concern. "Just the gold, or you, me, Quincy, and the gold?"

"All of us."

Holy Mother—he must be desperate! "This must be pretty important to you and Quincy," she challenged.

The muscle in his jaw tightened. "Yes."

Her eyes narrowed. "You're a spy, aren't you?"

He gazed stoically back at her. "Quincy has told you this?"

"Yes. I thought something was funny concerning that gold. But you surprise me. I wouldn't have thought you'd take sides."

"I don't." His features remained somber. "The Crow is for his own side."

"But you ride with the Union."

"I ride for the side that is right."

"But now you and Quincy need my help."

He nodded.

*Well, well, well,* she thought. So now they were so desperate they were willing to come to her for help.

"Why me? Why not ask Bold Eagle for his wisdom?"

"I have given this much thought." His eyes refused to meet hers now. "It must be you. You are the most experienced in matters of this kind."

"Well, maybe," she agreed.

They sat for a moment in silence, thinking.

"What is your answer?"

"I'm still thinking." Closing her eyes, she mulled the situation over in her mind. If she thought hard enough, she could come up with a way out to get them and the gold out of camp without arousing suspicion, but why should she? Well, the money, for one thing. The sisters could use it, and she wasn't doing anything anyway.

But she was going to make him beg for her help. Her services didn't come cheap. If getting the gold out of camp, undetected, was that important, he was going to have to sweeten the pot a little.

"Well?" he prompted.

"Maybe I could think of something, but I want more than a fourth of the gold."

Creed tensed, the expression in his eyes grave now. "A fourth of the gold—that is the bargain."

"Then I'm not interested." Snuggling deeper into the buffalo robe, she closed her eyes, feigning sleep.

"I am not through speaking."

"I'm through listening."

The mission could use that gold, but if he was desperate enough to ask her help, he'd cough up more.

When he said nothing, she sighed, wishing for the hundredth time that she had been more careful in her dealings. Look where her talents had landed her: half-frozen and in the company of two men whom she still wasn't entirely sure she could trust.

Finally he spoke again. "Quincy has told you of our mission?"

"Yes—you're an Indian Northerner."

"Well, I'm gaining ground. It wasn't long ago you said I didn't look like an Indian, period."

"I've never meant you didn't look like an Indian—I only meant you don't act like an Indian." Her eyes focused on the skins lining the walls of the lodge. "At least not all the time."

"And you do not speak like a woman of the cloth, Miss McDougal." Their eyes met, and she could see he was censuring her again.

"So, you and Quincy are involved in the war," Anne-Marie murmured. Her situation was even more serious than she thought. "Where does that leave me?"

Shrugging, he smiled. "It leaves you just as desperate as Quincy and me."

"Maybe, maybe not. I know you were sent after that gold, so you might as well tell me why, because I'm not going to cooperate with you unless you do—and then I still might decide not to cooperate."

Creed thought about this a moment. He could continue to lie to her, or he could tell her the truth. The truth would make his job easier, but could he trust her? He wasn't sure.

"Are you a southern or northern sympathizer, Miss McDougal?"

"To be honest, I've never given the war much thought." She had no brothers or father to send into battle, so she viewed the war differently than others.

Thinking about it now, she thought the war was pointless. Thousands of men were losing their lives for a conflict that in her opinion could never be resolved by force. Man had to want to treat his fellowman with respect and dignity; no one could make him do it.

"If you were to think about it, whose side would you be on?" he prompted.

Her eyes now met his straightforwardly. "Man's side, Mr. Walker."

Drawing on his cigar, he was quiet as he studied her. For some impractical reason, he sensed that she could be trusted. Maybe it was the look in her eye right now, or the mulish set to her chin when she spoke of causes that concerned her. Whatever it was, he decided to utilize it.

"Quincy and I were on our way to pick up the shipment of gold when I rescued you from the jail wagon."

"I never saw Quincy," she countered.

"He rode ahead of me. We were to meet within the hour when I encountered you being chased by the Comanches. That is why I had such meager provisions the night I rescued you."

"Quincy had your supplies?" That would explain why he had been traveling so light.

Creed nodded. "He carried our supplies."

"And you were on your way to pick up the gold?" The irony of it made her laugh. "Then that explains why it was loaded and waiting on the buckboard."

"No. I don't know why it was loaded and waiting on the buckboard. The banker knew we were on our way to get it, but he didn't know when we would arrive."

"Whose gold is it?"

"It was donated by a group of wealthy California investors in the northern cause. The money will enable the North to continue fighting. Quincy and I were sent to pick up the gold and bring it to our commander in Louisiana."

Anne-Marie understood men's belief in a single cause, but a hundred thousand dollars was a whole lot of belief for any cause.

"Why would investors from California donate such a large sum specifically to the Union Army?"

He smiled, finding her naïveté refreshing. "Let's just say the 'investors' like their present affluent lives, and they don't care to lose them."

"Then the gold wasn't donated because the investors have a true sense of right and wrong, they gave it because they're looking out after their own selfish hides. It's a matter of greedy men wanting to dominate other men and having enough money to do it."

Drawing on the cheroot, Creed watched the play of emotions on her face. Anger, resentment, a sense of injustice. It was surprising how astute she was when she wanted to be.

"That, unfortunately, is the case," he conceded.

Her jaw firmed with resentment. "It's not fair. The North should refuse to accept the money."

He shrugged. "In war, the end justifies the means."

"Then you think someone else knew about the gold and was in the process of stealing it when we broke out of jail?"

"It's a reasonable assumption, but I have no proof that is the case." He could see the wheels in her head beginning to churn.

"Who could it possibly be? Agents working for the South?"

"Maybe."

"A crooked banker?"

"Maybe."

"A crooked sheriff?" She snapped her fingers. "A crooked sheriff *and* banker? That's it! Streeter's sheriff and banker are nothing but low-down, cutthroat snakes."

"You are jumping to conclusions—but you could be right. At this point it doesn't matter. We have the gold."

"And that's exactly how it's going to stay. Whoever tried to steal the gold won't get a second chance. Although the purpose for the gold is deplorable, I refuse to let it fall into even more unsavory hands."

"Then you agree to help?"

Her eyes lifted expectantly. "Certainly, for one fourth of the gold and your promise that once the gold is safely in your commander's hands, you will personally escort me to Mercy Flats."

He stiffened. "I cannot promise this!"

"That's my condition. Take it or leave it."

His brows lifted. "Blackmail, Miss McDougal?"

She smiled. "Conditions, Mr. Walker."

Creed knew she had him. He needed her help. Not just him, but the whole damn northern cause needed it.

"All right. I accept your conditions."

"Good. When do we start?"

"Bold Eagle says there are four men waiting on the outskirts of camp. They must have followed the buckboard tracks. They know we're in here."

"The posse," she murmured.

"Led by a Mexican called Malpas."

"You know him?"

"I know of him."

Frowning, Anne-Marie recalled the dirty little man with the sparkling silver tooth who'd been following them. "The leader doesn't appear to be overly bright."

"A man doesn't have to be brilliant to cause trouble."

"Well, why don't I just go out there and demand to know who they are and what they want? If they're after the gold, I'll just tell them they can't have it."

Creed was amazed and disturbed by her amount of spunk. "I don't think so. Your neck's too pretty to have it wrung off like a Sunday-dinner chicken."

He got slowly to his feet when he saw her energy was draining. "We will speak of this again later. Now you must rest."

"Yes—but come back tonight," she mused. "Meanwhile I'll think about our situation."

As the flap closed behind him Anne-Marie was curious about what had prompted his gentleness. By all rights he should have been angry with her.

As Creed emerged from the tent he motioned for Berry Woman who was tending the fire.

"You wish to speak to me, Storm Rider?"

Creed's eyes darkened with anger. "You are to see to the white woman's well-being."

"But I do, Storm Rider—"

"If," Creed continued, "the woman leaves again, I will hold you personally responsible."

"The woman does as she wishes—" Berry Woman said.

He interrupted, his voice sharp now. "Hear me, Berry Woman. If any further harm comes to her, you will answer to me." Turning on his heel, Storm Rider walked off.

Berry Woman's features were sullen as she watched him go.

Anne-Marie slept deeply, and when she awoke, she felt stronger. When Bold Eagle's youngest wife brought the evening meal, she was able to sit up to eat, then spent more than an hour combing the tangles from her hair.

Amid her loud protests, Spirit Cloud smeared another smelly coating of oil on her face. By the time Creed made his next visit, she felt almost normal again.

"You are looking much better," he observed as he sat down beside her pallet. They exchanged smiles. "We should give thanks for our sturdy stock."

"We should. And you have to admit your life hasn't been dull since you rescued me," she teased, aware that she was actually flirting with a man.

"I cannot imagine the word 'dull' will ever be associated with you." His gaze measured her flushed cheeks appreciably.

"I guess not." Her eyes dropped away quickly. It wasn't like he had said she looked pretty or anything, not with all this horrible grease on her face, but it almost sounded that way.

"After you deliver the gold, where will you go?" she asked.

"To rejoin my company in Louisiana."

For a moment Anne-Marie felt a sense of letdown— almost as badly as the time Father Luis had given her a newborn colt and it had died during the night. She had cried for hours, and when a second colt was born a few days later and Father Luis again offered her the animal, she refused to take it. She wasn't prone to be a crybaby, especially over things that couldn't be helped, but when she liked something, she liked it.

"Have you decided on a plan?"

"Not yet, but I'm thinking."

"I'll return tomorrow," he said. "Meanwhile do not venture out on your own again." His eyes swept her. "Do I have your word you will not leave?"

Sighing, she gave her word. She'd learned her lesson. She wasn't going anywhere without him.

When he'd gone, she lay back on the pallet and closed her eyes. It seemed he was on her mind a good deal lately. When he'd rescued her from the jail wagon, she'd thought he was as savage as the Comanches. Even at first, during his lengthy silence, she had sensed a difference between Creed and a savage—between Creed and any man she'd ever met.

Now that she had been among his adopted tribe, she realized how different they were from what she'd expected. She understood the importance of family to the Cheyenne from the things Creed and Elk Woman had told her. She had heard the laughter, she'd seen the teasing camaraderie, the loving concern shown small children. She was impressed by the tribe's warmth and closeness.

She stared out the smoke hole at the top of the tent. What was it about Creed Walker the man that made her pulse race when he was around like she was coming down with something real bad? What was there about him that made her want to follow him to Louisiana, made the thought of never seeing him again once the gold was returned so disturbing? She'd never so much as looked at a man twice, so what made him so special?

When she dropped off to sleep, she was still wondering.

# Chapter 10

"Ben!" the sheriff bellowed. "Gall dern it! Get in here!"

Ben Parnell tossed the pail of water out the back of the jailhouse and hurried back into the office, cursing Anne-Marie McDougal with every step he took. Since he'd let that woman get away, his life hadn't been worth shootin'.

If he *ever* got his hands on that woman, he'd snatch her bald-headed for makin' his life so miserable. How was *he* to know that Adams fellow was lyin'? He had him sure enough convinced the woman had stolen his brooch!

"What do you want!" Ben shouted, tossing the bucket into a corner.

"Run this down to the telegraph office." Ferris handed the deputy a piece of paper with a scribbled note on it. "Have Mae send it off to every lawman in a hundred-mile area."

Ben glanced at the brief message.

SHERIFF———,
IF WOMAN POSING AS NUN IN THE COMPANY OF A
BLACK AND A CROW INDIAN IS SEEN IN YOUR AREA,
APPREHEND IMMEDIATELY. AUBURN HAIR, GREEN
EYES, 14 HANDS HIGH. WANTED FOR THEFT AND JAIL-
BREAK.

"You think this is really gonna help, Ferris?" Malpas and his men had been chasing the trio for days, and
the gold was still in their hands.

"No, I'm sending it 'cause I don't have another
blessed thing to do, Ben!" Ferris mocked.

"All right, all right, you don't have to get so testy."
Ferris had been as cross lately as a heifer standing on
her own teat. "Seems to me a black man, a nun, and
an Indian traveling together shouldn't be that hard to
spot. If you ask me, which nobody ever does, that'd be
a sight kinda hard to overlook."

"Well, now, if you'd stop working your jaws and think
about it, Ben, don't you just suppose those three might
of had enough *brains* to split up so's they wouldn't be
so damn noticeable!"

Ben frowned. "Well, I allow that's possible—I
guess."

Snorting, Ferris stalked back to his desk. "That's
mighty big of you, Ben. Mighty big."

Ben's chin jutted out with resentment. "So, I ain't
perfect!"

"You gonna go send those telegrams, or do you plan
to take root where you're standin'?"

"I'm goin', I'm goin'," Ben mumbled, starting out
the door. "But for the life of me I cain't see what good

it'll do. Ain't *no one* seen hide nor hair of them out-
laws, and I don't likely think they're gonna.''

If anyone was to ask Ben Parnell, which nobody ever
did, that gold and those three were long gone.

Creed stepped from Anne-Marie's lodge the next
morning and walked straight to Quincy's tent.

Thoughts of this woman who had suddenly entered
his life were beginning to trouble him. He found himself looking forward to their daily matches of wit. The
woman was not only beautiful, she was intelligent. It
was not the quick-wittedness of a con artist that attracted him, although he found that aspect of her in-
triguing, but rather it was her appeal as an independent
and rational woman that fascinated him. He knew many
women, but none like this one.

Quincy glanced up from cleaning his rifle as Creed
entered his tent. Noting the lines creasing Creed's forehead, he grinned. ''How's the good sister this morning,
brother?''

Seating himself opposite his friend, Creed lifted his
hands to the fire. ''She is anxious to move on.''

''Is she now?'' Quincy mused. ''And what about
you?''

Creed's frown deepened as his gaze centered on the
bandage wrapped tightly around his thigh. To all who
asked he vowed he was recovering, but his strength was
slow to return. ''The wound does not heal swiftly.''

''I wouldn't be too concerned,'' Quincy consoled.
''Spirit Cloud says these things take time.''

''I do not have 'time.' '' His tone was short now.
''We have been delayed too long as it is.''

''I could go on,'' Quincy offered.

"No, it is too dangerous to travel alone with such a large amount."

Spitting on the rifle butt, Quincy polished it to a deep shine with his sleeve.

"And there is the matter of the men waiting outside the camp," Creed noted.

"Hmmm." Quincy looked up. "Haven't figured out a way to escape the illustrious members of Streeter's posse yet?"

"No," Creed admitted.

"What does Bold Eagle suggest we do?"

"I do not want to involve Bold Eagle any deeper in this matter. The tribe is small, and the people have already endangered their welfare by taking us in."

"You don't think Bold Eagle would insist on helping? You two are blood brothers, aren't you?"

"Yes. It is I who am reluctant to accept my brother's help." There would be no question of Bold Eagle's help if Creed chose to ask.

"One moonless night, and those four men could disappear never to be heard from again," Quincy mused. Two strong braves with freshly honed blades would see to that.

"No, this is not good. I will seek other ways to evade my enemies."

"Hmmm, the woman's safety wouldn't have anything to do with this, would it? I thought you would be more concerned about the mission than about her." Lifting the barrel of the gun, Quincy peered through it.

"My concern is for all who are involved."

"We could always leave the woman in Bold Eagle's care, then come back for her later. That way all we'll have to worry about now is the gold."

"No," Creed objected shortly. "The woman would not accept it, and I have given my word that once the gold is delivered, I will see her safely to Mercy Flats. It will be far wiser to enlist her help in this matter. She is, at this moment, thinking of a way for us to elude the enemy."

Glancing up, Quincy frowned. "Are you serious?"

"She is wise in the ways of deception," Creed maintained stoically. "She has given her promise to help, and I have accepted it."

"But we've never had to ask a woman's help before—"

Creed's eyes fixed on the fire as he interrupted. "We have not been in so grave a situation before."

Quincy had never known Creed Walker to rely on anyone, much less a woman. "Are you certain there isn't another reason why you're willing to jeopardize the mission by bringing her along?"

Creed's eyes turned coldly determined. "If you are implying that anything exists between the woman and myself, you are wrong. I think of only what is best for all concerned, nothing more."

Getting to his feet, he left the tent, leaving Quincy to wonder just how far he *would* go for this woman.

*There is nothing between the woman and myself,* Creed told himself as he limped across the open communal area to the lodge of the leader of the Heviqsnipahis or Burned Heart band.

Bold Eagle looked up as Creed sat across the fire from him.

"Your wound is better, my brother."

Creed nodded. "Soon I will be able to leave to complete my mission."

"This is good. And the woman?"

"She is eager to leave also, my brother."

"This is also good."

They sat for a while in companionable silence, savoring the peace and shared friendship. As a courtesy, Creed waited for Bold Eagle to break the silence.

"What does my brother wish for my warriors to do concerning Storm Rider's enemies waiting on the hillside behind our camp?"

"I have not decided the men's fate," Creed acknowledged. "If they are killed, more will come to take their place, and the Burned Heart band will cease to exist."

"This is not possible," Bold Eagle scoffed. "The Cheyenne are strong, and the Heviqsnipahis most of all. Tell me what must be done, and it will be, for I owe you my life as well as the lives of my people."

*How do you explain to someone the power of the white man?* Creed thought as he listened to Bold Eagle recount the many coups his band had taken against the white settlers. How did he tell this noble Cheyenne that his days were numbered? That when this war ended, there would probably be more and more whites encroaching on the vast plains of Texas. That if the posse were eliminated, more would take their place until Bold Eagle's band would vanish like the large herds of buffalo that used to dominate the plains.

"I do not want the men killed," Creed repeated.

"Then we must trick them," Bold Eagle decided.

"This is good."

Bold Eagle nodded. "I will help think of a plan, my brother."

"I, too, will think—and I will consult the woman."

"The woman?" Bold Eagle bit down on the stem of his pipe, hard.

"She is cunning—like the fox."

She is trouble, like the *wolf*, Bold Eagle thought as Creed rose to leave.

But he graciously refrained from saying so.

Late that evening Creed returned to the visitor's tent. Anne-Marie had just finished bathing. She sat close to the fire braiding her auburn tresses. The flames from the fire caused her hair to come alive with a fire of its own. Her doeskin dress clung damply to her soft curves, and Creed felt a disturbing tightening in his groin. He had seen her in various conditions, but tonight she looked like a proper Indian wife waiting for her husband.

She glanced up to see him standing proud and powerful above her, and she was suddenly assaulted by feelings so strong that her heart started to pound. They stared at one another in silence until a fire log broke in two, shattering the stillness.

Seating himself opposite her, Creed crossed his legs, gazing at the flames. Anne-Marie could tell by his manner that he was troubled tonight, and wondered if he, too, felt the strong pull developing between them. She spoke first.

"How are you?"

"Well, and you?"

"Better," she answered. "Thanks to you." Lowering her eyes to the flames, she tried to keep from staring at him. He was so handsome—exceptionally so this evening. "You've saved my life three times now. I will forever be in your debt."

"It was my duty." His tongue twisted in the lie, because suddenly he knew that he had gone after her the third time for a reason beyond that of simple human compassion.

"Well, thank you anyway," Anne-Marie said quietly. For just a brief moment, as Creed entered her lodge, she had felt that he was seeing her as something more than just a troublesome burden. She had felt his dark eyes on her, almost sensuously touching her, and her body had responded shamelessly.

"I want to leave now." The words escaped her mouth before she realized it.

"I await your plan."

"Well, we could just have Bold Eagle's warriors tie the posse up until we can get away."

Creed silently laughed at the idea of Bold Eagle's warriors tying men up, but his features remained somber as he answered her, again surprised at her gentleness even toward those who would harm her. "This is not possible. Once they were freed, they would track us. They would send others to retaliate for their humiliation. We must find a more clever way to leave without bringing harm to either ourselves or my brothers."

"Have you spoken to Bold Eagle?"

"Bold Eagle will do as I ask."

"It would be easier for the three of us to escape if we didn't have the gold to worry about."

Creed's expression sobered. "The gold goes with us, or we do not leave."

"But if we—"

"We do not leave without the gold."

Well, talk about stubborn! Anne-Marie's eyes locked with his. "All right. But it's not going to be easy," she warned.

"I ask only that you do your best."

Creed knew she had the cunning to get them out of this. He would do everything within his power to see that whatever plan she chose would be swiftly carried out. Getting slowly to his feet, he extended his hand to her in a gesture of friendship.

Placing her hand into his, Anne-Marie felt the same magnetic current between them.

Confusion momentarily clouded her features as she quickly broke the contact, for she had seen the answering desire in his eyes.

Before she could speak, the tent flap closed, and she was alone, still reeling from sensations too strong to ignore.

Morning dawned. Creed and Quincy had spent the night talking, but they had failed to come up with their own plan for escape. They had thought of several means of diversion, but there was always an obstacle, either involving the gold, Anne-Marie, or in most instances, both.

"I still say we leave the woman here," Quincy argued. "It's the only smart way to handle this."

Creed's answer was the same. He had a one-track mind when it came to the holy imposter. "No, and we will discuss it no more."

"Well, we better come up with something, and pronto." Resignation was evident in Quincy's voice. "The band wants to move on, and Bold Eagle can't be happy about that posse camped under his nose."

The men glanced up as the flap to the lodge opened and Anne-Marie stepped inside. "I've got it!" she declared in a breathless voice.

"Got what?" Quincy's eyes took in her nun's attire. She was once again dressed as the demure sister he had seen in the Streeter jail.

"I've got the plan." She addressed Quincy, but her eyes found Creed's.

Quincy frowned. He dreaded this. He glanced to Creed for a way out.

"She is the best in her field."

Quincy's brows lifted dubiously. "Her field being?"

"She cons people. She's good at it."

"I don't know, Creed—"

Creed overrode his protests. "Tell us of this plan of yours."

"Well, it's lengthy." Seating herself opposite the men, she took a deep breath, then began. "What I'm about to say may sound farfetched, but from my considerable experience with matters such as these, I think it's the only way out of our situation. We'll need Bold Eagle's help—maybe he should be here for this?"

Creed didn't want Bold Eagle involved until he could decide the plan's worthiness. "You will tell me of your plan first."

"All right." She glanced at Quincy. "Some of us might be leery about the specifics, but it's the only way to get us and the gold out of here. Once we're out, there's an old abandoned mission not far from here." Her eyes searched Quincy's. "You know where it is. We were talking about it moments before Bold Eagle's warriors found us."

Quincy agreed that he knew of the mission. He had seen it many times in his youth.

"We'll be safe there until Creed regains his strength.

Then we can deliver the gold to your commander, and I can rejoin my sisters.''

Creed nodded for her to go on. ''What is this plan?''

Anne-Marie quickly began to outline her strategy. As she talked on in a rush she could see disbelief creep into Creed's expression and outright horror in Quincy's.

''You must be kidding,'' Quincy choked out when the plan was laid out. He glanced incredulously at Creed, who was staring at Anne-Marie as if she had lost her mind.

''This plan—I am not sure. . . .'' Creed hedged, but when he looked into her emerald eyes and remembered his promise that he would go along with anything, he knew, though the plan was peculiar, he would do as she asked. ''You are certain this plan will work?''

''I know it will! It's positively brilliant; some of my best work,'' she said, glowing.

''You're both crazy,'' Quincy declared, ''and I refuse to have anything to do with this. Why, we'd be struck dead!''

''It is your wish to see your wife and children again?'' Creed inquired.

''Yes, but—''

''Then we will do as she says.''

Quincy's mahogany features paled to almond. ''Oh, Lord have mercy on our souls!

Anne-Marie thought he was overreacting. The plan was brilliant, he'd see that once it was under way. ''You know of a better way?''

Quincy had to admit that he didn't. But what she was suggesting was impossible. The way their luck was going the last thing they needed was to stir up a bunch of evil spirits! ''I don't like it, Creed, I think we'd be setting ourselves up for more trouble than we ever thought about!''

"No one said you had to like it," Anne-Marie consoled, patting him soothingly on the arm. "Besides, it'll be over before you know it."

*Oh Lordy, Lordy Lordy,* Quincy agonized inwardly as he followed Creed out of the tent.

What was she getting them into this time?

# Chapter 11

Bold Eagle looked up from repairing arrows to find three pairs of eyes staring at him. "Bold Eagle welcomes his friends to his lodge." He motioned for the three visitors to sit on the buffalo robes encircling the fire.

"We have decided on a plan, Bold Eagle." Creed's eyes cautioned Anne-Marie to keep silent.

"And the three of you agree to this plan?" Bold Eagle questioned, keeping his eyes on the woman.

Smiling, Anne-Marie nodded.

Bold Eagle directed his gaze to the black man.

Reluctantly Quincy nodded his head affirmatively.

"Tell me of this plan."

"It is one that will take a great deal of courage, my brother, for it goes against the teachings of Heamma-wihio."

Bold Eagle visibly paled at these words, for if he went against the Wise One Above, he would be doomed forever to walk the Hanging Road or the white man's Milky Way. However, Storm Rider had saved his life, and the lives of his people. Now Storm Rider was asking the same favor returned; Bold Eagle could do no less than listen.

"Continue, I am listening."

As Creed unfolded Ann-Marie's plan Bold Eagle's features grew more and more distressed.

"I am to understand you want my people to prepare your bodies for burial, transport them out of camp on a travois, and place them on sacred platforms?"

Creed's gaze met his brother's unflinchingly. "This is what I ask."

"Before you are *dead*?"

Creed nodded soberly.

"You ask too much, Storm Rider! It is said that the ghosts of the people waiting to be escorted to the Hanging Road walk between the scaffolds as they wait for Heammawihio's signal."

"I am aware of the Cheyenne beliefs," Creed continued, "but I have thought it through, and there is no other way to escape without causing pain to my Cheyenne brothers."

Bold Eagle shook his head. "I am not certain my people will help."

"We need the help of the Heviqsnipahis if we are to be successful," Creed stated.

Silence, heavy and foreboding, settled upon the visitors and their host. Only the fire emitted warmth. As the silence grew Anne-Marie decided she would try to convince Bold Eagle that it was in his best interests to let the plan go forward. Turning all her feminine wiles upon the noble savage of the plains, she began, "Chief Bold Eagle, may I have permission to speak?"

Although women were allowed to give counsel among

the Cheyenne, Bold Eagle was still taken aback at the boldness of this woman.

Bold Eagle glanced at Storm Rider and saw that his gaze, resting on the woman's face, was filled with trust and something else. If Storm Rider trusted this woman, then he would permit her to speak.

At Bold Eagle's nod Anne-Marie turned her full attention to convincing the chief of her plan. Gathering up her habit with one hand and pointing to the wedding ring on her left hand, she forced herself to speak slowly.

"I know that you, Noble Chief of the Burned Heart band, are aware that I am a representative of God." She glanced at Creed, silently asking for his forgiveness for this one more small lie.

At the chief's nod she continued, "I am here because God wills it. My God and your Wise One Above speak as one. You have learned this from the black robes." She looked at him for confirmation.

The chief nodded again.

"I wear this robe and ring as a symbol that I am one with the One Who Is Above. He will let no harm come to me or you, for I am in his good graces."

Bold Eagle turned his attention to Creed. "Do you agree with her words, my brother?"

"Yes," Creed said simply.

Bold Eagle gave him a piercing look and then returned his gaze to Anne-Marie. Creed had the distinct impression that the chief wasn't buying it. However, Bold Eagle had a problem: he had to rid himself of this problem; Anne-Marie had given him a way to do so without loss of face, and at little danger to his band.

As the sun sank lower Creed, Anne-Marie, and Quincy used their persuasive powers to convince the

chief of the Heviqsnipahis that the plan, though unorthodox, was sound, and there was no other viable solution to the situation.

"Let it be so," Bold Eagle finally conceded with a
heavy sigh.

*And may Heammawihio look the other way.*

As he promised, Bold Eagle executed the plan. That
afternoon he called the council together and explained,
with Creed's help, the steps needed in order to make it
a success. The council was dubious, but willing to help
Storm Rider and his friends. The next morning the plan
was set into motion.

"I'm telling you, I don't like this." Quincy was visibly trembling as he was wrapped in buffalo hides and
strapped onto a wooden rack. Just the thought of being
buried alive gave him the willies.

"The hours will pass swiftly," Creed assured from
across the tent where Berry Woman and other Cheyenne
women were busily wrapping his body in buffalo hides.

Quincy panicked as the women cinched the straps
around him tighter. "I can't move my arms!"

Creed smiled. "You're dead, Quince. Your arms
aren't supposed to move."

"Oh Lord!" How did he ever let himself get talked
into this? Quincy was in agony.

"You have the knife, don't you?"

"What good's a knife gonna do me when I'm bound
up like a Christmas turkey, my body wrapped in buffalo
hides, and ropes are lashed so tight around me I can't
move?"

"You don't hear Anne-Marie complaining, do you?"

"Of course not," Quincy snapped, "it was her idea."

"And a splendid one it is, you'll see." Anne-Marie bravely made her way to the waiting pallet and calmly lay down with her hands against her sides. With a serene smile, she closed her eyes and gave herself over to the women.

"Well, I just want you to know," Quincy's muffled voice complained beneath the hides, "that this is the most idiotic idea anyone claiming to be of sound mind has ever come up with!"

"Too late to think about that now." Creed's pallet was raised and placed upon the shoulders of four Cheyenne warriors.

Quincy audibly groaned as his pallet was also raised onto the shoulders of two other warriors.

Creed felt rather than saw Anne-Marie's pallet being lifted and carried by the Cheyenne. He felt her reach out to him, and he sensed that she was asking for his reassurance.

He willed her to know his thoughts, then closed his eyes and gave himself to the One Who Lived Underground, Ahtunowhio.

"Hey, looka there." Ollie elbowed Butch as activity in the Cheyenne camp picked up.

"What do you make of that?" Butch asked as Malpas struggled to see through the clouds of dust that had suddenly enveloped the Indian camp.

"Looks to me like they're leaving," Malpas grunted. *And damn well time!* Another hour and his boots would be frozen solid to the ground.

"See the black and the nun?" Rodrigo peered around the other men's shoulders.

"Yeah, and the Indian?" Butch cut in.

"Malpas see *many* Indians," Malpas replied sharply, "but he does not see the black or the woman."

"What should we do, boss?" Ollie tried to see over his boss's shoulder down into the suddenly active camp.

"We watch . . . and wait to see which way they go." Malpas spat a stream of tobacco on the crusted snow. "They must now come out into the open. When they do, we follow the buckboard."

"But, boss, I don't see a buckboard," Butch argued.

"Did you see it leave?" Malpas flared. As the three shook their heads negatively he continued, "They will not *leave* the gold. They will take it with them, and when they do, we will follow and get it back."

Four pairs of eyes watched as the Cheyenne went about striking camp.

"Oh, yeah. Right, boss. They wouldn't leave the gold."

They continued to watch the activities, their eyes focused on the burial procession that slowly wound its way out of camp.

"Well, will you look at that?" Ollie whispered. "A bunch of 'em must've died off."

"Could be that's why they're strikin' camp, boss," Butch fretted. "Could be there's a sickness down there like the pox or something, and the whole tribe is dyin' off."

"Could be," Malpas said thoughtfully, "or could be just some old people whose time has come."

"I don't think so," Ollie said. "Warriors are carrying the dead. See." He pointed to where the medicine man walked in front, carrying weapons. "Them's not just old people."

"So?" Malpas said absently. He wasn't interested in the burial detail; what he was interested in was the buckboard, and right now all he could see was women tearing down the lodges.

A thought suddenly occurred to Ollie. "You don't suppose that could be that bunch we're chasin', do you, boss? After all, we haven't seen hide nor hair of those three since we arrived. Those Injuns could have took a notion to finish them off."

"*Basta!* Enough!" Malpas roared. "You are *muy estúpido*! And if it is them," he added as an afterthought, "*qué importa*, who cares, all I want is the *oro*."

Frowning, Ollie studied the slow-moving procession. "I don't know—we might oughta check it out, *jefe*."

Rodrigo was still trying to recover from digging up the witch, and just the thought of going into an Indian burial ground made him sick. "I'm not going anywhere near those travois."

*"No es necesario,"* Malpas stated emphatically. "The Crow, the woman, and the *negro* are still down there. They are not fools. They would not leave the gold. We wait."


As the sun blazed down on the scaffolds Anne-Marie began to have second thoughts. The black habit was turning her body into an oven. She lay for a moment, listening to the wind keening through the trees.

If she only had some water, she thought, and then remembered that a buffalo stomach full of water was hanging just a few feet below her. Food was also left on her scaffolding to provide nourishment for walking the Hanging Road.

The men had the weapons secured to their scaffolding so that they would be able to hunt for their nourishment as befitting courageous warriors.

Right now all Anne-Marie wanted was to leave this smothering cocoon, but she remembered Bold Eagle's warning. They mustn't leave until well after dark, when the moonless night would effectively cover their escape.

She could barely hear the tepees being dismantled, but she could feel the wind that had sprung up. It rocked her scaffold and caused the buffalo stomach and parfleche to thump loudly against the sides of the poles.

If one was afraid of ghosts, she thought, this could be one's undoing. Quincy's earlier fear of Eulalie came to mind and she wondered how he was handling the situation.

Quincy wasn't handling it well. Like Anne-Marie, he was aware when the wind had come up.

Unlike her, he did not find the swaying of the scaffold comforting. Instead he imagined it to be an irate ghost, shaking the poles and demanding that the living vacate the premises.

Each time his rifle banged against the side of the pole, he had to restrain himself from slashing his way out of the robe that had him wrapped tighter than an Egyptian mummy, and run. He didn't care where, so long as it was away from here. Oh, Lord have mercy. Would this day never end?

Creed lay quietly on his scaffold, awaiting the darkness. The pain in his thigh was intolerable. He'd known, even before he'd accepted the plan, that it would take a toll on his wound. The leg was swollen, pressing tightly into the buffalo hides.

The sound of his rifle thumping against the pole was as comforting as the knife he held in his right hand.

Closing his eyes, he saved his strength for the ordeal that still lay ahead.

# Chapter 12

Four riders sat atop a rise surveying the deserted land before them.

"Well, that's the last of 'em," Ollie mused to no one in particular.

"Yeah, that's the last of 'em all right," Butch echoed.

"This we cannot be so sure!" Malpas snapped. "We have not seen the wagon carrying the gold. Where is the damned wagon!"

"It ain't come out, boss," Ollie pacified. He was gettin' right down pissed over the way the boss was makin' out like they was all stupid or something. If Malpas hadn't seen the blasted wagon, how was they supposed to have seen it! "We've been watching for hours, and that buckboard ain't left that *camp*."

"*Es la verdad, jefe,*" Rodrigo put in. "We watch ver' close."

"Well, it's got to be down there somewhere," Malpas grumbled. "It couldn't have just disappeared into thin air."

Spurring his horse forward, Malpas headed toward

what had been a Cheyenne camp only an hour ago. The other men halfheartedly reined in to follow.

When they arrived at the site where the camp had been, it was hard to imagine that over a hundred people had lived there not three hours before.

Not one scrap of debris was seen. Several horse tracks, as well as two-pole tracks, led off to the southwest, but there was no evidence of a buckboard.

If Malpas had not seen it with his own eyes, he would not have believed that there had once been a buckboard. But he trusted his own eyesight and, grudgingly, that of the idiots with him.

"Spread out and check every inch of this ground!" Malpas ordered as the men sat their horses, looking at a loss as to what they should do.

"Maybe they burned the buckboard," Butch offered when he thought about the monumental task Malpas had commanded them to do. Why, they couldn't search every inch of this ground. That'd take days!

"*Estúpido!*" Malpas exploded. "This is what we must find out! The wagon, it had iron to hold it together, no? Iron does not burn. If we find iron that is not burned, then we know our eyes do not play the tricks upon us." He pointed to several mounds of smoldering ashes, and his eyes narrowed in on Ollie. "You and him"—he motioned to Rodrigo—"go sift through the ashes."

Turning to Butch, he ordered, "You, I want you to ride to where they buried them Injuns, and look for any sign of tracks."

Butch stared back at him vacantly. "Buckboard tracks?"

Malpas spat on the ground with disgust. "No, *estúpido, monkey* tracks."

"But, boss," Butch argued, "we didn't see no one come near that place once those dead people were put on those platforms—"

"The *carro* couldn't have vanished into thin air. GO!"

Reining his horse, Butch reluctantly started toward the burial ground, but he didn't like it. Not one bit.

The sound of approaching hoofbeats startled Anne-Marie. *Just be calm,* she told herself. *You're perfectly safe.* No one would dare desecrate a Cheyenne grave, not even one of these scroungy-looking men.

As Butch's horse walked beneath Quincy's scaffold Quincy began to shake uncontrollably. The unconscious trembling movement of his body, plus the rising wind, caused the scaffold to sway as if an evil spirit had set up housekeeping on the premises.

Slowing his horse, Butch shaded his eyes with his hand as he looked up, studying the platform.

Clamping his teeth together, Quincy tried to still the quaking, but his efforts were in vain. As the silence below him grew more pronounced he shook harder.

Squinting, Butch focused on the pulsating platform, a knot the size of a horse collar forming in the pit of his stomach. Was the wind making that platform shake like that, or—

He jumped, startled, as something dropped to the ground, sounding like a shotgun blast in the eerie silence.

*Oh Lordy, Lordy Lordy,* Quincy thought as every

tooth in his head began to rattle. He'd never see his Floralee again. His babies would never have their papa bounce them on his knee, ever again.

If these men got their hands on him, there'd be nothing left of John Quincy Adams but a bunch of bleached bones for the buzzards to roost on.

When the platform began to oscillate, Butch had seen enough. He wasn't gonna tangle with one of those heathens' spirits for anyone—Malpas included.

Wheeling his horse, he beat it back to camp.

"See anything?" Malpas asked as Butch came thundering up.

"Nothing, didn't see a thing—just some weapons dangling off them spooky-lookin' platforms."

Frowning, Malpas took off his hat and scratched his head. "No sign of the *carro*?"

Butch looked him straight in the eye and lied through his teeth. "I looked everywhere. No buckboard, just dead Injuns."

Malpas's eyes centered on Ollie and Rodrigo, who were busy poking sticks among the rubble of various campfires. "Well, now, you just ride back up there and help yourself to those weapons. No sense in letting good weapons go to waste."

"Huh-uh. Not me, boss."

Malpas glanced up. "What do you mean, 'Not me, *jefe*'?" He thumped his chest authoritatively. "Malpas, *he* gives the orders!"

"Yessir, you do, but I ain't going back up there."

Butch rode off, and Malpas stared after him, astounded. What had gotten into the fool? No man disobeyed Malpas, especially a pissant like Butch Fernado!

The sun had been down for over an hour when all the campfires and surrounding areas had been checked for remains of the buckboard or the gold. Nothing was found.

At the end of the day the men were dirty, cold, hungry, and frustrated, Malpas most of all.

"This I do not understand. How can a *carro* of *oro* just disappear"—he snapped his soot-covered fingers weakly—"like that?"

"Beats me," Ollie admitted. "All's I know is I need a drink and a decent night's sleep before we face Streeter and break the news we let the gold get away."

Butch shuddered at the thought. They thought they had trouble before. Streeter would lay an egg when he found out they'd let that gold slip clean through their fingers.

Rodrigo remained silent. Frankly he had had enough of this job. He agreed with the *gringos*. The only thing he wanted right now was a decent meal and an oversized bottle of tequila.

"There's a town some five miles from here. We go there where we will rest," Malpas announced.

"We don't go back and tell Streeter what's happened?"

Malpas's eyes narrowed into viperous slits. "We tell Señor Streeter *nothing*. Do you understand?" Malpas had not been made the fool! The *oro* was out of sight; it was not out of Malpas's grasp!

"Sure, boss, whatever you say," the others agreed wearily.

"The gold, it is here, somewhere." Malpas's gaze wandered around the barren campsite like a hungry animal. "And Malpas will find it."

As the four riders rode past the burial platforms, Rodrigo crossed himself.

"One *momento*!" Malpas called as he suddenly swerved his horse and urged it up the incline to the entrance of the burial ground.

"Oh hell," Ollie groaned. "He's gonna make us go after those weapons."

"I ain't going near those platforms," Butch vowed. He wasn't going to say he'd seen one move 'cause they wouldn't believe him, but a team of wild boars couldn't get him back in there. "If he wants 'em, he can get 'em himself."

Anne-Marie lay frozen as once more the sound of riders approached. She willed her heart to remain in her chest.

This was even worse than when she and her sisters were in the jail wagon being chased by Comanches. Now, as then, she silently began to recite the litany. *Holy Mary, Mother of God, pray.* . . .

*Oh Lordy, they're back again,* Quincy realized as he heard a horse pause by his scaffold. *They aren't going to give up!* The plan wasn't going to work! Adrenaline rushed to his tightly bound limbs, and he started shaking again.

Below, he could hear someone working to loosen the rifle tied around his platform.

"See, such fine weapons, men. They will make Malpas very happy," Malpas taunted.

"I wouldn't touch those if I were you," Ollie called out. "This here's those Injuns' sacred ground, and they wouldn't take lightly to you disturbing their dead."

Scoffing at such a display of sniveling, Malpas continued sawing. "See, rifles, and knives with long shiny blades, and—"

He suddenly glanced up to see one of the bundles starting to shake. His eyes grew wider as the body started to jerk back and forth.

"See," he said lamely, "such nice knives . . ." His voice faded as a low, wailing moan was emitted from the bundle.

Aghast, Malpas hurriedly ripped the rifle from the leather thong and wheeled his horse around, kicking it into a fast gallop.

As he burst out of the clearing he nearly collided with Ollie's horse, who was stationed well out of the area.

"Out of my way, *idiota*!" The Mexican ordered as he plunged his horse down the steep incline.

"What the hell's wrong with him?" Ollie shouted as he fought to control his shying horse.

"Who knows," Butch grumbled. If you asked him, they all needed their heads examined.

It was getting late when Anne-Marie finally heard a familiar voice below her.

"Anne, it's Creed. I'm going to cut you loose now."

She felt the ropes give way, and moments later her pallet slowly lowered to the ground.

The hides were stripped away, and she shivered at the sudden chill she felt when her sweat-drenched body was exposed to the cold night air.

"Are you all right?" Creed whispered.

"I'm fine, and you?" She tried to wring feeling back into her hands as she viewed his badly swollen thigh. "Your leg—it looks awful."

He followed her gaze. "Lying there for hours without moving was hard on the wound."

"I'm sorry," she murmured. She hadn't thought about the effect her crazy plan would have on his injury, but the plan seemed to have worked. Giving a quick look around, she saw no sign of the four men. "Do you think they've gone?"

"You two all right?" Quincy asked as he hurried toward them.

"We're okay," Creed assured in a hushed tone. "Let's get out of here."

Quincy didn't have to be invited twice. He'd had all of being buried alive he wanted.

"Bold Eagle better be where he said he'd be," Quincy worried aloud as the three struck off in a northwesterly direction under a cloak of darkness.

"He will," Creed said.

*He'd better be,* Anne-Marie thought.

# Chapter 13

As three figures rounded a bend in the road, riders moved from the shadows. Kneeing his horse forward, Bold Eagle rode to greet his brother.

"You have survived your ordeal," he greeted as the figures drew closer.

"We have survived it." Creed studied the blood-soaked bandage wrapped tightly around his thigh. The wound was throbbing from the arduous walk.

Black Earth and Two Belly brought along a fresh horse. A moment later Berry Woman appeared leading the buckboard.

Slipping from her horse, she ran quickly to Creed's side. "You are most ill, Storm Rider—you cannot continue this madness," she pleaded. "It is not wise!"

Anne-Marie looked away when she saw the unconditional love in the young maiden's eyes. Creed responded to her, softly cradling the girl against his broad chest.

Quincy was busy examining the buckboard. He had to hand it to Bold Eagle: he'd never seen a slicker operation in all his born days! Breaking down the wagon, then hauling the parts—plus the gold—out of camp on a travois right beneath the posse's nose was brilliant all right, even if a woman had masterminded it.

Berry Woman helped Creed to the back of the wagon as Quincy and Anne-Marie climbed aboard. Securing the horse to the back of the wagon, Black Earth and Two Belly dropped back.

"You will rest?" Berry Woman fretted over Creed as she stretched his leg out in the bed of the wagon.

"My sister clucks like a mother hen," Bold Eagle scolded. "Come, we must move on before we are noticed." He rode to the back of the wagon, where his eyes met Creed's. "You will be at the mission?"

Gritting his teeth against pain, Creed nodded. "We'll remain there until I am able to ride."

"I will send herbs, fresh kill, and water."

"Thank you, my brother."

Leaning forward, Berry Woman whispered into Creed's ear. He nodded, and she returned to her horse.

Turning their horses, the small party rode off.

Quincy picked up the reins. "Well, I've got to hand it to you, Miss McDougal. The plan went off smooth as my grandmother's Christmas pudding." He chuckled, imagining the looks on the faces of Streeter's men. "I'll bet that posse is still shaking their heads and wondering what happened."


At one time Santa Belle mission was a lovely sight; now the buildings lay in ruins. Low adobe structures adorned with red-tiled roofs dotted the hillside. However, years of neglect could not detract from the beauty of the twelve arches, some tall, some short, some semicircular, and others majestic and narrow. Their grandeur was still breathtaking.

The outer buildings were crumbling to the ground, but the mission's beauty and serenity still showed through the rubble. Though it was early, the walls of the courtyards were already overgrown with wild bougainvillea and honeysuckle vines, which nearly obscured the living quarters. Anne-Marie could imagine what a magical place the gardens must be in the summertime, when the heady scent of Castilian roses, lilies, and myrtle bushes with sweet-smelling leaves and starry white flowers filled the air with an aroma as sweet as honey.

High above in the old tower, a bell swayed in the gentle breeze. Its clear tones reminded Anne-Marie of all the mornings a bell much like this one had awakened her and her sisters for morning prayers. Scampering into their clothes, they had raced giggling to the chapel, to be detained at least once by a stern-faced nun who reminded the impetuous McDougal sisters that young ladies never ran, they walked. A pain so deep she could hardly bear it flooded over her when she thought about those happy, carefree days with her sisters. Would she ever see them again? She was beginning to lose hope.

"It doesn't look like much," Quincy noted as his dark eyes studied the crumbling ruins. "But I guess it'll keep the rain off our heads."

"Yes, I guess it will," Anne-Marie agreed without much spirit.

Leaving Creed asleep in the wagon, Anne-Marie and Quincy set out to explore the main building. As they entered the dim interior Anne-Marie wrinkled her nose at the musty-smelling alcoves. What few pieces of furniture had been left behind were either damaged or broken. All were covered with inches of dust.

As they entered the kitchen with its vaulted roof, she sighed with relief to note the chimney was intact and the kitchen stove still there. It was a huge, monstrous contraption, but at least they would have hot water and a more convenient way to cook their food—if they could find any. She hoped Creed and Quincy were more resourceful in that department than she.

"Lord have mercy," Quincy murmured as they roamed the empty corridors. Walls, some seven feet or more thick, with innumerable rounded stones sunk into the clay floors. They passed through the baptistry and into the large sanctuary.

Light streamed down through a long, narrow, horizontal window, illuminating the reredos with its nine statues in various niches. The altar was resplendent and elegantly carved with winged heads of cherubim. Pieces of the altar candles still remained, waiting to be lit for prayers.

A bat darted from the high ceiling, startling Quincy and Anne-Marie. They ducked for cover and Quincy's eyes grew round as he huddled closer to Anne-Marie.

"This place gives me the jebee's."

"What's the jebee's?" she whispered.

"Lord, I don't know, but I've got them."

"It's not so bad." Anne-Marie moved on, with Quincy following close behind. Returning to the kitchen, she parted a layer of thick cobwebs and peered down a black column of steps leading to the cellar.

"Now if you're thinking of going down *there*, you can just get that clean out of your head," Quincy told her. There was a limit to what he'd do!

"You're such a ninny," she chided. Searching for a light source, she spotted a candle stub lying near the base of the first step. "You have matches with you, don't you?"

"No, ma'am." His answer was too automatic for Anne-Marie to believe him.

"Quincy," she rebuked. "I know you have some, now give them to me."

"Ma'am, you don't want to go down there," he argued. "It's dark and dirty, and who knows what's at the bottom?"

God knows, he didn't want to speculate on what might be crawling around down there—or even worse, slithering around down there—on its belly.

"You don't have to go if you don't want to," she told him, hoping to allay his fears. The old mission seemed spooky only because it was so quiet. Dark cellars didn't bother Anne-Marie. When she was small, she had fetched potatoes and rutabagas for Sister Delia from the cellar nearly every day.

"There could be something to eat down there," she reasoned. "Something the former occupants might have left behind."

"By the looks of the place there's been no one here for years," he countered.

But her mind was made up. "We're wasting time. Give me a match."

She watched as Quincy reluctantly fished a sulfur-tipped match from his vest pocket and handed it to her.

Striking the match on the sole of her shoe, she lit the candle stub, brightening the narrow stairway with at least enough light to see the way down.

"Oh." Quincy's eyes grew rounder. "I wish you

hadn't done that.'' Edging closer to Anne-Marie, he cringed as the sound of scampering feet ruptured the silence.

"It's just some old mice. They won't hurt you." Hitching up the hem of her skirt, she stepped down a couple of stairs, then turned to look back over her shoulder. "Are you coming?"

When he didn't answer, she continued in a peeved tone, "You don't have to, but if I should find something, I'll need your help carrying it up."

"What we need is two or three torches instead of one little candle," Quincy muttered. "Ma'am!" he said pleadingly. "Why don't you just forget all about looking for something to eat. Anything you'd find would be rotten by now, anyway."

Lord have mercy. If she *were* to find anything, he'd be afraid to eat it. The last thing they needed was a good case of the gripe! "Why don't I just go out and see if I can find us some wild berries—"

He jumped back, startled again as a mouse darted up the stairway and shot between his legs.

"Oh, dear Lord," he agonized when he saw Anne-Marie was already halfway down the stairs. She wasn't listening to a word he said! His pappy had taught him to be a man, and a man wouldn't let a woman go down in an old dark hole by herself, but this was one time when John Quincy Adams was sorely tempted to go against his upbringing; sorely tempted. Drawing a shaky breath, he started down the stairs behind her.

Candlelight danced across the walls as Anne-Marie stepped deeper into the dank cellar. The sound of dripping water could be heard in the distance.

Cool drafts of musty-smelling air threatened to extinguish the candle, plunging the stairway into total darkness.

"Don't let the candle go out!" Quincy hissed.

"I'll try not to."

Pausing at the bottom of the steps, Anne-Marie lifted the candle higher, trying to see. It was black as the ace of spades down here. "See anything?" she whispered.

"Nothing." Lord Almighty, Quincy couldn't have seen a speeding locomotive if it had been coming straight at him. Squinting, he slapped blindly at something that zoomed by his ear.

Drifting deeper into the vault, Anne-Marie noted the cellar wasn't as large as the one in Mercy Flats, but it was adequate.

As she moved the light slowly along the walls, her eyes searched the premises, looking for anything edible. It appeared as if nothing had been left behind.

Boy, it *was* spooky down here.

A man's voice shattered the silence.

"What are you two doing?"

Quincy's muscles went limp at the sound of Creed's voice. Anne-Marie's hand shot out to support Quincy as his tall frame slumped against her.

"What are you two doing down here?" Creed repeated as he stepped off the bottom step to join them.

"What are *you* doing down here?" Anne-Marie rebuked, half-shaken herself at the unexpected intrusion. "I thought you were sleeping."

"I was, but when I woke up and found you both gone, I thought I'd better look for you." His eyes roamed the dark interior. "What are you searching for?"

"I thought the former occupants might have left

something we could eat,'' Anne-Marie murmured. ''You never know where a sister might have stored food.'' Lifting the candle higher, she moved the light slowly through the inky interior. Her hand paused, swinging the light back to the left a little more when she thought she detected a small chamber in the very back of the room.

''Do you see anything?''

''It looks like a room or something.''

''We're *not* going in there,'' Quincy warned.

Ignoring him, Anne-Marie held the candle out in front of her and moved toward the small chamber, her habit rustling in the shadowy darkness.

Quincy glanced at Creed. ''That woman is going to give me the trots before this is over.''

Brushing aside a layer of cobwebs, Anne-Marie lifted the heavy bar blocking the entrance to the chamber. As she slid the bar aside it rattled noisily on its rusty hinges, creating an ominous sound throughout the small chamber.

Using her slight weight, she shoved against the door. The hinges groaned at the disturbance, but refused to budge. Stepping around Quincy, Creed laid his shoulder against the wood and heaved.

The door slowly swung open, yielding an even blacker void.

The three stood for a moment, peering into the gaping edifice.

''See anything?'' Anne-Marie whispered.

Creed edged closer. ''Nothing. Hold the light higher.''

Quincy hated this. He had no desire to enter that spooky room, but even less desire to stay outside alone.

The three pressed close to each other and entered the stale-smelling chamber. Inside, it was even blacker.

Anne-Marie moved the light along the walls as their eyes anxiously roamed the tight quarters. The room appeared to have no apparent purpose.

"Just more storage room," Anne-Marie announced, to Quincy's relief.

Sinking back against a ledge, Quincy fumbled in his back pocket for a rag to wipe his brow. This place was worse than the old witch's house and that Cheyenne camp put together.

His hand suddenly froze as it brushed something. Sweat rolled down the sides of his face, and his heart pumped faster. He hadn't felt what he thought he'd felt, had he?

No, sir, he surely hadn't. No, sir, he was just imagining. . . .

Wiggling the fingers on his left hand, he suddenly went sick to his stomach. *Oh Lord.* There was a hand other than his own trying to get into John Quincy Adams's back pocket.

Lunging forward, he startled Anne-Marie, who screamed and dropped the candle, catapulting the room into all-out darkness.

Amid the high-pitched frenzy, Creed dropped to his good knee in search of the candle. "Silence!" he roared when his companions' screams ballooned to full-blown hysteria.

Their noise died away at his authoritative command, and the room echoed with an uneasy silence.

"Quincy?" Creed snapped.

"Yes, sir?"

"Where are the damn matches!"

"In my pocket."

"Hand me one."

"I can't see."

"You don't need to see! Reach in your pocket and hand me a match!"

A sound of rustling cloth followed, and they heard Quincy striking the match. The smell of sulfur filled the small chamber. The candlewick caught, again flooding the room with light.

Anne-Marie turned on Quincy crossly. "Why did you scream like that?"

Unable to find his voice, Quincy could only motion with his eyes to look over her shoulder.

Her gaze followed along with Creed's and she swallowed back a gasp. Skeletal remains were perched on the ledge behind Quincy, the skulls grinning devilishly at them.

Quincy jumped back. "Oh, Lord have mercy," he cried. "I *knew* we shouldn't have come down here! We're in big trouble this time!"

Creed moved the candle slowly along the ledges, trying to keep a semblance of calm. The light revealed skeletons reclining in various positions throughout the room.

The deceased, all dressed in monks' attire, appeared undaunted by the appearance of unexpected guests.

Pressed tightly against Creed's back, Anne-Marie fought the urge to panic. She didn't scare easily, but sharing quarters with dead monks was something she could do without.

"We're in some sort of burial vault," Creed mused as he moved to examine the remains more closely.

Quincy groaned. "Don't touch those bones!" Lord,

they were going to get these spirits all riled up and they'd not get out of here alive!

"They're dead, Quincy," Anne-Marie reminded.

"I know they're dead! That's what bothers me!"

"They can't hurt us," Anne-Marie consoled, then added with more conviction than she really felt. "They can't hurt us. They're *dead*."

"Oh, mercy, mercy, *mercy*." Quincy wondered what he'd done to deserve this misery?

"They can't hurt us—but I don't think we should disturb them." Anne-Marie couldn't tear her eyes away from the macabre collection. "Don't you agree, Creed?"

"I agree."

Moving as one, the three began backing out, keeping a close eye on the chamber's occupants.

Once they were clear of the room, Creed quickly closed the door and slid the rusty bar back into place.

Exchanging looks of relief, they turned and beat a hasty path back up the stairway.

Within days, life settled into a pattern at the mission. Each morning Anne-Marie was up before dawn. Meals were meager, consisting mostly of a thin gruel made from the last of the provisions, and whatever Bold Eagle's braves had left on the doorstep that day.

After breakfast each morning Anne-Marie dressed Creed's wound and rebandaged it, using strips of petticoat that she had washed and hung out to bleach dry in the sun. To her delight, Creed's health gradually began to show signs of improvement.

Each new day brought a new and wondrous discovery for Anne-Marie. She found a contentment with Creed that she hadn't known was possible. At times she wondered if she was falling in love. The thought was so unlikely it made her laugh, but at other times she would try to analyze her frightening new feelings. She decided she felt the way she did about Creed Walker because he made her feel like a woman.

It wasn't anything he said, but more the way his eyes fixed on her at times, following her as she went about her work. His gaze would lock with hers, and there was something indefinable in his dark eyes.

But at other times he looked at her as if she had lost her mind. Like the night she was invited to read her poetry. She had warned the men that she was only a novice poet, and her attempts were amateurish at best, but they had insisted she recite something, so she had complied.

"Are you sure?" she asked, afraid she would bore them to tears. Nights were long at the mission, and entertainment was as scarce as hen's teeth, but that night the men were in a charitable mood.

"Go ahead," Quincy invited. "Recite something for us."

Glancing at Creed, Anne-Marie sensed that he wasn't necessarily the poetic type, but he seemed agreeable. "Well," she began, drawing a fortifying breath, "I'm not very good."

"You have to be better than either one of us," Creed acknowledged.

They sat on the floor in the kitchen, around the huge cook stove. The fickle spring weather had turned balmy, but there was still a chill at night. May was right around the corner, and Anne-Marie found herself longing for the time when the air would be perfumed with honey-suckle, bougainvillea, and jasmine.

"I wrote a poem about robins once. Would you like to hear that one?" she asked.

The men agreed that her poem about a robin would be fine.

"All right." Clearing her throat, she began.

" 'The Robin,' by Anne-Marie Lynell McDougal.

"The robin hopped, the robin sang,
The robin fell, and broke his wang.

"He got right up and chirped some more,
Until a bolt of lightning struck him to the floor."

She took a deep breath.

"The robin—"

Creed lifted his brow. "Broke his 'wang'?"

Her face clouded. "I told you, I'm not very good."

*That* was when he looked at her as if he doubted her sanity.

Later that night the conversation returned to the gold. Quincy had hidden the buckboard in the mission court-yard beneath a growth of tangled vines, but Creed was uneasy with the arrangement. He thought the gold should be stored in a safer place, and he argued that the buckboard was their only means of transportation should they be forced to leave on short notice.

Quincy agreed with him, but he didn't know where

else to put it. Once again Anne-Marie supplied the logical solution.

"Why not store the gold downstairs?" She glanced at Quincy, aware he wasn't comfortable with the idea of sharing the mission with its past inhabitants who resided below the kitchen floor.

Way below.

When Quincy grasped what she was suggesting, his rebuttal was swift and emphatic. "Down there with those corpses?" He shuddered. "I'd sooner *eat* the gold!"

"But think about it, Quincy. What better way to assure that the gold will be safe? No one but us knows the room's there, and even if the posse should find us, they'd never discover that room."

"That posse isn't going to find us." Quincy stated.

"They might."

Quincy shook his head. "Huh-uh. Malpas isn't smart enough to keep looking. I'll wager he's given up and gone home."

"I wouldn't be so certain about that," Creed observed.

"Are you siding with her?"

"Yes, because she's right, Quince. That gold isn't safe where it is."

Quincy had noticed that Creed supported Anne-Marie's suggestions more and more lately. He'd noticed the looks passing back and forth between those two, and it made him nervous. When a man and woman looked at one other like that, it only meant one thing: trouble with a capital T.

"Now look, you two." Quincy knew what they were up to and it wasn't going to work. Anne-Marie wouldn't be strong enough to carry the gold to the cellar by herself; Creed was babying his leg so he wouldn't reopen the wound. Who would that leave to move the gold down there?

John Quincy Born Sucker Adams, that's who.

"I'm not going near that cellar, so don't even ask me." And this time he meant it.

Sighing, Anne-Marie got up to stir the fire.

As the silence lengthened, Quincy grew more determined. He knew what they were doing; they didn't fool him. They were trying to make him feel guilty about not being more protective about that gold, but they were wasting their time.

That gold was safe right where it was.

There hadn't been a sign of that posse for days, so they might as well move on to another subject.

"Do you have another poem to recite?" he inquired solicitously of Anne-Marie.

"No. That was the only one."

Well, he couldn't say he wasn't relieved. That robin thing was bad.

The silence grew. Creed lay back, closing his eyes as he listened to the night birds calling back and forth in the courtyard.

"You're not going to shame me into that cellar," Quincy told them. He wasn't going down there in that dark hole again. "It isn't like the gold is in any danger now."

Moving back to the pallet, Anne-Marie sat down, gathering the hem of her skirt between her legs. Loosing the pins from her hair, she absently ran her fingers through the thick mass.

A slow warmth crept into Creed's groin as he studied

her movements from beneath hooded lids. Candlelight caught the fiery highlights and he found himself wanting to run his own fingers through it and smell her sweet feminine scent. His gaze moved to her mouth, and the heat burned hotter.

Anne-Marie looked up to see him staring at her. Color suffused her cheeks as she quickly looked away. The curve of her ankle beckoned to him from beneath the hem of her skirt. Her inexperience should have quelled his desire, but it only made the heat more blistering. It had been too long since a woman had shared his bed.

As she lifted her eyes again their gazes touched. His sultry eyes ignited new and mysterious feelings inside her, feelings she was powerless to explain. She was hot, then cold. Her mouth was dry, then she needed to swallow. She wanted to move closer to his comforting presence, yet she felt the need to run.

She imagined how nice it would be to lay her head against his broad chest and feel the steady beat of his heart. She wanted him to hold her tightly, to whisper to her the way he had to Berry Woman.

She wanted him to teach her things, things that only a man could teach a woman. She thought that at this moment he looked very kind, like someone who would understand all the curious feelings raging inside her.

''Oh, *all right*!'' Quincy had suffered enough! The pressure was too much! They weren't going to let up until he moved that damn gold!

Startled, Anne-Marie and Creed broke eye contact, watching as Quincy stalked to the door, jerked it open, and left.

Glancing at Creed, Anne-Marie frowned. "What got into him?"

Shrugging, Creed got slowly to his feet. "He must have changed his mind about moving the gold. He'll need my help."

"No!" Scrambling to her feet, Anne-Marie searched for her boots. "You are going to sit here and let that leg heal." He wasn't going to undo all she had managed to accomplish the past few days. *She* would help Quincy move the gold.

Before Creed could argue, she followed Quincy out the door.

# Chapter 14

Ferris Goodman sat across the table from Loyal Streeter in the Gilded Dove saloon Thursday afternoon. The men had been talking for over an hour, and it seemed to Ferris that Loyal was restless. He kept toying with his whiskey glass, glancing nervously at the door.

"Relax, Loyal, Malpas is gonna show up any minute now."

"Where the hell is he?" Streeter barked.

"We're gonna get the gold back," Ferris assured him. "It's just takin' a little longer than expected."

Loyal tossed down another whiskey. "It's like the earth opened and swallowed that Indian and woman alive."

"There's a Cheyenne camp the other side of Brittle-branch. Fifty or so tepees—"

"You think they went there?" Streeter blanched at the thought. Malpas would never confront a band of Cheyenne. The Mexican was loco, but not that *loco*.

"That's what I'm thinkin'."

"They'd be crazy to do that—unless the Crow's in cahoots with the chief."

"Well, you never know. If the Indian's desperate enough, and I'd say right about now he is, he might try anything to save his neck."

"Maybe—but I'm still puzzled about what part the black has in this. And why the Indian was with the woman."

Loyal signaled to the bartender for another refill. "I don't know, but you can bet your life the Indian's not worried about the black or the woman right now. He's protecting his own hide."

Ferris frowned. "You don't think those three might be tied in together someway? They couldn't have known about the gold—could they?"

Shrugging, Loyal tossed down another drink.

"Naw, those three couldn't have known about the gold," Ferris said with conviction.

"Where the *hell* is Malpas?" Loyal glanced at the doorway again. He knew he should have insisted that Ferris put someone other than that thickheaded Mexican in charge of the posse.

Goodman's face clouded. "I haven't heard from him, but that's a good sign. He must be onto something or he would have been back by now."

Shoving out of his chair, Streeter tossed a coin on the table as he reached for his hat. "Time's running out, Goodman."

"I know that." Ferris had seen newspaper accounts of the war. It didn't look good for the South. They weren't going to be able to hang on much longer. "You're not thinking of doing anything crazy with that gold, are you, Loyal?"

Loyal paused. "Crazy? What kind of fool question is that?"

"Nothing, just wondering." Ferris had his reasons for asking. He'd seen the look in Loyal's eyes lately, that greedy look he got sometimes when he was hatching a plan. He didn't know what Streeter had in mind, but it was a pretty safe assumption that the Confederacy wasn't going to benefit from it.

Loyal's voice was tight now. "If you haven't heard from Malpas by sundown, send someone out to find him."

"If that's what you want."

"That's what I want."

Loyal strode angrily across the saloon and out the bar's swinging door.

Yes, Ferris thought. Whatever Loyal was up to, you could bet it was no damn good.


"You have family, Quincy?" Anne-Marie asked as she stacked another bar of gold between a monk's legs. Quincy seemed so tense she thought that talking might help.

"Yes, ma'am."

"A wife? Children?"

"Yes, ma'am. One—three."

"One wife, three children?"

"Yes, ma'am."

Anne-Marie bit back a grin as he jumped, smothering a curse as his hand accidentally brushed one of the monks'. "Guess you'll be glad when the war is over and you can go home," she mused.

Wedging a bar between the shoulder blades of a skeleton and the wall, Quincy smiled. His tone was wistful now. "Yes, ma'am, I sure will be."

"How old are your children?"

"Too old to be without a papa. Floralee has all she can do to care for young'uns and keep food on the table." Quincy often agonized over his family's welfare. It was hard enough for a woman to be alone with three babies, but the war made it even more difficult.

"I'm sure your family misses you." Anne-Marie barely remembered her papa, but she remembered his voice. Loud and spirited, the kind of voice that made you smile when you were around Irish McDougal. She remembered Mama saying Irish had created many an evil thought among women in his younger days. But it was Mary Catherine McCurdy who had won the fiery Englishman's heart.

"I've heard it said the war can't last much longer," Anne-Marie observed quietly.

"Yes, ma'am, sure don't think it can."

Anne-Marie paused to catch her breath. "You're still worried about the gold, aren't you?"

Quincy met her gaze solemnly. "I'd just as soon it was in the commander's hands," he admitted.

"It will be, just as soon as Creed's able to travel."

"Well," Quincy said as he hid the last bar on the stack. He was mighty relieved to have the gruesome job finished. "I hope you're right."

"Why wouldn't I be? We got rid of that posse, didn't we? They haven't a clue as to where we are right now."

"Yes, ma'am—maybe it's safe, all right."

She hated it when he just "yes ma'amed" and "maybe'd" everything she said to death. His superficial answers meant that he didn't agree with a word she said.

"What're your plans once you and your sisters are back together again?" Quincy asked as they simultaneously slid down the wall to rest a spell.

"Well . . ." Anne-Marie thought before answering. Before their arrest, she and her sisters had planned another scam near Dallas. She supposed that once they were together again, they'd execute the plan. "I guess we'll visit friends in Dallas," she said vaguely.

"You ever thought about settling down?"

"Like—married, settling down?"

"Yes, married, settling down. Like having kids, that sort of thing."

"No."

"No?"

"No."

Quincy leaned back, smiling, stretching his long legs out before him.

"What are you grinning at?" She knew he was grinning at her; she just didn't know what he found so amusing.

"You're downright funny, ma'am."

"I don't mean to be." And she resented the implication. Having a congenial personality was one thing, but being the butt of someone else's joke was another.

"How old are you?" he asked.

"Twenty-two."

"Twenty-two." Sighing, Quincy recalled the days of his youth, not that he was old. Thirty-one wasn't ancient, but he'd seen better days.

Anne-Marie returned to his earlier observation. "Why am I funny?"

"Pretending not to have an interest in the opposite sex."

"I don't have!"

He closed his eyes, his grin widening. "Yes, ma'am."

"Don't 'yes ma'am' me! What would make you think I have any interest in the opposite sex?" The very nerve of him, accusing her of something so absurd!

Quincy looked downright smug as his white teeth flashed in the dark. "I've seen the way you look at Creed, and I've seen the way he looks back at you."

"You're just imagining things." She turned her back, put out with him for saying things like that. She didn't look at Creed any certain way, and he certainly didn't go out of his way to look at her.

"He's pledged to Berry Woman," Quincy said quietly.

"I know that." If she knew nothing else, she knew *that*. Someone went out of their way to remind her everywhere she went. Her voice suddenly assumed a small and childlike quality. "Do you think he loves her? I mean, the way a man really loves the woman he plans to marry?"

"Well, that's hard to say. Creed never mentions her, but then, that doesn't mean much. Creed doesn't talk about his personal life."

"Yes, I suppose men don't talk about things like that—not the way women do," she admitted. If it were she and her sisters, they'd sit up half the night talking about such things, but men were different.

The tantalizing image of Creed's unclothed body lying naked on Eulalie's kitchen table popped into her mind.

*Really* different.

"Don't you think a man should love a woman so much it wouldn't bother him to talk about her?" she persisted.

If Anne-Marie loved someone that much, it wouldn't bother her one whit if the whole world knew it.

"Yes, ma'am," Quincy murmured, thinking about his Floralee. "A man should love his woman enough to talk about her, that's for sure."

"Then why doesn't Creed talk about Berry Woman?" Anne-Marie didn't like to think about Creed being in love with another woman, but if he was, she was curious as to why. Berry Woman's life and his were so different now. They were both of the same heritage, but Creed had learned the white man's way. Was it possible he wanted to return to the Indians' way of life? "Maybe he doesn't really love her."

"You don't know much about the Crow, do you?"

"No," Anne-Marie admitted. "Nothing at all, really." She'd seen Indians all her life, and she had heard tales about how they not only fought each other, but also had to fight to protect their territory from a variety of enemies, including miners, settlers, and soldiers. But that was about all she knew.

Quincy's expression sobered. She might be twenty-two, but she was awfully innocent and he felt sorry for her. "The Crow's ideal of marriage is one between a man near Creed's age with honors to his name and a girl Berry Woman's age who is no clan or kin relation."

Anne-Marie's heart sank. "Really?"

"Really."

"But—"

"Miss McDougal. It doesn't matter if he loves her or not, he'll marry her," Quincy told her gently.

Meeting his gaze, Anne-Marie's eyes couldn't hide her emotions. "But why—if he doesn't love her?"

"No one but Creed can say if he loves her, but Creed

has given his word to his blood brother, Bold Eagle. Nothing"—Quincy's eyes searched hers; he hoped to make her understand—"and no one can alter his pledge."

"But you *admit* that Creed may not be in love with Berry Woman?"

Anne-Marie didn't know why that should make her so happy. Whether he loved her or didn't love her, Quincy had just said Creed would marry her regardless.

Getting slowly to his feet, Quincy dusted off the seat of his breeches. "Won't do any good to dwell on it, little one. As soon as the war's over, the marriage will take place."

Anne-Marie stood up and hurriedly stuck the lid back on the Wells Fargo box, refusing to look at him now.

Laying his hand on her shoulder, Quincy tried to console her. "Nor will it do any good to brood about it, child."

It was impossible for Anne-Marie to hide her feelings. Someone once said that a woman's eyes never lied. "I wouldn't brood about any old man."

She turned away, biting back tears. "Especially someone named Storm Rider."

"See, it's much better today." Anne-Marie studied Creed's bandages, proud of her handiwork. After only a few days at the mission, the wounded leg looked much better, although she'd had to remind Creed several times a day to keep his weight off it. He was anxious to deliver the gold to his commander, and she'd had to remind him repeatedly that they would do so in no time at all, if he would just show some patience.

"We'll be forced to leave soon," she teased as her

eyes centered on the dwindling pile of makeshift bandages. "My petticoat's up around my waist now."

Creed's sober eyes focused on Anne-Marie as she
wound the clean bandage neatly around his leg. Her
hands were small and her touch was as light as a hum-
mingbird. The past few days had produced a different
side of Anne-Marie McDougal. A softer, more vulnerable side he found disturbing. In the beginning he had
thought her more man than woman with her rowdy ways
and rapier tongue. Now he realized that he had been
wrong. She would honor the man she chose to marry
and bear children with.

Creed had begun to think about the time he would
take Berry Woman as his wife. The war would be over
soon, and Bold Eagle would be anxious for the ceremony to take place.

Creed had learned the white man's ways and many of
those ways he found practical. Like the white man,
when he married, he desired a woman with gentle ways
and quiet strength. He would be her weakness.

This woman would come to him in her need when no
other could comfort. To her husband, she would give
her body, her deep and abiding love. Together, they
would become one heartbeat, one soul. Apart, the other
would find no pleasure in being, take no joy in the
rising sun. Without the one, the other would cease to
exist.

"There now." Anne-Marie drew him back to the
present as she patted the bandage into place. "All finished."

He smiled, resting his hand upon hers. "Your touch
is gentle."

Turning aside, she prayed he wouldn't hear the way

her heart was pounding. It pounded a lot lately when he was near. "Would you like to see some pictures I found this morning?" she asked.

"Pictures?"

"Yes, I found them in one of the chambers this morning." She left the kitchen, returning shortly carrying two large canvas paintings.

Propping them against the wall, she considered them a moment, then turned to gauge Creed's reaction. Admittedly the pictures were unusual in content, but the artist's efforts were not in vain. "What do you think?"

Creed's eyes traveled quizzically over the two canvases. One painting showed a dilapidated house, the other an eroded field. "Odd."

"Aren't they, though? I suppose a sister—or a monk—must have painted them in their spare time." She suddenly broke into a grin. "Let's play a game."

She could practically hear his mental groan, but there was little else to do. The dishes were washed, Quincy was off hunting, and it was a long time until noon. She and her sisters had played the game she had in mind often to while away the hours.

"What kind of a game?" he asked slowly, skepticism lacing his voice.

"We'll each make up a story about the pictures. Whoever concocts the best story wins."

A smile played at the corners of his mouth. "And the prize?"

She thought for a moment, then smiled. It was impossible to best her when it came to making up stories. "Whoever loses cooks the evening meal."

Leaning forward, he whispered, "I don't want to

play games. I'd rather just look at you.'' Laying his hand across hers, he viewed her prettily flushed features.

When she realized that he was staring as her again, her color deepened. Why did she get so darn flustered every time he looked at her!

His features clouded. ''My touch disturbs you?''

''No.'' She glanced away, uncomfortable with his close scrutiny. ''I . . . it's just that I've never . . .'' Drawing a deep breath, she confessed in a rush, ''I haven't been around men very much.''

The corners of his mouth curved with amusement.

''You're laughing at me,'' she accused.

His repentance was swift. ''I do not laugh at you. I find you most charming—a little stubborn and rebellious, but nevertheless feminine and sweet.''

Her heart sprang to her throat, and she suddenly felt as though she was going to suffocate.

He reached for her hand and held it, his eyes drawn to hers. ''Being with a man is not so frightening.''

When she didn't look up and refused to answer, he placed his fingers beneath her chin, forcing her to meet his gaze. ''I frighten you, little one?''

Yes, he frightened her. He aroused feelings in her that she knew she was not supposed to feel. She didn't know anything about the man-woman kind of love, but it seemed to her she was on the verge of falling right smack into the middle of it. What other explanation could account for the havoc he wreaked inside her—and it was *evil* havoc because when he looked at her, her mind was filled with lust—yes, plain old lust. Sister Agnes had warned of the consequences of such feelings. She knew her thoughts would eventually get her in terrible trouble, because Sister Agnes always said they would. But here she was, aching for this man's touch, lusting after him like a common . . . common lusting person!

His voice took on a husky timbre as his hand closed over hers, comforting her. "I would not hurt you."

"It's just that . . . my thoughts are sinful when we are together," she confessed.

"I have many of the same thoughts," he whispered back.

She looked up, and they exchanged forgiving smiles.

Sighing, she gazed back at him, wondering why her feelings were so wrong when they felt so right. "I don't understand. If our Lord doesn't want us to feel this way, why does he place such temptation in our paths?"

Smiling, he tenderly brushed aside a strand of her hair, his fingers reluctant to relinquish the silken strand. "I do not presume to be so wise. I know only that my heart is filled with wonder at your words."

She couldn't look at him now. "What words . . . what did I say?"

His gaze softened. "You said that your heart is filled with temptation."

"But I didn't say for whom," she reminded him quickly. Perhaps if she didn't voice the source of her sinful thoughts aloud, then her transgressions would not be so grave.

Bringing her fingertips to his mouth, he pressed his lips against the back of her hand, gazing deeply into her eyes. "There is no need for you to speak a name. I know of whom you speak."

The touch of his mouth on her skin was electrifying. Closing her eyes, she allowed herself the iniquitous indulgence of the blissful moment. The upheaval he caused within her went against everything she held sacred, yet strangely enough she was beginning to feel less shame. His lips, supple and provocative, were torturous on the back of her hand. Had she been bolder, she knew where this moment would lead. If a kiss on the back of her hand could have such a devastating effect, she was reasonably sure he would spare her no mercy were they alone, in bed. . . .

Shattered by the disturbing images that seemed to come unbidden to her mind, she broke away, springing quickly to her feet.

"Do not run from me, Anne-Marie," he called softly as she bolted for the door. Ignoring his pleas, she fled from the room.

Yet he knew where he would find her.

Following, he found her in the sanctuary, kneeling before the lighted candles. With head bowed and hands clasped tightly together, she appeared to him as an almost saintly picture of contrition. For a moment anger and confusion overshadowed his own turbulent emotions. Did she feel—sinful—because of her feelings for him? Was she ashamed because he was Indian? Because they were of two different worlds?

His anger dissipated as he watched her kneeling before the altar. A shaft of sunlight slanted through the narrow, horizontal window above Anne-Marie. It caught the lustrous glint of her hair, bathing her in a ghostly radiance. The scene before him took on an ethereal quality. She looked so small—so vulnerable—so much in need of being protected, cared for—and loved. He wanted to be the one to do all those things for her.

Tensing, Anne-Marie clamped her eyes shut tighter as his voice drifted softly to her from the back of the room. "Why do your feelings for me frighten you so?"

"Because I don't *want* to love you," she whispered brokenly.

Her admission echoed hollowly in the chapel. She hadn't fully realized until this moment how deeply she loved him—but she did. She loved him more every day, and she couldn't help herself. What would Amelia and Abigail think when she told them of her foolishness? Would they laugh at her, tease her, tell her how silly she—the levelheaded one—was being?

"Love is nothing to be frightened of," he chided gently.

"It is—for me it is."

"I, too, have felt this power between us," he confessed.

"Doesn't it bother you?"

"At first it did, when I thought you were a nun."

"And now?" She held her breath, afraid he would say he was falling in love with her and terrified he wouldn't.

Moving up to the altar beside her, he knelt, his wounded leg causing him to grimace. His close proximity unnerved her even more. He was so virile, so powerfully male. She wanted to touch his bare chest, to explore all the tight ridges of muscles she knew lay beneath his buckskin shirt—

*Sinful, sinful, sinful!* she thought. God was going to strike her dead here and now for thinking it!

"Don't touch me," she warned, for she knew if he

did, all her efforts to cleanse herself of wickedness would be in vain.

"Speak to me of your fears, Anne-Marie."

"I'm not afraid to love," she babbled. "I just don't want to love you—" She broke off, sobbing, then opened her eyes quickly to see if she had hurt his feelings. She couldn't tell; she might have. She was being awfully direct.

His tone revealed no particular emotion now. "Would it be insensitive of me to ask why?"

Opening her eyes a crack, she saw that he was smiling at her again.

"Until you came along, my life was happy."

He sighed. "And I have made you unhappy."

No, he hadn't made her *unhappy*. Considering all the agony she had put him through, it was the other way around. But he had taken away her contentment, whether he'd meant to or not, and she wanted it back. She wanted her life to be like it was before, when all she wanted or needed was her sisters.

"*I* have made you unhappy?" he pressed when she failed to answer him. "This is not my intent."

She whirled to face him. "What about Berry Woman?" she said harshly.

For a moment he looked as if his future wife had completely slipped his mind.

"Remember Berry Woman?"

"Yes, what about her troubles you?"

"You are supposed to *marry* her, that's what troubles me! How can you sit here and ask me why I don't want to love you when you know you couldn't love me even if you wanted to—which you might not," she babbled, for fear he would think she was, again, being too presumptuous.

Why did he make her so blasted indecisive! It unnerved her just to be near him.

"I do not *love* Berry Woman," he protested. "Our marriage is an arranged one, nothing more."

She stared back at him, barely able to maintain her civility. "And what is that supposed to mean?"

"Anne-Marie." Over her soft protests he took her hand again. His eyes spoke of his great desire for her, but she refused to see it. "The Indian and white man's way are not alike. Among Crow, fidelity is extolled, but a constant man can be ridiculed."

Her heart was breaking at this revelation. Breaking! "What are you saying? As a Crow, you can have as many women as you want?"

"Well—"

"That's disgusting!"

"We cannot have as many wives as we want," he hastened to add, as if that would make a difference. "But a man can have—lovers."

"That's—absolutely revolting!" she sputtered.

His jaw firmed. "It is the Crow way."

"Well, it isn't my way." She stood up, glad they'd had this conversation. It had not only cleared the air between them, but it had cleared her head where he was concerned. She would share a cup of cornmeal with another woman, but never the man she loved.

And most certainly, she would never share Creed Walker.

"Do not run from me again," he warned, impatience

tinging his voice now. She was as elusive as the wind. Here one moment, gone the next.

But Anne-Marie refused to listen anymore. She fled from the chapel, slamming the door on her way out.

# Chapter 15

Supplies began to run critically low. Creed and Quincy knew it, but neither seemed inclined to do anything about it. As promised, Bold Eagle had kept them supplied with fresh meat, but Anne-Marie needed flour and cornmeal—something that would stick to a man's ribs. She had to deal with the problem daily, while Creed and Quincy seemed content to eat the thin gruel she prepared each morning, noon, and night without comment. Game was scarce and rhubarb wasn't in yet, so that left only chokecherries and wild turnips as staples.

"Don't wander away from the mission," Creed had told her on various occasions, and at first Anne-Marie obeyed. Now she was seriously considering going against his wishes. If Creed or Quincy wouldn't do anything about seeing that they were properly fed, she guessed it would be up to her. Besides, Creed's wound would heal faster if she had some medicinal salve. But she'd need money for her venture, and she knew of no money except the gold coins hidden in the mission cellar. One single coin would never be missed, and even if it was, it wouldn't make that much of a difference.

Besides, it would be for a worthy cause. They had to keep up their strength. The gold would never reach the commander's hands unless they delivered it, and they couldn't deliver it if they were emaciated and half-starved, she convinced herself.

The decision made, she planned to start off early the next morning right after she finished dressing Creed's wound, and was confident he wouldn't miss her.

"What are your plans for the day?" Creed asked. His hands brushed hers as he handed her his empty plate. He touched her a lot lately, always spontaneously, but with enough feeling to heighten her awareness of the strong, sensual pull between them.

"Nothing," she lied. "I thought I might look for mushrooms."

Alarm entered his dark eyes. He was helpless to protect her if trouble should arise.

"You are to stay close by," he warned.

"How far could I go?" she reasoned. The paths surrounding the mission were overgrown with weeds. It would be all she could do to find her way out.

On the way to the mission they had passed the small community of Brittlebranch. The town wasn't more than an hour's ride, so if she left now, she'd be back well before dinnertime, and Creed would never know she'd gone. Oh, he'd be angry when he discovered she had disobeyed him. But his anger would fade once he enjoyed the wonderful meal she'd cook from the provisions she'd purchase with the one gold coin that would never be missed.

The plan was simple, and she could pull it off with

her eyes closed. She would be in and out of Brittle-branch before a cat could give itself a bath!

"Well." Quincy got up from the table to hand her his plate. "I'm going fishing this morning."

She dunked the plate in a pan of hot water. "Fishing?"

"Yes, I spotted a little stream about a mile up the road. I thought I'd try my luck at getting us a fish for our supper tonight. 'Course," he added wistfully, "a nice fat catfish is going to be mighty tasty, but there won't be any corn bread or fried potatoes to go with it."

*Don't be so sure about that,* Anne-Marie thought smugly. There just might be a big pan of corn bread, some nice creamy butter, and a huge pan of fried potatoes waiting when he got back with his fish.

But she played right along. "And with what do you plan to catch a fish? You don't have a fishing pole, a string, or even a hook."

"Why, ma'am." Quincy held up both his hands. "I have two of the finest fishing poles the good Lord ever created." Grinning, he walked out of the kitchen. She heard him whistling merrily as he struck off for the stream.

Rinsing the last plate, Anne-Marie laid it on the countertop and then wiped her hands on her skirt. "What do you plan to do this morning?" she asked Creed as he prepared to leave.

"I found part of an old ax in one of the outbuildings. The blade's rusty, but I should be able to chop enough firewood to last for a couple of more days. By then we should be able to move on."

"Be careful," she cautioned, "and don't break open

the wound again. It's just now beginning to heal properly.''

Smiling back at her, he rose to leave, and as he did so his backside brushed hers, triggering that strange tingling deep inside her again. She wished he wouldn't do that. She didn't understand the crazy feeling, and she wasn't entirely certain she cared to.

The moment he was out of sight, she raced out of the kitchen and down the cellar stairway. Sliding the heavy bolt aside, she lit the candle stub, took a deep breath, and entered the dank chamber. Then taking one gold coin from the skeletal remains of a monk, she slipped it into her pocket, turned, closed the heavy door, slid the wooden bar back into place, and raced back up the stairway.

Blowing out the candle, she laid the stub on the first step and firmly shut the door. Leaning against the wooden frame, she paused for a moment to catch her breath. *So far, so good.* Giving a hurried glance to the back of the mission, she breathed a sigh of relief when she saw that Creed was already engrossed in chopping wood.

Now all she had to do was get to town and back by dinnertime.

The ride to Brittlebranch was pleasant. It was a beautiful spring morning and Anne-Marie was tempted to dawdle. But she couldn't, she reminded herself. She must complete her errand and return to the mission as quickly as possible.

A gentleman in a passing buggy tipped his hat to her and she returned his smile as the buckboard rolled merrily along the road. The last thing she needed was to draw attention to herself. She must be careful to hurry about her purpose and remain as inconspicuous as possible. A passing stranger would think that she was merely a lowly sister on her way into town to purchase supplies for a mission—which was nearly true.

As she entered Brittlebranch several more men tipped their hats, bidding her a pleasant morning. Nodding demurely, she acknowledged their greeting solemnly. There wasn't much stirring in town this morning, but then it was early and most people were still at home. The schoolteacher stood outside the schoolhouse, ringing the bell for late arrivals.

Driving straight to the mercantile, Anne-Marie climbed off the buckboard and quickly disappeared inside the store.

The proprietor glanced up as the sister entered. Smiling, he walked toward her. "Morning, Sister."

Anne-Marie nodded. "Good morning, sir."

The shelves were adequately stocked despite the war. Anne-Marie quickly went about gathering the needed supplies. She lingered before the sugar, thinking how nice it would be to have some, but decided on a jar of honey instead. Selecting six nice plump apples from a barrel, she placed them on the counter beside her other purchases.

When the clerk saw that she had finished, he turned from where he was busy stacking canned goods and began to total her selections. "That about do it for you?"

"Yes, this should be sufficient. Thank you." Anne-Marie fished inside her pocket and handed him the gold coin.

Gilbert Kinslow looked at it closely, but he made no comment.

''You're new around here,'' he observed as he boxed her purchases.

''Yes.'' A pretty, small porcelain music box caught her eye. It was lovely and she still had plenty of money left over from her purchases, but she didn't dare buy it. Creed would understand the need for supplies, but he wouldn't understand a foolish whim like a music box.

''Right pretty, isn't it?'' the clerk remarked when he saw that she couldn't take her eyes off the trinket.

''Yes, that it is,'' she agreed.

''Make you a real good price on it,'' he offered. ''Stocked it for Christmas, but with the war and all, I didn't have any takers.''

''It is lovely.'' Anne-Marie picked the box up to admire it more closely. The detail was exquisite.

''Quality craftsmanship,'' the clerk observed.

It was indeed; the finest Anne-Marie had seen. Amelia was fond of doodads and she would love the music box, Anne-Marie thought. Before prudence intervened, she hurriedly laid the box beside her other purchases.

The clerk's brows arched curiously. ''You don't want to know the price?''

''I'm sure it will be fair.'' Anne-Marie glanced anxiously out the window. ''Add it to my other purchases, please.''

''Be glad to. I'll even wrap it for you,'' the clerk said obligingly.

''Thank you, that's most kind of you—if it won't take too long.'' Anne-Marie's eyes returned to the window again.

''Looking for someone?'' The clerk tore off a sheet

of heavy, brown paper and began to wrap the delicate box carefully.

"No—oh, would you stick in a few pieces of the peppermint candy?" she asked. Creed and Quincy would like the special treat.

The front door opened and a woman holding the hand of a small child entered.

"Morning, Mrs. Bigelow."

"Morning, Mr. Kinslow."

The young woman began browsing while Gilbert completed Anne-Marie's order. Handing her the large box, he smiled. "Be glad to carry this to the wagon for you, Sister."

"Thank you, sir, but that isn't necessary. I'll manage on my own."

Emerging from the store a moment later, Anne-Marie glanced up and down the street before hurrying to the wagon.

A speck of violet hanging in Harriet's Millinery caught her eye. Her footsteps slowed as she viewed the exquisite finery displayed in the window.

Drawn closer to the window, she admired the beautiful garment. The dress was lovely, to be sure. White grenadine with lavender-edged ruffles and puffs, narrow matching mantle, and a hat of rice straw with violet and white plums.

Slipping her hand into her pocket, she closed her fingers around the remaining coins left from her purchases. She had more than enough to buy the gown. After all, she had gotten the music box for Abigail, and Amelia would surely feel slighted if she didn't receive a similar token of her sister's affection.

Impulsively her hand closed around the doorknob and

she entered the shop. When she emerged from the millinery a few minutes later, she was carrying a large box tied gaily with a red ribbon around the middle.

Storing the box beside the mercantile box, she lifted the hem of her skirt and was about to climb aboard the buckboard when a steely hand closed around her shoulder.

She glanced up, and her heart sank as she looked into the cold hard eyes of Malpas.

"Morning, Sister."

"Are you sure you haven't seen her?" Creed paced the kitchen floor at the mission, his frustration mounting. For over two hours he had searched for Anne-Marie, but she was nowhere to be found. When he returned to the mission for dinner and found her missing, he had immediately begun to search.

"I saw her the last time you did," Quincy told him for the hundredth time. "This morning at breakfast."

Creed's features were strained as he strode back to look out the window again. "Where in the hell could she be?"

Shaking his head, Quincy had to admit that her disappearance had him stumped. He had spent the last two hours scouring the gardens and the surrounding area, and there wasn't a sign of her anywhere.

"Have you checked to see if the buckboard's here?"

Quincy frowned. He hadn't, but then he hadn't thought there was a need to. "She wouldn't have taken the buckboard! Not after all the times she's been warned to stay close to the mission." He frowned. "You don't think—"

"With her, you don't know." Creed started for the

door. When he discovered the buckboard and one horse were missing, he swore furiously beneath his breath.

Quincy kept quiet. When Creed was this angry, keeping silent was the only sensible thing to do.

"I'll have to go after her," Creed said.

Quincy was about to tell him that he didn't have to find her. The gold was safe in the cellar and their assignment wasn't threatened. But he still kept silent. He knew no matter what he said, Creed would go after her.

"We had better get started. It'll be dark soon," he said instead.

"No, you stay with the gold." Creed's eyes met Quincy's and a look of understanding passed between them. "She's my responsibility."

Nodding, Quincy quietly accepted the fact that Anne-Marie was becoming a whole lot more to Creed than a responsibility.

"For the last time I don't *know*." Anne-Marie stared straight ahead, determined to die before she told Malpas where the gold was hidden.

"*Señorita,* you are most unwise." Malpas paced before her, hands clasped behind his back, looking pensive. The *mujer* was stubborn, but Malpas had yet to meet his match. His voice dropped menacingly. "You will tell me, or I will be forced to cut out your tongue!"

"Then I for sure couldn't tell you," Anne-Marie said stubbornly, jutting her chin out. She prayed he wouldn't hear the way her heart was thumping against her rib cage in fear.

"Ohhhh, the *mujer* has an obstinate *disposición*! Malpas, he appreciates a sense of humor, but I'm afraid he must resist the urge to laugh." The Mexican's eyes were steely. "You will tell Malpas, *señorita*. Where *is* the gold?"

"I don't know where it is."

"You lie!"

She stared straight ahead.

Ollie and Butch exchanged uneasy looks. Malpas was red-faced again, and that meant he wasn't going to let up on the woman.

"The *oro* and the *indio*—where are they?"

"I haven't seen them recently."

"You lie!"

She stared straight ahead.

Swearing now, Malpas paced faster, his eyes narrowing into viperous slits. "I will cut off your tongue and make you point the way!" he vowed.

Anne-Marie kept her eyes resolutely fixed to the branch of a tall cottonwood. Her hands were bound firmly behind her back, which ached from the awkward position. Until Malpas had begun his interrogation, she had been gagged.

Butch pointed out the obvious. "She ain't gonna tell us anything."

"Yeah, but leastways we know we caught up with 'em again," Ollie noted. "It was a sure stroke of luck that we were still in town this morning."

The liquor had been good and the women so obliging that Malpas had lingered longer than planned. Another hour and the woman would again have escaped their clutches.

"Are we *mujers*?" Malpas sneered.

Butch shifted on his haunches, pouring the remains of his coffee into the fire. "We ain't women, boss, but

if she refuses to talk, there ain't much we can do about
it.''

"Oh, no, you are most wrong, *Señor* Butch.'' Malpas spit, then wiped his mouth on the sleeve of his shirt.
''There are ways to make her tell us what it is we wish
to know.''

Rodrigo stirred uneasily. They had been at this for
days, and they were getting nowhere fast. "I don't
know, boss—''

"Do we not know of ways to loosen her tongue?''
Malpas prodded.

The men looked at each other as understanding
dawned in their eyes.

"I agree with Butch, boss, but . . .'' Rodrigo preferred using other methods. After all, she was a woman
and a woman of the cloth. He wasn't a religious man,
but it did seem risky mistreating a nun.

Anne-Marie's eyes darted from one man to the other.
Her heart was throbbing so painfully against her ribs
that she could barely breathe. *Stay calm,* she told herself. *Stay calm.* No matter what they said or did to her,
she would never tell them where Creed and the gold
were! Nothing they could do would make her further
endanger Creed's mission. She had caused him all the
trouble she was going to.

"Pissants!'' Malpas spat on the ground with disgust.
"I will *know* where she has hidden the gold!''

Anne-Marie struggled to free her hands as Rodrigo
grasped her by the arm and dragged her to a waiting
horse. Screaming, she bit and fought him until he
stuffed the gag into her mouth to shut her up.

Manhandling her into the saddle, he mounted behind
her.

"What about the Indian?" Ollie called. If the Crow knew she was missing, he'd be sure to come after her, because she knew where the gold was hidden.

Malpas climbed off his horse and removed a pick from his saddlebag. Lifting the horse's left foot, he pried the shoe off.

"But, boss," Butch complained, "the horse will go lame."

"We do not ride far," Malpas grunted. "Malpas make sure the *indio* will find her."

With a sinister look he climbed back on his horse, and the four riders left the camp in a thickening cloud of dust.

# Chapter 16

It was nearing dark when Creed entered Brittlebranch on foot. The storefronts were dark, the shops closed for the day.

Piano music filtered from the saloon as he slipped through the shadows on the sidewalk. When he saw that the clerk in the mercantile was just locking up, his pace quickened.

Gilbert Kinslow glanced up, startled when confronted by a pair of cold, hard black eyes. For a moment he couldn't find his voice as he stared back at the Crow.

Nodding solemnly, the Indian spoke. "I am looking for a woman."

"What sort of woman?" Gilbert asked. *Good Lord.* He couldn't help him. The Indian would have to find his own women.

"Small, pretty, dressed in a nun's habit. Have you seen her?"

Gilbert's brows lifted. "The sister?"

"Then you have seen her." Creed was relieved his guess was accurate, but when he got his hands on Anne-

219

Marie McDougal, she'd rue the day she disobeyed his orders!

"Yes, she was in earlier in the day. Bought some staples and a music box," Gilbert said.

Creed stared at the storekeeper unflinchingly. "A music box?"

Gilbert nodded. "Yeah, a right pretty one, porcelain—real dainty like—"

The Crow interrupted. "Did you see where she went after she made her purchases?"

"Yes."

"Where?"

"To the millinery."

A muscle tightened in Creed's jaw. *Where* was she getting the money for this burst of frivolous shopping?

"She came out later carryin' a big box. Must've bought someone a nice dress," Gilbert theorized. "Them sisters are always doin' nice things for folks!"

*A dress? A music box* and *a dress?*

"And then?" Creed probed.

"Then I don't know where she went," Gilbert admitted. "Mrs. Bigelow needed some kerosene, and I had to go to the back room to get it for her. When I looked out later, the sister's buckboard was gone."

Thanking him, Creed slipped back into the shadows. *A music box and a dress,* he thought, fuming. He was going to wring her neck! Having that kind of money meant only one thing. She had gone against his orders and had dipped into the stash of coins. She had done exactly what he had told her not to do.

At the edge of town Creed quickly located the tracks of a buckboard and four riders. The trail was easy to read—too easy. One of the horses had a missing shoe.

It appeared as if whoever had taken her wanted to make certain that Creed followed. The Crow's features hardened stoically as his hand settled around the handle of his knife.

Creed knew who had her, and he knew he would go after her.

His eyes, the color of black coal, darkened with fury as he thought about the consequences she would face because of her reckless actions. But his fury was tempered with fear—a fear that he wouldn't reach her in time. Something stirred within him, an emotion deep and disturbing. What was it that he was feeling for this woman?

Slipping back into town, he waited until the opportunity presented itself, then quickly untied a horse from the railing in front of the saloon and walked it quietly out of town.

"Where is the *oro*!"

"I don't know!" The lie barely escaped Anne-Marie's parched throat now. For hours she had been lying beside a pit, her hands bound to stakes in the hard ground. Excruciating pain racked her body, and she was faint with hunger.

But Malpas refused to concede defeat. *"Señorita,"* he cajoled, "you have only to answer my simple *pregunta*. Once you have spoken the truth, Malpas will give you some nice warm tortillas, beans, and something to quench your most terrible thirst!"

The Mexican's swarthy features wavered above Anne-Marie, but she was barely conscious of him.

"See the pit," he urged. "See, it is filled with many

large lizards. *Many* large lizards. Iguanas, *señorita*. Have you ever heard the word 'iguana'?''

Bile rose to Anne-Marie's throat at the mention of lizards. She hated lizards.

''If you do not tell Malpas what he wishes to know, he will have no choice but to throw you into the pit of iguanas. This would not be so nice. This would spoil the *señorita's* whole day, *sí?''*

Anne-Marie felt herself growing dizzy. His threats seemed to be coming at her through a fog. Somehow it no longer mattered what he was saying. She was so filled with fear that she was paralyzed.

Jerking her to a sitting position, Malpas grasped her by the shoulders and shook her until her teeth rattled. ''The *oro*? Where is it? *Speak!''*

Anne-Marie tasted blood as the crack of his hand across her cheek shattered the silence. Shaking her head weakly, she dropped back to the ground, welcoming the blackness about to consume her.

The Mexican's voice lowered ominously. ''You are most stubborn, *señorita*. Now you have pushed Malpas's patience to the limit.'' He straightened, his eyes focusing on the pit. ''Perhaps if Malpas gives you time to reconsider your ill-advised ways, you will have a change of heart.''

Barely hearing his voice, Anne-Marie swam in and out of consciousness. Nothing mattered anymore. She was going to die. She was going to be thrown into a pit full of lizards and be eaten alive. *Creed,* she thought. *Where are you, Creed?* He would know that she was gone by now, but would he look for her? Her heart ached with the realization that he might not. He had no reason to further jeopardize his mission in order to save her from the consequences of her own willful ways. The gold was safely hidden in the mission cellar, and she would *die* before she would let this evil man know where it was—but oh, how she prayed Creed would look for her.

"Boss, don't you think she's had enough? She ain't gonna say where that gold is."

Ollie had watched the past hours' proceedings with cautious interest. He was as contemptible as the next man, and he didn't want Malpas to think he was getting soft, but it went against the grain to see a woman treated this way. His eyes traveled over Anne-Marie's supple body, and he felt a familiar tightening in his groin. Women were made for a man's enjoyment, and it seemed a pity to mistreat one like this. There was other ways to handle a woman—more pleasurable ways than this.

"Why don't you turn her over to me? I'll make her talk," he offered.

A little sweet talkin' and a lot of lovin', which Ollie knew he was good at, might convince the little lady to have a change of heart.

Malpas glanced up, sneering. "*You* can make the woman talk?"

Ollie wet his lips as his eyes ran lustfully over Anne-Marie's young, ripe body. Oh, yes, he could make her talk. But he had to be careful not to show his hand. If Malpas thought for a moment that he would treat Anne-Marie with anything but merciless cruelty should she refuse to cooperate, the boss would never let him have a chance at her.

Malpas was not stupid. He saw right through Ollie's plan. Ollie was known for his endurance in a woman's bed. Generously endowed, he could no doubt provide the woman with hours of exquisite pleasure, or so Ollie always boasted, Malpas thought sneeringly. But Butch now—Butch took no pleasure in his women. He was interested only in his own physical gratification. If the only way to loosen the woman's tongue was to turn her over to one of the men, then Butch would be the logical choice.

Malpas viewed Anne-Marie's slender form lying before him and his own animal instinct flared. After Butch was finished with her, he would take his turn.

"Whaddya say, boss?" Ollie looked back at Malpas expectantly. "Want me to have a try at it?"

"No, I think this is a job for *Señor* Butch."

*"Butch!"* Ollie exclaimed with disgust. Butch, dad-blastit, could barely find his fly with both hands!

Butch looked up from the foot of a mesquite tree where he lay swigging on a bottle of tequila. His hand paused as he drew the bottle to his grimy mouth.

A wicked grin formed on the Mexican's lips. *"Sí,* you, *señor,* Butch. You will make the woman tell us where they have hidden the gold."

Butch glanced at the comatose woman lying on the ground in a small pitiful heap. *"Now?"*

Malpas's eyes moved back to Anne-Marie. "Now," he announced dispassionately.

"But she's as cold as a well digger's ass in January!"

"But you will revive her, *sí?"* Malpas mimicked. With a wicked laugh, he found himself anticipating the hour when it would be his turn with the woman.

Ollie's face went sullen. "What about the rest of us?" It wasn't right to leave him and Rodrigo out of the fun. After all, they had frozen their butts off just like Butch and Malpas in pursuit of the gold, so it was only fair that they share in the spoils.

Turning away, Malpas walked toward the stream. "When Butch and Malpas are through with the woman, you and Rodrigo can do what you want."

Grinning, Butch stood up, eager to get down to business. "I'll need the tent, amigos." He and Rodrigo exchanged ill-tempered looks as Butch's grin widened. "That is, unless you wanta watch."

In a rare burst of courage, Ollie found his tongue. "No, dammit. It's been you first every time, Butch! This time it's gonna be me! 'Sides," he added placatingly as Butch advanced toward him, "she's still out cold. You don't like your women limp as a rag. 'Member, you always said you like your women to be feisty."

Butch stopped, the threatening scowl on his face fading.

"I'll just go in and warm her up a bit for you—you know, get her good and stirred up, then when you get a go at her, her blood'll be runnin' hot!"

That did make a lot of sense, Butch thought, studying Ollie through narrowed eyes. He had no patience for rousing lethargic, dishrag-limp females! He liked 'em rough and ready to go!

"Might not be a bad idea at that," he mused aloud, rubbing the dirty stubble on his chin. Then, too, he could finish that bottle. Warm him up so's he'd be in good performin' shape!

"Well, guess it won't hurt nothin'," he growled. "Might as well save her the best for last," he taunted. "If I went in first, she'd be spoiled for the rest of yous anyway." He lumbered away to his spot under the tree and picked up the tequila bottle. "But hurry up, I wanta get some shut-eye!"

Rodrigo stalked off, rolling up in a blanket beside the campfire.

Alone now, Ollie's eyes focused on Anne-Marie's unconscious form as the painful throbbing in his groin grew more insistent.

"Well, well. Looks like it's just you and me, little lady," he murmured.

Bending over, he scooped up Anne-Marie's limp form and began carrying her toward the tent. Once inside, he laid her down on a dirty striped blanket and began to pull off her habit.

He smiled down at her, his fetid breath near her face. "We'll just see how long it takes for you to tell old Ollie where you've hid that gold."

He laughed, the evil sound ricocheting throughout the camp.

"I'll wager it won't take long."

An hour before dawn Creed lay on his belly outside the perimeter of Malpas's camp. His eyes, alert and watchful, searched for any sign of Anne-Marie. A mockingbird called to its mate in the distance.

The moon slid low, casting yellow light on the two primitive-looking shelters that had been hastily erected in the cleared area. The cooking fire had dwindled to glowing red embers.

With catlike furtiveness, Creed stealthily crept toward the camp. His ears were sharpened for any unusual sounds, but the camp's occupants appeared to be sleeping. He wondered where Anne-Marie was, and his stomach knotted with anger when he thought of the way she had fallen into the Mexican's trap.

Four unsaddled horses stood amid a thick grove of cottonwoods on the right of the camp. Pulling himself slowly along on his elbows, Creed inched closer, his body silently skimming over the hard ground.

His eyes fell upon the large pit dominating the clearing, and he frowned. It was a large hole, measuring a good twenty by twenty. A stake and the dusty footprints beside the pit revealed mute testimony of earlier activity.

Rage welled deep inside the Crow as he thought about Anne-Marie's fate. Her foolish actions might well have gotten her killed this time.

Focusing on the nearest tent, Creed elbowed closer. Buckboard tracks led straight to the clearing. Malpas had made certain that Creed would have no difficulty following them.

The mockingbird called again as the Crow slithered closer.

Inside the tent, Ollie slowly pulled his breeches back on. His gaze focused resentfully on the lithe beauty who lay on the blanket, the slender curves of her naked form faintly visible in the eerie night light. His features remained sullen. The plan had not gone as anticipated. For over an hour he had sat in the tent, trying to think of a way to bring her around. Once she was conscious and got a taste of his manhood, she'd be beggin' for more. She'd gladly tell him where that gold was just to have him love her up one more time.

But waking her up was growing more difficult by the minute. Several times Butch had shouted to him to hurry up. He was getting tired of waiting, he said. Any minute he might storm through the tent flap and discover Ollie's failure. Ollie couldn't let that happen! No matter what he tried, Anne-Marie lay still and silent. He had punched her several times and nudged her with the toe of his boot, all to no avail. She had fainted into deep unconsciousness. Even worse, Ollie realized his passion was fueled only when a woman was at least awake. And when she wasn't a religious woman. That didn't hardly seem right. He'd never attempted *sexo* with a completely unresponsive companion. Been plenty who hadn't necessarily been willing, but at least they had some life to 'em. Always made it more fun.

This woman had not fought. This woman had not even opened her eyes when he had stripped her bare, telling her in the crudest of terms what he planned to do to her.

This woman had not even heard his threats.

Hearing her soft moan, he sat up straighter. Well, it was about time she was comin' around. But then she grew silent again and seemed to fall back into unconsciousness.

Ollie was just plain disgusted. By now his ardor had wilted like a pansy in the boiling sun. He was aware that for some time now, Butch, Rodrigo, and Malpas had been standing outside, listening for the woman's screams for mercy.

Ollie couldn't afford for them to find out that not only had he not been able to back up his frequent boasts of masculinity and make Anne-Marie talk, he hadn't even been able to wake her up!

No screams begging for mercy. Not even a whimper.

What was he going to do? Malpas and Butch would never let him hear the end of it!

This was awful.

Sitting down, Ollie tried to think of a better plan. And it'd better be fast, he thought, cracking his knuckles. He wouldn't be able to face Malpas and the men. When they learned what a washout he was, Malpas would call him a woman and buy him a dress next time they were in town. What was worse, he'd make him *wear it*!

Sweat formed on Ollie's forehead. He wouldn't let that happen. He couldn't let Butch and Malpas think he couldn't handle a woman!

Getting back to his feet, he slapped his hands together, calling out loudly. "Where *is* the gold, woman?" Clapping his hand over his mouth, he imitated in a high-pitched whine, "I'll never tell you!"

Smacking his hands against his thighs, Ollie roared, "Tell me, woman! Tell me, or I'll beat you to death!" Falling to the ground, he thrashed about, imitating feminine squeals of agony.

"Let me *go*, you ruffian!"

"You will tell me where the gold is!"

"No, never!"

"You want more?"

"No, please! No! Please, someone help me!"

The tent vibrated with the supposedly violent scuffle taking place inside. Ollie rolled on the ground, crashing and thrashing around the tiny space, his voice swelling and falling as he portrayed both victim and aggressor.

At last Anne-Marie began to stir. She lifted her head, struggling to find the source of the commotion. At first she couldn't recall where she was or what had happened.

"Shut up, woman!" Ollie roared, unaware that she had awakened.

"Help me, help me! Someone help me!"

Frowning, Anne-Marie watched as Ollie rolled around on the ground, taking on like a madman.

"Don't you touch me again! No, please!" he wailed.

"Where is that gold?"

"You can kill me, but I'll never tell you!"

The tent quaked, threatening to collapse from all the violence.

*What in the world* . . . ? Anne-Marie groggily shook her head to clear away the cobwebs.

The moment the noise inside the tent erupted, Creed froze. His eyes steeled and his hand went for his knife.

Three men suddenly appeared in the clearing, drawn to the fracas. Creed watched as the men crept closer to the canvas, drawn by the dramatic sounds coming from within.

Suddenly a woman's screams rent the night. Creed recognized the agonizing screech of Anne-Marie. He sprang forward, knife in hand, and in one long leap, the Indian charged the Mexican Malpas, who was creeping closer to the tent opening.

But Malpas, though taken by surprise, quickly recovered. In a matter of moments he, Butch, and Rodrigo had the Crow disarmed and pinned to the ground.

Anne-Marie's screams had startled Ollie and he turned from his pretend scuffling to commence the real thing. Before he could blink, though, the struggle outside the tent caught his attention. Rolling to his feet, he crept to the opening and peered out, seeing Butch and Rodrigo tying up an enraged Creed Walker.

It hadn't been an easy capture—even for three of them. Their hats torn off, Ollie and Rodrigo were panting hard and bleeding from several scratches on their faces. Malpas had conveniently stepped aside after his men came to his rescue and let them wrestle with the Crow. Now he stepped forward, sticking his chest out arrogantly. He would show this impertinent Indian who was boss! *You do not mess with Malpas!*

Emerging from the tent, Ollie made a big production out of buttoning the front of his pants. "What's all the racket, boss?" he asked innocently.

Malpas grinned wickedly. "It seems we have captured our prey, *Señor* Ollie."

Butch sat on the middle of Creed's back, holding him down as Rodrigo tied the Indian's hands and ankles with a thick twine.

"You want me to let up on the woman?" Ollie asked.

"Has she told you anything yet?"

"No, not yet. I was just gettin' started real good."

Malpas looked at the Indian, his eyes narrowing with thought. "Perhaps force will no longer be necessary, *Señor* Ollie. Perhaps if the *indio* is willing, he will keep the woman from further harm." He laughed, showing his horselike teeth in the flickering firelight.

"Let the woman go," Creed demanded in a tense voice.

"I shall, my good friend, I shall. The moment you tell me where the *oro* is."

Creed struggled to sit up, but Butch slammed his head back to the ground.

Squatting, Malpas leaned over Creed. "Now, tell Malpas where is the *oro*?"

"I'll take you to it," Creed grunted. "Just let the woman go."

"No. You must tell Malpas where it is. He will go and get it himself."

"That isn't possible." Creed knew he would have to show the Mexican where the gold was hidden personally. If Malpas showed up at the mission alone, Quincy would defend it with his life. The gold was not worth either Anne-Marie's or Quincy's life. "I will have to take you," he said in a controlled tone.

Malpas spat on the ground in disgust. "You are a stubborn man, as stubborn as the woman." He straightened, growing weary of the games.

Creed twisted, trying to see around the Mexican into the tent. "Let the woman go, and I will take you to the gold," he repeated.

"*Silencio!*" Malpas started to pace, fury a tight knot in his stomach. It seemed he could not do this in a reasonable manner. The *indio* and the woman wanted to play rough. Very well, Malpas wanted the *oro*, and he was willing to play rough. Very rough.

"Gentlemen," he announced. Ollie, Butch, and Rodrigo glanced up. "*Señor* Ollie, bring the woman out here."

Ollie looked hesitant. Anne-Marie wouldn't look roughed up enough. He was afraid his sham would be swiftly exposed once they set eyes on her. He'd be the laughingstock of Texas! He would just as soon they concentrated on the Indian and kept Anne-Marie in the tent.

"Uh, I don't know, boss. Why don't we just forget

about her. We've got the Indian now—he knows where the gold is. Besides," he added, hooking his thumbs in his belt loops and thrusting his chest out pompously, "I was pretty rough on her and she's a little upset—if you know what I mean!?"

"*Upset?*" Malpas roared. "Why should Malpas care if the *mujer* is upset! Bring her to me!"

Chagrined, Ollie lifted the tent flap, fully expecting Anne-Marie to meet him with fire in her eyes and a rock in both hands. Steeling himself, he held his arms protectively in front of his eyes as he entered the tent.

Inside, Anne-Marie sat huddled in a corner, clutching the dirty blanket around her, shaking with cold and fright, too disoriented to search for her clothes.

When the flap opened, illuminating Ollie's stocky form in the dim campfire light, her heart thumped painfully against her chest. She had heard the shouting and commotion outside, but didn't know what it was about. She supposed it was Malpas and his men having a drunken argument. Now they were coming for her again!

"Don't you come near me, you—you bastard!" *Forgive me, Lord and Sister Agnes, but that's what they all are.* She clutched the blanket more tightly.

"Here," Ollie whispered, shoving her clothes at her. "Put your clothes on." He paused, staring down at her trembling form. "I could drag you out bare-assed nekkid, but I'm being a gentleman, and don't you ferget it."

"You touch me and I'll knock your slimy, pissanty head off your pissanty shoulders!"

"Uh, look." Ollie lowered his voice. "Keep your voice down—"

"Keep my voice down!" Anne-Marie interrupted hotly. "Why should I? Listen, you greasy son of a drunken sodbuster and saloon whore, if you so much as touched me, Creed will tear your black heart out and make you eat it!"

Ollie swallowed, looking over his shoulder uneasily. He'd suffered plenty under Malpas's cruel and overbearing leadership, but he'd seen the power behind the Indian's steel-eyed gaze.

"Uh, that's just what I want to talk to you about," he said in a pleading tone.

"Talk to me about what!" She glared back at him heatedly. "If you dared to so much as—"

"See," Ollie continued, still talking low, "that's just it. I didn't do anything, but . . . but . . . I'd like to . . . well . . . kind of like to ask that you don't tell Malpas and the boys that."

"Don't tell them *what*?"

"Don't tell them, I, uh . . . didn't . . . uh, you know . . ." His voice faded to an embarrassed whisper.

"Don't tell them you . . . didn't . . ." Anne-Marie repeated. Then, understanding dawning: "*You'd* better not have—"

"Shhh, pipe down!" Ollie begged. "They kin hear you!"

"Get out of here!" Anne-Marie ordered. "I want to put my clothes on, and if you know what's good for you, you'll tell those other low-down, vulgar, stinking smelly varmints they had better leave me alone, too!" She raised her voice louder. "And I don't care if they do hear me!"

Ollie backed out of the tent, and in a few minutes

Anne-Marie heard him tell Malpas the woman would be out shortly.

"You did not break her legs? She can walk?" Malpas jeered.

"Well, I guess she can," Ollie admitted.

"Then tell her to hurry up. Malpas grows weary of his wait!"

"Ahh, my lovely." Malpas surveyed his captive smugly when Anne-Marie finally emerged. "You had a most pleasant evening, no?"

Staring coldly back, Anne-Marie retorted, "I've had better."

Snickering, Malpas pointedly grinned at Ollie. Then beginning to pace, he clasped his hands behind his back. "Our good friend here"—he motioned behind him with a curt nod—"has also refused to tell us where the *oro* is hidden."

It was then that Anne-Marie saw Creed. Giving a small cry, she started to run to him, but Malpas stepped in front of her, blocking the way.

"The two of you are most *obstinado*. You must stop this. Malpas grows weary of your games."

"I haven't refused to tell you where the gold is hidden," Creed said. "I said I would take you there."

"No, Creed." The words escaped Anne-Marie in a rush. She didn't want him to tell where the gold was because of her.

"Untie me," Creed continued, "and I'll take you to where it's hidden."

"Why do you not just tell me where it is, and I will go myself?" Malpas was not this stupid. The *indio* had set a trap for him. The *negro* at this moment was waiting for Malpas to walk into it.

"I'll have to take you," Creed persisted.

Malpas glared at Anne-Marie. "And you have not yet changed your mind?"

Her jaw firmed. "No."

"Ah, then you leave Malpas no choice, my fair *señorita.*"

Motioning to Butch and Ollie, he gestured toward the pit. "The woman will lead us to the *oro* while the *indio* waits. In there."

Butch and Ollie's eyes widened. "In the pit, boss?" Butch asked incredulously.

Malpas's eyes hardened. "In the pit."

Images of the giant lizards crawling around below surfaced in Anne-Marie's mind, and she felt faint again. Straightening, she arched her back and took a deep breath. She wouldn't faint again. Not now!

"If I have not returned by daybreak, you will abandon the campsite, leaving the *indio* to die a slow, torturous death," Malpas ordered. "You will then meet me in Streeter, where we will return the gold to Señor Goodman to return to Señor Streeter."

*Now,* Malpas thought smugly, *who was the smartest?*

Over Anne-Marie's screams, Butch and Ollie dragged Creed toward the pit.

"Don't put him in there!" she pleaded. "I'll tell you where the gold is!"

But Malpas no longer trusted her. No, she would *lead* Malpas to the *oro* if she wanted her lover to live.

"No!" Anne-Marie screamed. "Don't throw him in there!"

Oblivious to her cries of desperation, Ollie and Butch dragged Creed toward the pit. Rolling him onto his side,

Butch grinned as he placed his large boot in the middle of Creed's back, then shoved hard.

Anne-Marie turned away, screaming as Creed tumbled down the steep incline. Moments later she recoiled at the sound of iguanas moving about, their thick, hard bodies brushing one another in their quest to greet the new arrival.

Seizing Anne-Marie by the arm, Malpas dragged her to the horses Rodrigo had saddled and waiting.

"Now, my lovely, you will *show* Malpas where the *oro* is."

Swinging her into the saddle, he grabbed the reins of her horse and quickly mounted his own animal.

"Don't we need a buckboard for the gold, boss? It'll weigh the horses down," Ollie shouted.

"*Sí*, this is good, *Señor* Ollie. If Malpas mind not so busy, he would have thought of this. You will get the buckboard and bring it to the mission. Butch, you stay here and make sure that our *indio* friend"—he chuckled—"is comfortable."

"*Sí*, boss."

"Again, if we have not returned by daybreak," Malpas ordered, "we meet in Streeter. The *indio* is to be left in the pit. *Comprendo*?"

Butch nodded. "*Comprendo*, boss."

Wheeling their horses, the riders departed with the sound of thundering hooves.

# Chapter 17

By sunup, Quincy was pacing the kitchen floor. Creed had left the mission hours ago, and he still wasn't back. That could mean only one thing.

Trouble.

If he had found Anne-Marie, he would have been back by now. Or he had found her and he couldn't get back. He had encountered trouble, possibly in the form of the posse.

Muttering under his breath, Quincy pulled on his jacket, then exited the mission through a side entrance.

If he lived through this, it would be a miracle.


Three riders rode hard through the early light. Anne-Marie was so intent on getting back to the mission and giving Malpas the gold so she could return to Creed that she was barely aware when the sun came up. In her mind, she saw over and over again Creed being pushed into the pit and heard the iguanas crawling toward him.

Biting back a sob, she clenched the reins harder, willing herself to stay calm. With Rodrigo riding ahead and Malpas behind, there was no way she could escape.

As the mission came into sight Anne-Marie wondered what she would tell Quincy. She was heartsick that her carelessness had once again not only endangered the men's mission but their lives. Quincy's concern for Creed would override his instinct to protect the gold, but Anne-Marie now began to fear for Quincy's life. What if Malpas decided to kill Quincy once the gold was in his hands?

Choking back another sob, she realized that the McDougal luck, which had never failed her, was about to run out.

The horses were lathered and breathing heavily as the riders approached the mission.

*Quincy, please don't shoot,* Anne-Marie prayed as she rode straight to the overgrown gardens near the kitchen door.

Quickly dismounting, she held her breath as she made her way through the tangled thicket. Overhead, a crow cawed harshly, further fraying her already ragged nerves.

Malpas and Rodrigo dogged her steps, their hands resting on the handles of their guns.

"The *negro*," Malpas whispered. "Where is he?"

"He was here," Anne-Marie answered. "I don't know where he is now."

Malpas scowled darkly. "If you speak the lie, he is a dead man."

*Please Quincy, be gone fishing,* Anne-Marie prayed. Or maybe he had decided Creed needed help and had gone to look for him. She prayed that this was the case as her hand reached for the handle on the kitchen door.

Undoing the wooden latch, she stepped inside. Except for the embers still smoldering in the mammoth stove, there was no sign of life. Behind her, she could hear Malpas breathing with exertion.

"Quincy?" Anne-Marie called. Her voice echoed back to her. When there was no answer, she called again. "Quincy?"

Moving through the kitchen, she hurried toward the cellar door.

"Where is the *negro*?" Malpas demanded.

"I don't know," Anne-Marie returned.

"He is hiding," Malpas said.

"No, he wouldn't hide. Maybe he went to look for me. I've been gone a long time."

Malpas, visibly uneasy, motioned for Rodrigo to stand watch at the door.

Kneeling in front of the cellar doorway, Anne-Marie searched for the candle. Locating it, she struck a match, and light flooded the narrow stairway.

Wings fluttered overhead as she descended into the bowels of the mission, Malpas close on her heels.

"It would not be wise to try to trick Malpas," the Mexican warned.

"It's no trick. This is where we hid the gold."

Malpas did not like the dark hole. He batted a cobweb. He was not the coward, but he preferred to see his enemy.

Anne-Marie wound her way down the dark staircase. A cool, musty scent rose to assault their noses. Upon reaching the bottom, she hurried to the partially hidden door and quickly slid the wooden bar aside.

"What is this you do?" Malpas barked behind her.

"I'm getting you the gold! This is where we hid it."

The Mexican's eyes darkened with suspicion. He smelled a trick. A most nasty one.

The door creaked as it slowly swung open to reveal an even darker abyss.

Straining to see around Anne-Marie, the Mexican squinted into the blackness. "It is dark in there."

Dampness surrounded them as they entered the chamber. The flickering candlelight cast supernatural shadows on the walls, revealing the grinning skeletons. Lifting the candle above her head, Anne-Marie allowed the light to play along the skeletal remains of the monks. She heard Malpas's sharp gasp.

"We thought the gold would be safe here," she said.

"*Sí,*" the Mexican replied, his voice wavering now.

"Well." Anne-Marie stood back. She would lead him to the gold, but she wasn't going to gift-wrap it for him. She pointed to the empty Wells Fargo box sitting on the floor. "There's the box it came in."

Malpas looked at the crate, then at the gold wedged between the monks' bones. Suddenly his greed overrode his fear of the dark, and swallowing, he reached for a bar, grasping it quickly.

Working feverishly now, Malpas stacked the bars of gold in the wooden crate. Occasionally an angry curse escaped his mouth as his hand brushed too close to a skeleton, but his greed for the gold pushed him on.

When all the bars had been retrieved, Malpas fastened the lid on the crate, shouting for Rodrigo.

Rodrigo appeared in the doorway, gun trained on Anne-Marie. His eyes widened at the sight that greeted him.

"Quick!" Malpas panted. "Help me carry the *oro* up the stairway."

"*Sí,*" Rodrigo returned lamely, his eyes trained on the skeletal remains.

The two men grunted and struggled up the stairs, lugging the heavy crate between them. Moving through the kitchen, they dragged the crate across the floor and outside.

Extinguishing the candle, Anne-Marie laid it on the step, then hurried after them. When she emerged from the mission, the men were already sticking the bars of gold into their saddlebags.

"You have the gold. Can I leave now?" she asked, anxious to return to Creed. Could he still be alive? He just had to be! She suppressed a shudder of repulsion, picturing him in that pit of lizards. How would she get him out? Could she overcome her intense fear to help him—assuming he was still alive?

"Malpas does not care what you do," Malpas said cruelly. He laughed, his evil voice piercing the air. "I have the gold—many more *señoritas* will come to Malpas now! We have no time for you!"

Tying the empty crate onto the back of his saddle, Malpas swung onto his horse. He leered down at Anne-Marie, tipping his sombrero to her. "*Gracias, señorita.* You have been most helpful."

Giving another maniacal laugh, he spurred his horse, and the animal sprang forward. Rodrigo, wheeling his animal, fell in behind him.

Anne-Marie watched as the two riders disappeared, kicking up a thick cloud of dust. Racing back to her horse, she mounted and rode swiftly to rescue Creed.

It was late when Anne-Marie arrived back at Malpas's camp. The moon lit her way as the horse thundered into camp.

"Creed?" Anne-Marie fell on her stomach, peering into the gaping pit.

*Dear Lord, please don't let them have eaten him.*

"Are you still in there?"

"Yes, I like it so much I hated to leave."

Incredulity and relief spilled over inside her. His voice didn't sound as strong as it should, but it was his voice. He was alive!

"I can't believe it." She peered deeper into the pit, squinting to find him. Nausea threatened when she saw the dim outline of the giant lizards. "I can't see you!"

"I'm on a ledge just to your right."

"The lizards didn't eat you?"

"You don't know anything about iguanas, do you?"

"No—and I don't want to."

"They spit on me."

"What?"

"They spit on me," he repeated.

"Why would they do that?"

"That's their nature."

"Oh. How far down is the ledge?"

"Maybe ten feet."

She thought for a moment, wishing it wasn't pitch-black, wishing she had a torch of some sort, wishing she had a rope, wishing she'd never gone after that silly cornmeal in the first place!

"Hold on, I'm coming after you."

"No! Don't do anything foolish." Creed's voice echoed back to her. The last thing they needed was for both of them to be trapped.

"I'm coming down. You stay right there."

"Anne-Marie! I said no! You could hurt yourself!"

Aware that what she was about to do was perhaps the

most foolish thing she'd ever done, and perhaps the last thing she'd ever do, Anne-Marie dropped a leg over the side of the pit and searched for a foothold. The toes of her boots scraped the sides until she found a niche. Testing its strength, she shifted her weight to one side, blindly groping for a second hold with the other boot.

"Turn around, and go back," Creed ordered.

"Don't boss me around." Step by agonizing step she made her way down the side of the crevice. Twice her foot slipped and she caught her breath, terrified by the thought of what lay below.

"Be careful," Creed urged as he watched her body slowly descending into the pit.

Hand over hand she lowered herself, scraping her knuckles against the sharp rocks that cut into her hands. She prayed that if she reached the shelf, she wouldn't knock them both to the bottom. Her rasping breath echoed harshly against the rock walls of the pit.

"You do know there are lizards down here," Creed warned. He glanced in the bottom of the pit. "Big ones."

"I know."

"You're afraid of lizards."

"I know, but I've grown accustomed to your face and I hate the thought of it being eaten off."

"I can take this as a compliment?"

"Sort of." Grunting, she gradually made her way down the wall of the shaft.

"You're not thinking, Anne-Marie." Creed knew her fear of lizards, and he didn't see how she was going to overcome it long enough to be of help. If she panicked, they would be in worse shape than they already were.

"Go get Quincy—"

"Don't talk to me. I have to . . . concentrate."

She continued her descent, searching for footholds and handholds, knowing that if she thought too much and too long about what she was doing, she would be lost.

"Careful." When her foot touched the ledge his hand shot out to steady her.

"Creed?"

"I'm right here." His hand grasped her ankle as he pulled her down beside him on the ledge.

"Creed? Oh, *Creed*!" His chest felt as solid and reassuring as she remembered. Burying her face in the curve of his neck, she held tightly to him for a moment while she caught her breath. "I thought you would be dead," she whispered.

He held her close, relishing the feel of her small body against his.

"How are we going to get out of here?" She pressed tighter, seeking his quiet strength, agonizingly aware of the lizards, who were trying to claw their way up the sides of the walls. She turned to look down, but his voice stopped her.

"Don't look down."

"But, Creed, the lizards . . ."

Shielding her from the sight, he turned, pointing to a ledge several feet above their heads. "See that ledge?"

She nodded.

"If I can make it up there, I can get us out of here."

"But your leg—"

"If I can get to that ledge, I can get us out," he assured her.

Anne-Marie viewed the ledge some fifteen feet above

her head, then said quietly. "You can stand on my shoulders to reach the edge."

"Anne, I'd crush you."

"I'm stronger than I look," she alleged.

He drew a long breath. At this point he couldn't argue. "All right. What are you wearing?"

"The habit."

"Take it off."

"What?"

"Take off the dress."

Balancing on the ledge, she carefully drew the dress off over her head and handed it him, never once thinking to question his command. "Here."

"Now remove the remainder of your petticoat and anything else you're wearing that has any strength to it."

"Honestly?" This really did seem an unusual request.

"Honestly."

She did as he said. When she was finished, she stood naked, her cheeks flaming as his body brushed hers.

Turning aside, he stripped out of his shirt and pants and she heard the sound of cloth tearing.

"What are you doing?" Shivering, she crossed her arms over her bare chest.

"Making a rope." When he was finished, he had assembled a length of cord he hoped would be sufficient. "Are you ready?"

Anne-Marie hesitated, glancing down at the lizards, then quickly up again. "I'm ready."

"Good girl. You'll have to prop me up. We'll need to work together on this."

"Just tell me what you want me to do."

"First, I want your promise that if I start to fall, you'll let go of me. I don't want you falling with me."

She felt dizzy. "I don't want that either."

"I want your word, Anne-Marie." His hands found her face in the darkness. "For once in your life, do what someone tells you."

"You have my word," she promised. "I won't fall in a pit of lizards—even for you."

"Be careful, and stay close to the wall."

Through a series of gyrations, they managed to get to their feet. Creed leaned heavily on her, and she realized he was hurt worse than he was saying.

Balancing on her shoulders, Creed hefted himself up on the ledge. Anne-Marie watched, trying to support his bare buttocks so he would exert as little weight on the injured leg as possible. The minutes ticked by with agonizing slowness.

Leaning down, he extended the rope to her. "I'm going to pull you up. Hold on as tight as you can."

Nodding, she grasped the makeshift rope and held on tightly as he eased her slender form upward.

When she reached the ledge, he quickly tied one end of the rope around his waist, then tied the other end around Anne-Marie's.

"Hold on tight."

He didn't need to remind her. She planned to.

Overhead, stars dotted the sky as he began to skim the wall of the pit. The rim of the pit edged closer, but the remaining twenty feet may as well have been a hundred, Anne-Marie thought.

She lost track of time. Her muscles screamed with the pull of the rope, and the tips of her fingers were bleeding from gouging into the sides of the jagged rocks. The only thing that kept her going was the knowledge that Creed was hurting worse than she. If he could keep going, then so could she.

"You all right?" he grunted.

"I'm . . . I'm okay, just keep going," she panted.

When Creed reached the edge of the pit, he held on to it for several minutes, then hoisted himself over the rim. Grasping her forearm tightly, he heaved her over the edge, and they collapsed in an exhausted heap.

Drained, they lay on their backs staring at the sky for several moments, the only sound coming from their labored breathing and the rustling in the bottom of the pit of restless lizards.

"You . . . all right?"

"I don't know," she gasped. "I feel like I've been caught in a buffalo stampede."

"Have you ever seen a herd of buffalo?" he asked.

"Once. What about you? Oh, of course you have. You're Indian."

Their breathing gradually returned to normal.

"Watching a herd of buffalo on the run, seeing the dust boil up, hearing the thunder, feeling the earth move beneath pounding feet—it's the most powerful thing I've ever experienced," Creed admitted.

She rolled over, propping herself up on her elbows so she could look at him.

"Do you realize that all we've done in the short time we've known each other is get into trouble?" he asked.

"I believe I have noticed that."

He smiled as his hand came out to cup her cheek. "My friend the priest once told me that in China when a man saves the life of another, the one must serve the other until the debt is paid."

She grinned, a warmth rushing through her. "Are you saying you have to serve me until a debt is paid?"

His fingers slipped into her hair as he pulled her face down to his. His lips were warm and supple on hers. When she opened her eyes a moment later, she saw a warm smile curving his lips.

"You're laughing at me again."

Creed studied her in the moonlight. Her face was dirty, scraped, and bruised. Her lustrous hair curled wetly around her cheeks and trailed over her shoulders in damp strands. She looked as if she'd been dragged behind several buffalo, but he was certain she'd never looked more desirable.

Twining her arms loosely around his waist, she held him. Her eyes closed to savor the rare moment, relishing the feel of his powerful muscles rippling beneath bronzed skin.

"You look very pretty," he said softly. His eyes traveled possessively over her.

"Thank you." She knew she looked a fright, and she knew he knew it, but a man had never told her she looked pretty before.

Creed reluctantly pulled away, his eyes searching the clearing around them. "I'd better get a fire started and then see what I can do about finding you something to wear."

Shock jerked her upright. Embarrassment sent her fleeing to a nearby rock from where she could hear Creed's laughter.

"Why didn't you remind me I didn't have a stitch on!"

"It's not something a man necessarily wants to remind a woman of.'' Chuckling, he set about gathering branches for the fire, oblivious to his own nudity.

Peeking out from behind the rock and watching his strong masculine form, Anne-Marie told herself she was sinning again. Badly this time. ''Aren't you going to put any clothes on?''

''I don't have any.''

''Well . . . maybe there's something in the saddlebags.''

''It's possible.''

''Turn your head.''

''What?''

''Turn your head. I'll see if there's anything useful.''

''I've seen you already, Anne. In fact, I've seen you more than once.''

''Then you don't need another look.''

''What I need and what I want are two different matters. Stay where you are. I'll search the saddlebags.''

Resting her head against the boulder, Anne-Marie studied the stars. Here she was, in the middle of nowhere, stark naked, with a man she'd almost given her life to save . . . and she was embarrassed. For the first time Anne-Marie McDougal, who had invented a thousand schemes to dupe a thousand men a thousand ways because she thought they deserved everything they got, was spending her time trying to come up with a way to keep a man with her.

''We're both crazy, you know that?'' she called.

''Speak for yourself.''

''*Turn* your head.''

He walked toward her, dressed in a pair of trousers. Handing her a shirt and a pair of buckskin pants, he smiled. ''You're in luck.''

Dressing quickly, Anne-Marie folded back the shirt sleeves and rolled up the cuffs. She looked down at the trousers—not too bad a fit. A little big, but then, Creed's own hips and thighs were slim. She blushed again, realizing his body had been inside those very pants. Unbidden, wicked images darted through her mind. She knew they must be wicked. If Mother Superior could read her mind, she knew she would tell her they were!

Creed was busily feeding dry twigs into a bed of coals when she finally stepped from behind the rock.

"What about the gold?" he asked.

Sighing, she joined him beside the fire. She dreaded telling him that despite their efforts, Malpas had won. "It's gone. That vile man and his partner took it all."

The telltale muscle flexed in Creed's jaw. "What did they do to you?"

"To me? Nothing . . . much."

He turned, his eyes searching hers. "I heard your screams."

"Oh . . . you mean when I was in the tent?"

"Yes, when the one they call Ollie had you—before I got there—"

"Oh, that. Well, that . . . that vile, smelly creature stripped my clothes off, but he swore he didn't do anything to me. In fact"—Anne-Marie chuckled harshly—"he begged me not to tell the others he hadn't."

"They didn't . . . ?" His voice faded with relief. "No."

His features sobered. "Are you certain?"

Color flooded her face. "I'm positive!"

Relieved, he glanced away. "What about Quincy?"

"I don't know where he is. He wasn't at the mission when we got there."

Staring into the fire, Creed turned pensive.

"I think he's probably looking for us," she said.

Nodding, Creed fed more twigs into the fire.

"You heard Malpas say who is behind stealing the gold, didn't you?"

He nodded.

"Someone by the name of Loyal Streeter. Apparently he and the sheriff are working together."

"It appears that way."

She made him look at her. "What are we going to do about it?"

Tossing the last of the wood into the fire, Creed stood up. "Nothing."

"Nothing!" Springing to her feet, she grabbed to secure her pants as she stood with her legs slightly apart, hands on her hips. "What do you mean, nothing? We can't just let this Loyal Streeter person get away with stealing the gold! What about the North? What about your duty? What about Quincy?"

Turning, Creed walked away, leaving her to wonder what about *her*. What was going to happen to her!

# Chapter 18

Quincy returned to the mission late the following day, tired but relieved to find Creed and Anne-Marie safe. Having spent twenty-four hours searching for them, he had begun to despair that they'd be found alive.

"The gold?" he asked, fearing he knew the answer.

Shaking her head, Anne-Marie turned away, busying herself at the stove. She couldn't stand to see the disappointment in Quincy's eyes.

For days, Anne-Marie brooded about the gold. She realized that if it hadn't been for her, the gold would still be safely in their hands. Creed appeared to take the loss better than Quincy. Quincy's pride was wounded because he had been sent to do a job and had failed.

Creed had driven the buckboard back to the mission. The supplies she thought invaluable only a day ago lay on the counter untouched. The large package with the bright red ribbon and the porcelain music box wrapped in heavy brown paper were hidden beneath the wagon seat so Anne-Marie wouldn't be reminded of her folly.

Now they waited. Anne-Marie wasn't certain why.

Creed's leg was almost back to normal, and yet no one talked about leaving.

Late one evening a storm came up. The wind rattled the old windows of the mission and whistled down the chimneys. Thunder rolled overhead, and lightning lit the kitchen as bright as day.

As if they didn't have enough trouble, more arrived as they were about to go to bed. The sound of an approaching rider brought Creed and Quincy quickly to their feet.

*Who could it be?* Anne-Marie wondered, frightened. If Malpas had returned, she hoped Creed would shoot him this time. She was *sick* of that man and his evil ways. Absolutely sick of him. Because of him, Creed's mission had failed, and the North would suffer even more.

Stepping away from the window, Creed went outside to greet the rider. He was met by a solemn-faced Bold Eagle.

"What brings my brother out in such a storm?"

Rain pelted from the sky and thunder rolled as the chief of the Heviqsnipahis faced them astride his war pony.

"Bold Eagle bears bad news, my brother."

Creed's smile faded as Anne-Marie came outside to stand beside him. "What is this news my brother brings?"

Emotions played across Bold Eagle's features. Pain, anguish, deep sorrow. "Bold Eagle brings his brother Storm Rider sad news of Berry Woman."

Laying her hand on Creed's arm, Anne-Marie stood beside him as Bold Eagle struggled to keep his voice dispassionate.

"Is Berry Woman ill?"

Bold Eagle's composure broke now, overcome by the heavy burden he carried within his heart. "My sister is gravely wounded."

Anne-Marie felt Creed tense. "When did this happen?" His voice was barely audible above the wind and thunder.

Straightening, Bold Eagle fixed his eyes beyond Creed, his features contorted in pain. *"Haneseeva."*

"Yesterday? How?"

Bold Eagle's face and body revealed the strain of the past few hours. His shoulders were stooped, and he looked much like a defeated man.

"Berry Woman was digging wild roots. When Plain Weasel heard her cries, he ran to help her, but there was little he could do." His voice broke. "My sister happened upon a *nahkoheso*—she was not swift enough—" His voice broke again as he recalled the horror Plain Weasel had described when he found a mother bear, in an effort to protect her cub, tearing at Berry Woman's tender flesh.

"I'm so sorry." Anne-Marie moved forward to comfort Bold Eagle, but he drew back, preferring solitude. He looked straight ahead as another thunderous explosion split the sky.

Turning back to Creed, Anne-Marie saw he was standing, head bowed, trying to absorb the severity of Bold Eagle's words. Finally he lifted his eyes and met his brother's solemnly.

"I am deeply saddened, Bold Eagle. Thank you for making the long ride in the storm to bring me this news."

"The Wise One works now to spare my sister's life—but you must know of this somber occurrence."

"Berry Woman is strong," Creed told him.

Nodding, Bold Eagle turned his horse slowly and rode into the worsening storm. When Anne-Marie turned after watching him depart, Creed was gone.

Stepping into the chapel later, she found him sitting in front of the railing, knees crossed, studying the large cross on which a replica of Jesus hung. She knew by small things Creed had said that the Crow had a strong religious faith.

Quietly seating herself beside him, she shared his grief in the lonely silence. Berry Woman was young to consider the possibility of death. Many times in Anne-Marie's years, she had been troubled by the subject. She and Sister Agnes had shared many long talks about dying and about eternal life. She'd never completely understood the premise—it all seemed so vague and uncertain to her. But over the years she had gained a sense of peace about the matter. And tonight, sitting in the chapel listening to the rain and thunder, she felt no fear. Instead she felt a gentle peace for Berry Woman. If a power so strong could create the sun and the moon and the thunder and the lightning and the wind, then that same power could welcome a lovely young maiden into the folds of His love.

It was a long time before Creed finally broke his silence. Anne-Marie waited, respecting his sorrow.

"I know very little about your God." He spoke quietly, his voice lacking is usual assurance. "Why does He permit these things to happen?"

Sighing, Anne-Marie studied the image hanging on the cross before the altar.

"I don't think He brings bad things upon us purposely. Sister Agnes thinks our hurts and happinesses are all a part of life. She says if we didn't hurt, then we'd never know the full degree of happiness."

"I do not understand this way," Creed confessed.

"No one understands," she consoled. "He doesn't ask that we understand, only that we accept what is put upon us."

"I want to go to her, yet I cannot."

"Why not? Quincy and I can look after things here."

"No, I cannot further endanger my mission. The gold is my mission. I must deliver it to my commander. You have accepted many things in your life," he pondered. She had spoken of losing both parents when she was very young. He understood the strong bonds she had formed with her sisters, for he too had felt that bond with Father Jacob and Bold Eagle. Yet at this moment, confronted by death, he could not feel the forgiving spirit that she had in her heart.

Outside, the wind howled, and rain lashed angrily at the mission, almost as if venting its own rage at the unfairness of it all.

"You do love her, don't you?" Anne-Marie knew her timing wasn't the best, but the words slipped out.

He took a long time to answer. "Bold Eagle is my brother, and I would have honored my brother's wishes."

She turned to face him now, her eyes shining in the flickering altar candles. "She is still alive, and there is the matter of miracles."

"These miracles you speak of—do you believe they happen?"

"Sometimes—not always, but if we both pray hard enough, the Lord might see fit to answer our prayers."

"Then we must pray."

Getting to their knees, they bowed their heads and closed their eyes.

"Creed?"

"Yes?"

"You do love her? I mean, not just fond of her like a brother would be for a sister, but you honestly, deep down love her?"

"If she is spared, I will marry her. I have given my brother my word. We have spoken of this before."

"But you've never said you were in love with her."

Creed's eyes returned to the cross and remained there for a long time. So many things filled his mind. So much had happened in so short a time. Did he love Berry Woman? He respected her very deeply, and he found her desirable, but the woman who sat beside him created a sense of longing within him he had never known before.

Anne-Marie reached for his hand and held it. They knelt side by side, hips touching, praying together until the storm passed and a thin, watery moon slipped from beneath the clouds.

Anne-Marie thought of how very much she loved him, and how she would feel if he were the one lying near death instead of Berry Woman. The resulting pain made her petitions to a higher power more urgently heartfelt.

Then they sat, hand in hand, until the cry of a rain dove ushered in a new day.

But not once did he tell her he was honest to God in love with the young Indian maiden.

* * *

Loyal Streeter patted his lapels as he watched the last of the gold being stored in the icehouse. "That's it, boys—handle it real easy," he purred.

Ferris Goodman stood beside him, watching the activity. When Malpas had appeared toting the gold, Ferris had been surprised. He really hadn't expected ever to see it again. But then Malpas had been promised a hefty reward for returning the gold.

"You done a good job, Malpas, good job—and you'll be rewarded for it," Loyal had promised.

"*Sí, señor.*" Malpas grinned.

When the last bar was safely tucked away, Loyal turned, leaving the gold under heavy guard. Walking toward the saloon for a celebratory drink, he appeared to forget Ferris for the moment.

Ferris quietly fell into step behind him.

"Mind if I join ya', boss?"

Grunting something that sounded to Ferris like, "Do whatever you want," Loyal headed for the Gilded Dove. He didn't take his customary table this afternoon, but headed instead to the bar.

Ferris noticed this. It seemed to him almost as if Loyal were trying to brush him off today. He didn't know why. After all, he'd gotten the gold back for him, hadn't he? He'd done his job.

"Whaddya drinking, Ferris?" Loyal asked him, more out of habit than courtesy.

Ferris said he'd have the usual whiskey.

The conversation was stilted as the two men stood at the bar drinking. Ferris knew something wasn't right, but he couldn't put his finger on it. Loyal should have been happy that the gold was back—and he was, to a degree. But it was a reserved degree.

"Guess you'll be wantin' to move that gold on to proper channels," Ferris remarked as he toyed with his whiskey glass.

Tossing the last of his drink down, Loyal didn't answer him.

After a few strained moments Ferris tried again. "I'll put a couple of men on it first thing in the morning. The quicker the gold is out of our hands, the quicker we can relax."

When Loyal still remained silent, Ferris continued, "Should be able to have it signed, sealed, and delivered by this time tomorrow night."

Signaling the bartender for another drink, Loyal reached into his vest pocket and drew out his watch. Checking the time with the Seth Thomas hanging across the room, he wound the stem and absently returned it to his pocket.

Ferris was positive that Loyal was ignoring him now. "Somethin' troublin' you, Loyal?"

Tossing down a second rum, Loyal glanced around the nearly empty bar, lowering his voice. "Uh, there's been a change of plans."

"Concerning the gold?"

"Yeah."

Ferris lifted his glass. This didn't surprise him. Loyal had been acting real antsy lately. "What's the change?"

"You've read the latest papers, haven't you?"

Ferris nodded. Richmond had fallen. Lee was making a desperate push to regain ground, but it looked grim.

"The South can't hold out much longer."

"Looks that way," Ferris agreed.

Motioning to the bartender, Loyal drew his handkerchief out of his pocket and mopped his brow. It wasn't ten o'clock, and yet it was already hotter than a smoking pistol.

"What're you tryin' to tell me, Loyal? That you're keepin' the gold?"

Ferris didn't know until that moment that he'd figured it out. Sure, that was what was eatin' Loyal. He'd been acting real strange all week, so his decision to keep the gold didn't come as a surprise.

"Can you think of any reason why we shouldn't?" Perspiring heavily now, Loyal mopped ineffectively at the sweat streaking the sides of his face. In his youth he had been a handsome man, but time and too much liquor had altered his features.

"I can think of one. The South is dependin' on that gold," Ferris returned quietly.

"With the war over, the South's gonna have to fend for itself," Loyal grunted. He'd worked his ass off for the Confederacy and had not heard one word of gratitude out of them.

"The Confederacy's in bad shape, Loyal. They'll need that gold to rebuild."

"Once the war's over, they'll rebuild," Loyal said shortly, signaling for another drink. It wasn't like him to drink so much this early in the day.

Pushing his glass aside, Ferris turned to confront Loyal Streeter. There wasn't anything he could do to stop him from keeping the gold, but by damn, Ferris's hide and Malpas's hide had been on the line, and he planned to see they'd get a cut of it.

"We want our share, Loyal."

Loyal looked up. "Of what?"

"Of the gold. I was responsible for gettin' it back for you, just like I said I would. If you're plannin' on keepin' it, then we split it three ways—you, me, and my men."

Taking another sip from his glass, Loyal considered the ultimatum. Ferris knew too much. Ferris would just as soon cross him as spit on him, he knew that. Loyalty flew right out the window when the chips were down.

"I promised you I'd pay Malpas and his men handsomely if they got the gold back."

"That ain't the case now. If you keep the gold, we want our cut."

"All right." Loyal tossed the last of his drink down, then set the glass back on the counter. "A third, three ways. In return, I have your word you'll say that the woman, the black, and the Indian were never found."

Ferris nodded. "You got my word."

Loyal smiled. "I thought you might see it that way." The men who'd stored the gold in the icehouse would be easy enough to pay off. A couple of bottles of rotgut whiskey and fifty dollars and they'd betray their own mothers.

"Then I guess we've got ourselves a deal."

They sealed the agreement with a gentlemen's handshake.

Smiling now, Loyal appeared to relax. "What're you planning to do with all that money, Ferris? You'll never have to work another day of your life."

Smiling, Ferris settled back, thinking about the cushy life that lay ahead. It was a shame, really, for the South, but that was life. You won some and you lost some. Ferris just happened to have won the big one. "Guess

I'll buy me that hundred acres I've been wantin' just east of town. Settle down, maybe find a woman who'll cook and clean for me—who knows, might even have me another young'un." He'd have to leave all that money to someone.

Elbowing him, Loyal winked. "Don't plan to work that land, do you?"

"No, don't plan to work it." Ferris grinned. "I'll just sit back and take it easy. Real easy."

Smiling, the two men jovially slapped each other on the back.

"We'll make the split first thing in the morning," Loyal promised as he got up to leave.

Ferris nodded. He'd wire the sheriff in Firebrand and turn in his badge tonight. A third of the gold would make him rich beyond his wildest dreams.

The two men left the bar together.

As Loyal entered his office later he motioned for his clerk, Jake, to follow him.

"You want somethin', boss?"

"Tell Skid Baker I need him."

Jake's brows raised. "The hired gun?"

Loyal nodded. "Have him here within the hour."

As Jake hurried off to do Loyal's bidding Loyal walked to the window. Striking a match on his thumbnail, he watched as Ferris walked jauntily toward his office.

*A third of the money,* he thought, sneering. *There's one born every minute.*

That night a strange thing happened in Streeter, Texas. There were four killings in the Gilded Dove saloon. Four. That was unheard of in Streeter, a town whose people prided themselves on law and order.

Ferris Goodman, the town sheriff for over fifteen years, was killed by a lone assailant who broke into the jail and shot him in cold blood.

The town was shocked.

Ferris Goodman was respected by almost everyone—why, he was even a close friend of Loyal Streeter, the town's honorable councilman. Not a single person could think of anyone who would want to harm a hair on Ferris's head.

Even more startling, over at the Gilded Dove, four drifters—a Mexican called Malpas and three of his men were shot to death in a ruckus over a card game.

Eyewitnesses swore the fight broke out so fast no one was able to tell who shot who. By the time the smoke cleared, the gunman had run out of the bar and disappeared.

Well, you just never know, do you?

Loyal Streeter, the town's honorable councilman, was so outraged by the violence, he ordered the town to shut down for a full day in deference to the deceased.

Like Loyal said, the citizens of Streeter were shocked by such brutality and they weren't going to put up with it.

# Chapter 19

Anne-Marie stored the last of the supplies in the buckboard with a heavy heart. She hadn't slept all night, anticipating the moment. Creed was strong enough to travel. They had agreed to leave at dawn.

She heard approaching footsteps, and her pulse quickened when she saw Creed coming toward her.

Smiling, he slipped his arms around her waist, drawing her to him. "You're up early," he murmured.

"I couldn't sleep."

A delicious warmth spread through her as he held her tightly for a moment. It bothered her to know that monogamy wasn't a Crow's strong point, but if he were her Crow, she'd change that.

"I hate to leave," she admitted.

Here with him she had found a sense of completeness.

Turning her around, he drew her closer to his broad chest. They parted reluctantly as Quincy came out of the mission whistling.

Creed ambled to the front of the buckboard to check the rigging as Quincy stored his gear in the wagon.

"Why the grim look?" Quincy teased when he saw Anne-Marie's troubled face.

"I don't know. I guess I should be happy that all the misery is finally about to end."

"Yes, ma'am. You'll be back with your sisters in no time at all, and I'll be home with Floralee and my babies." His grin widened at the happy prospect.

"I know you can hardly wait." Anne-Marie wouldn't have understood his feelings a few days ago, but now she did. The happiness she felt at the thought of being reunited with her sisters dimmed when she considered that Creed was about to be taken away from her.

In such a short time he had become a necessary ingredient in her life, an ingredient that she would miss. No matter how much she loved him, there was Berry Woman, and her own blood vow to stay with her sisters forever. Blood was thicker than water, wasn't that the old saying?

Even if the worst should happen and Berry Woman died, that wouldn't mean Creed would marry Anne-Marie.

Sneaking a longing glance at Creed, she reminded herself that leaving, no matter how painful, was right. She had become too dependent on a man.

There had been a time when she didn't think she needed anyone but her sisters—particularly not a man—but the hours she'd spent with Creed had shown her otherwise. She had discovered the power of love and how one man could bring alive feelings that she thought never existed.

Adjusting the bit in the horse's mouth, Creed walked back to where Anne-Marie was standing with Quincy.

"Well, that about does it."

"Is there any word on Berry Woman?"

Creed shook his head. "Bold Eagle knows I am leaving. He will send word—if the need arises."

Quincy nodded, anxious to be on his way. They had mapped out their plans the night before. Creed and Quincy would return to Louisiana to inform their commander about the loss of the gold, then deliver Ann-Marie to Mercy Flats.

Creed and Anne-Marie had not privately spoken of the time when they would part, but the unsettling thought hung over them like a gray shroud.

Casting a fond glance at the mission, Anne-Marie lifted the hem of her habit and climbed into the wagon. Adjusting her skirt primly around her knees, she kept her eyes trained straight ahead, fearing Creed would see the tears that threatened to give away her feelings. She had a hunch that he didn't like women who cried in the face of adversity.

Quincy climbed aboard and settled himself on the narrow seat. Scooting across the bench, Anne-Marie made room for Creed beside her.

When he was aboard, the three sat for a moment listening to the wind gently ringing the old bell in the mission tower.

"It's been real peaceful here," Quincy admitted with just a touch of regret in his voice.

Creed and Anne-Marie looked at one another, emotion deep in their eyes.

"I don't want to leave," Anne-Marie whispered, flinching when she saw Creed's jaw clench.

"I must leave—the gold is gone."

"Well." She sat up straighter, her spunk suddenly

returning. "Maybe not. No. We can't just leave like this," she decided.

"Anne-Marie—" Creed's tone was gentle, but determination was written all over his face.

"No!" she said again more forcefully.

Quincy mentally groaned. When she talked like this, there was bound to be trouble; they might as well count on it.

"We can't just let them beat us like this!" she exclaimed. "What are we—cowards?"

"Anne-Marie!" Creed wasn't going to discuss the gold again. It was gone and there was nothing he could do about it, short of getting them all killed.

"No, listen." Anne-Marie whirled to face him, her features animated. "I've thought of a way to trick Loyal Streeter out of that gold!"

Quincy groaned aloud this time. He didn't want to hear this, he didn't want to *hear* this!

"No, listen!" Anne-Marie pleaded when she could see that both men were going to be muleheaded about it. "It's a brilliant plan, really!"

"Yes, ma'am." Quincy remembered all too well her last brilliant plan. He still had nightmares about being buried alive by those Indians.

"Wouldn't it be nice if you could return to your commander bearing the gold instead of bad news?" she asked.

Creed and Quincy looked at one another, acknowledgment of the truth of her words creeping into their eyes.

"See! You know you would!" she cried.

"All right." Creed braced himself for the jolt. "What is this new plan?"

"Creed!" Quincy objected. They were *this* close to getting out of this mess by the skin of their teeth!

"We owe her the courtesy of listening," Creed reminded him.

"Why?"

"Because she's part of this, like it or not."

"I don't like it!"

"Then don't listen."

Groaning, Quincy wrapped the reins around the brake handle and waited for the worst. It arrived on a fast freight.

"Here's the plan." As Anne-Marie outlined her ideas Quincy shifted about on the seat, muttering under his breath. Rolling his eyes, he groaned and moaned as her new strategy came to light. Sweat rolled down his ebony face as he listened to Anne-Marie explain that she was sure that the plan would work. By the time she was finished, though, even Creed was skeptical.

"That could never work."

"Why not?" She gazed back at him expectantly. "I've hatched up schemes that were a lot less thought out than this one."

"It just won't work!" he reiterated.

"It will!"

"Where do we get the clothes?" The gold was gone. They were destitute.

Guilt flashed briefly across Anne-Marie's features. "I have some money left from the coin I took," she murmured.

Creed swore.

"Well, where would we *be* if I hadn't taken that one precious coin that will never be missed anyway?" she accused.

Creed and Quincy answered in unison. "Still in possession of the gold."

"Oh, you two. I knew you'd throw that up at me."

They sat for a moment discussing the pros and cons of the plan. To be sure it was unorthodox, but then so was she. Quincy was firmly against it, but after a while Anne-Marie began to win Creed over to her side.

"Well, it might work," Creed reluctantly admitted after he had thought about it, and it sure would salvage his pride if he could deliver the gold as planned. It was an insane plan, one fraught with danger, but it might be worth a try.

"No!" Quincy protested.

Creed and Anne-Marie looked at him and said in unison, "Yes!" and Quincy knew he was outnumbered.

"If this plan backfires, we're all dead."

"We know," Anne-Marie said, brushing off the possibility. She didn't have time to think about that now. "Okay, here's what we do. Quincy, there's a casket in the cellar. Get it and make sure the following items are in it." She rattled off a list.

"Lord have mercy," Quincy grumbled as he climbed back out of the wagon. The woman had clean lost her mind.

"Creed, I'll need some soot from the cook stove. Get plenty. There's a pail in the kitchen. You can use that."

Creed was uneasy about this part of the plan, and not fully convinced it would work, but he had to admit if it did, she was a genius.

"Streeter is a small town. It shouldn't take us long to discover where they've stashed the gold," Creed said.

"All right." She took a deep breath, smiling. "Gentlemen, we'll leave in exactly two hours. We make one brief stop in Brittlebranch to purchase appropriate clothing, then we proceed to Streeter.''

Scrambling out of the buckboard, she marched back to the mission, fire in her step now.

"Then, Mr. Loyal Streeter, we'll just see who's the smartest!''

Loyal Streeter was sitting at his desk when he glanced up to see a young woman standing in the doorway. Though she was dressed in widow's weeds, she was still a stunning sight to behold.

Getting slowly to his feet, he found it hard to take his eyes off this vision of loveliness. "Yes, ma'am. Something I can do for you?'' he asked.

"Yes, sir. I'm looking for Mr. Loyal Streeter,'' the young woman replied in a thick Georgia accent. Her voice was as sweet and melodious as a nightingale's.

Bowing from the waist, Loyal smiled. "Loyal Streeter at your service, ma'am.''

Taffeta rustled as the woman entered the office. The severe cut of the black gown couldn't begin to hide her delectable curves. Beneath the black veil covering her face, Loyal detected the hint of full, ruby-red lips. He felt his manhood twitch as he moved quickly to offer her a chair.

Thanking him, she seated herself, then continued, "I'm here to ask a great favor of you, Mr. Streeter.''

Loyal smiled, eager to do anything he could to help this tantalizing creature. Why, he'd walk through fire just for a taste of those luscious lips!

"Anything, Miss . . . ?'' He searched for a name, unable to recall if she'd given one.

"Miss Willingham. Lillie Belle Willingham."

Lifting her gloved hand, Loyal placed a kiss on the back of it.

"And what might I do for you, Miss Willingham?"

"I would like permission to make use of your ice-house," she replied.

For the briefest of moments Anne-Marie thought she sensed him tense, but he quickly regained his composure.

Loyal's smile faded. "The icehouse?"

"Yes," Anne-Marie said demurely. "I know it seems a most inappropriate request, but I'm afraid I'm just in an awful ol' predicament."

His smile quickly returned. "And what quandary is that, Miss Willingham?"

"Ma sweet, dear ol' daddy passed on yesterday, Mr. Streeter. He had been in ill health for some time, and I'm afraid—" She paused, lifting the hem of her veil to dab at the corners of her eyes.

"Permit me to offer you a cool drink of water," Loyal insisted. The heat was stifling and growing hotter by the minute, it seemed.

"Why, that would be most gracious of you, Mr. Streeter." She batted her long sooty eyelashes up at him.

"Jake!" Loyal barked.

The clerk's head appeared in the doorway. "You called me, boss?"

"Bring Miss Willingham a dipper of cool water."

Jake was back almost immediately with the requested item.

"Thank you evah so kindly." Anne-Marie drank

daintily from the dipper before handing it back to Jake with a grateful smile.

He grinned sheepishly, his ears turning fuchsia as he hurried out of the room.

"Go on, Miss Willingham. You lost your father . . ." Loyal prompted.

"Yes, yesterday, I'm afraid. My two servants and I are taking Papa's remains to be buried alongside Mama's in Georgia."

"Please accept my heartfelt condolences," Loyal soothed, reaching for her hand again.

"Thank you evah so kindly, Mr. Streeter. It has been a most dreadful time. Just evah so taxing on my strength. I am accustomed ta having my dear sweet daddy take care of just evahthing for me, and now . . . now . . . he's . . ." Overcome by emotion, Anne-Marie reached inside her pocket for a handkerchief.

"There, there, my dear," Loyal consoled. "You have encountered some trouble?"

"Yes, it seems—well, it seems indelicate to speak of, but due to the unseasonably warm weather that has set upon us, Papa's remains are putrefying more rapidly than we counted on. Georgia is still a good two days away, even though we're traveling by rail."

"Traveling by rail, you say?"

"Yayus, we are. Because of Papa's worsening condition, the engineer graciously agreed to stop here in Streeter for the night."

"The other passengers didn't complain?"

"Fortunately there are only a few others, Mr. Streeter. Two or three more and myself and my two manservants. No, the others haven't complained—but the odor is—well—most disagreeable.'' She wrinkled her nose primly.

''Well, I wish I could help, Miss Willingham, but the icehouse—''

Lillie Belle quickly laid her hand across the sleeve of his jacket.

''If you refuse me, sir, I have no other place to turn.'' Her voice broke with emotion, and to Loyal's dismay she began to weep.

''But, ma'am—''

''The casket would only take up a small area in the icehouse,'' she pleaded, ''and we'd be gone by early light.'' Her voice lowered to a sultry whisper. ''Please, do not refuse me this little bitty ol' favor. If Papa's remains aren't cooled down immediately, we'll not be able to continue on. Why, I'm afraid I will have to ask that you arrange for Papa's immediate burial if you can't oblige me, and I did so want to bury him next to my dear sweet mama. Papa would be so crushed if he knew he wasn't lyin' next to Mama. Why, he'd *nevah* forgive me. Nevah.''

Anne-Marie wrinkled her brow in consternation, blinking her eyes to hold back the tears. Sniffing loudly, she fumbled for her handkerchief again.

Loyal paled. His jaw worked as he mulled the idea over. He was caught in a dilemma. How could he refuse this lovely, sweet, innocent, young woman her touching request? Why, he'd be a cad of the worst sort not to help her out of her awful predicament. Then, too, he knew that Jebediah Powell, Streeter's only undertaker, was uncommonly squeamish for a man in his profession. Loyal knew he wouldn't relish the thought of burying a body as putrefied as Miss Lillie Belle said her papa was.

But then there was that little matter of the gold in the icehouse.

He bit his lip indecisively.

"My two servants will assume full responsibility for the casket," Miss Willingham assured him, seeing Loyal's internal struggle. "Because of the"—she paused—"unpleasant odor, they will carry the casket in and out so your men will not"—she paused again delicately—"be affected."

Loyal realized that she had him between a rock and a hard place. The gold was in the icehouse. No one but his trusted employees knew that, and he didn't want anyone else to know. If he let Miss Willingham store her papa's remains there, would it rouse her servants' suspicions? It was risky, to be sure.

Lifting her hand to her forehead, Anne-Marie feigned light-headedness.

"Are you all right, Miss Willingham? Perhaps you would like more water, or might I fetch you a refreshing sarsaparilla," Loyal offered. He was about to summon Jake again when she stopped him.

"Please, I'm just weak with hunger." Her voice sounded very small now. "I have eaten very little in the past few hours." She looked up at him. "You understand."

"Of course, Miss Willingham. Most understandable."

Loyal's mind raced. She was such a winsome creature, small and vulnerable. Perhaps he could make this one harmless concession.

She started to rise, then wilted weakly back into the chair.

"I must see to my servants' needs," she murmured. "One is blind, and the other, I'm afraid, has the mind of a small child. They look to me for their welfare." She sighed.

"Well, perhaps we can arrange something," Loyal offered. If one of her servants was blind and the other stupid, then surely there could be no danger in letting her use the icehouse. After all, as she said, it would only be until morning.

"Where are your servants now?"

"With Papa."

"On the train?"

She nodded, dabbing at her moist eyes again.

"Come then, Miss Willingham." Loyal offered her his arm and she stood up, placing her small hand on his wrist.

"Once we have your papa settled, you will join me for supper."

"Oh, I couldn't!" she protested. "I have imposed enough on your kind generosity!"

"Nonsense. I'll see that your servants are fed and bedded down in the barn for the night. Then you and I will enjoy a leisurely dinner in my private quarters."

"Well, if you insist," she said demurely, giving him her most radiant smile. "You are just evah so kind!"

Creed and Quincy sat up straighter when they spotted Anne-Marie returning to the train on the arm of Loyal Streeter.

"Damn." Creed murmured. "Looks like she's done it."

"Yeah, she's done it all right," Quincy murmured. He figured she'd done it up real good this time.

The two men were sitting on the floor of the rail car looking out. Anne-Marie had been gone over an hour now and they had begun to worry. Not that she needed to be worried about. The way she'd sweet-talked those two guards into telling her the gold was stored in the icehouse still had them slack-jawed.

Quincy glanced down at his clothes, feeling like a fool. He was decked out in flour-sack breeches and a gunnysack shirt. His only consolation was that Creed looked worse. Quincy wasn't able to look at him without bursting out laughing. Every exposed part of Creed's body was darkened with soot. He wore the same crude breeches and torn shirt as Quincy, except that he was barefoot. Anne-Marie had insisted that he be the "simple one."

Quincy had gotten off easier. He was merely blind.

As Anne-Marie and Streeter approached the rail car Creed could hear her laughter. Jealousy stung him like a knife. When he had seen her dressed in her fine gown and hat, he realized what a magnificent-looking woman she was. She would meet no resistance capturing the heart of any man she wanted. The realization had hit him hard. Until now Creed hadn't been sure what he felt for her, but he knew one thing. He'd kill Loyal Streeter if he so much as indicated anything other than compassion for her situation.

Approaching the rail car, Anne-Marie nodded solemnly at her two manservants.

"Tobias, Malachi."

The two men lowered their heads subserviently.

"We are in luck," she said. "Due to Mr. Streeter's

just evah-so-lovely kindness, he has graciously offered his assistance.''

Quincy nodded. ''I cain't see you, Mr. Streeter.'' He stared ahead of him sightlessly. ''But you'se surely a good man—a *gooood* man!''

Streeter nodded absently. ''You men can carry Miss Willingham's papa on up to the icehouse now. Afterward,'' Loyal offered, ''go around to the back of the jail and someone will feed you and show you where you can bunk down for the night.''

''Oh, thank you, Mr. Streeter, thank you. We shore nuf do thank you,'' Quincy intoned.

''Tobias, you are to help Malachi with his meal.'' Anne-Marie glanced at Loyal apologetically. ''Malachi hasn't quite mastered the art of feeding himself yet.''

''Yes'm,'' Quincy drawled. ''I do dat, missy. I shorely will!''

Loyal looked at the taller of the Negro servants in the growing twilight. His hat was pulled low over his face and he could barely see the man's features, but he did look to be a pitiful sight. Loyal wondered why people like Miss Lillie Belle Willingham kept his kind.

''Mr. Streeter has graciously invited me to take supper with him,'' Anne-Marie warbled, bestowing a winning smile on Loyal.

The muscle in Creed's jaw tightened as Anne-Marie slipped her arm back through Loyal's.

''Once Papa's in the icehouse, Tobias, you take Malachi and go over to the jail. Then you be sure that both of you get to bed tonight and get a good night's sleep, for we'll be leaving first thing in the mornin'.''

''Yes'm, we will, ma'am. Don't you worry one bit 'bout us!''

Creed and Quincy jumped out of the rail car as soon as Anne-Marie and Loyal turned to go. With Quincy loudly giving instructions to Creed, they unloaded the casket from the train and waited for Anne-Marie and Loyal to lead the way.

Positioning themselves on either end, the two alleged slaves followed behind their mistress as she led the way to the icehouse.

Loyal's armed guards lifted their rifles as the small procession approached. When they saw Streeter was among them, they relaxed their stance.

"Miss Willingham has asked permission to store her papa's remains in the icehouse," Loyal explained, when the two guards viewed the casket suspiciously, "and I have granted her wish. Unlock the door, Boyd."

Boyd did as he was told and the two guards stood back to let the two slaves carry the casket into the icehouse.

Creed's features were expressionless as he set the coffin down beside a stack of gold bars.

"It shore do smell cool and nice in here," Quincy drawled. "I bet it do look cool and nice in here. Is I right, Malachi?"

Malachi remained silent, maintaining his simpleton facade.

Groping his way, Tobias turned and led Malachi back out of the icehouse. The guards stepped forward to re-lock the door, then resumed their stance, rifles in hand.

"Well, I do declare!" Anne-Marie said, breathing a sigh of relief. "I do believe my appetite is returning. Shall we go to dinner, Mr. Streeter?"

"As you wish, my dear."

Turning her, Loyal Streeter walked her in the direction of the café, where his private dining quarters awaited them.

Once he was pointed in the direction of the jail, Quincy blindly stumbled his way along, dragging Creed behind him.

Glancing over his shoulder, Creed saw Loyal slip his arm around Anne-Marie's waist as they stepped up onto the hotel steps.

"The bastard!" he murmured.

"Land sakes, Malachi. Where you done learn language like dat?" Quincy taunted. "De missus, she done whoop you good if she hear you a-talkin' dat way."

"*Shut* up, Adams."

Quincy chuckled. "Yassuh."


Loyal Streeter was charming. During dinner, he entertained Lillie Belle with stories about Streeter, Texas, and the tragic deaths of five men that had recently cast a pall on their honorable town. The wine he served was a perfect complement to the roast pheasant, boiled potatoes, and string beans. In keeping with his idea of himself as a gentleman, Loyal made sure the supper was brief, because after all, Lillie Belle was still in mourning for her father. He would have preferred to spend hours with the charming Southern beauty or, even better, the night. But perhaps since Loyal had been so gracious, she might agree to return to Streeter sometime and dine again with him. Then, who knew what might happen? Loyal attracted his share of beautiful women, but this woman, Lillie Belle Willingham, would be a noticeable asset to a man in Loyal's position.

Yes, Loyal mused, he would try his best to get the

lovely Miss Lillie Belle to come back through Streeter someday.

"More wine, Miss Willingham?"

"No, thank you, Mr. Streeter. I do declare, I'm quite giddy as it is."

Rising from his chair, Loyal offered his arm to his tantalizing guest.

Accepting it, she stood up, bestowing a tremulous smile upon him. "You're evah so kind, Mr. Streeter."

As they stepped out of the hotel Loyal paused, smiling down on her. "Would it offend you, Miss Willingham, if I were to smoke in your presence?"

"Not at all, Mr. Streeter. My papa used to smoke after every meal."

Lighting a large stogie, Loyal inhaled, patting his rather portly middle. "Fine meal, fine meal."

"It was simply divine," she purred.

They strolled along the plank sidewalk, enjoying the cool night air. There were few people on the streets now, most having gone home to their families.

As Lillie Belle walked along she seemed pensive.

"Something troubling you tonight, Miss Willingham?"

"No, not really; I was just thinking. Perhaps I should check in on my two slaves."

"Oh, they're quite all right," Loyal assured her. "I have seen to their care."

"But if I could check on them for just a moment," she persisted. "They were my father's favorites, you know. I think that's why I feel so close to them."

"Very well," Loyal conceded. "If you insist."

"That would be evah so kind of you."

Loyal nodded to a passerby, who greeted him by his first name.

"Will you be coming this way again?" Loyal asked.

"I'm not certain of my plans once Papa's buried," she said.

"Well, Miss Willingham, I know that this has been a very unhappy time for you, but I've been thinking. The evening's been so pleasant, I thought perhaps on the way back, you'd agree to stop over in Streeter and take supper with me again."

"Oh, how nice of you to ask!" she exclaimed. "I'll certainly bear that in mind, Mr. Streeter. I shorely will!"

"You know you're a most compelling woman, Lillie Belle!"

Snapping her fan open, Anne-Marie stirred the air, stepping along a little faster. This portly ass was taxing her nerves.

"Where did you say my manservants were sleeping tonight?"

"They're comfortable," Loyal assured her.

"Yes, I know, but I think I would rest better if I could see them. I really would like to see them."

"Well . . ." Loyal thought it was a little late for socializing, but if she insisted . . . "If you wish."

Anne-Marie didn't know why, but she had an overwhelming urge to see Creed. Or rather to have Creed see her. On the arm of Loyal Streeter.

During supper, she had found herself comparing the two men. They were as different as night and day. Streeter's wealth and social status fell dismally short of Creed's quiet knowledge and good looks. If she were truthful, she'd admit she wanted Creed Walker to realize that men of great social prominence found her desirable.

Making the point that others found her attractive suddenly seemed of the utmost importance to her.

As they entered the barn they found Creed and Quincy reclining on a mound of straw.

As Creed got slowly to his feet his eyes locked with hers. For a moment they gazed at each other before his eyes focused on Loyal Streeter's hand upon her arm.

"Dat you, Miss Willingham?" Quincy stared sightlessly up at her.

"It's me, Tobias. Hope we're not disturbing you," she apologized.

"No, ma'am, you'se not disturbin' us. We's just relaxin' for a spell."

Lifting the hem of her skirt, she stepped around Creed, casting a coy glance in his direction. "Well, you certainly look well fed."

"Oh, yes'm, yes'm, we'se had real good eats," Quincy assured her. "Plenty o' beans and hardtack."

"How nice."

Her eyes, the color of emeralds, fixed on Creed's stoic features.

"And you, Malachi? Did you eat well?"

"He did, ma'am. He shore did," Quincy answered for Malachi, wondering what she was trying to do. If she wasn't careful, she was going to give them away.

Patting Creed on the shoulder, she turned to smile coyly up at Loyal. "They're such fine servants. If the South loses the waah, I just don't know what I'll do without them. Why, Tobias and Malachi are just like my children." She paused, smiling when she saw Creed scowling beneath the slouch hat.

"Mr. Streeter and I just had a long, nice dinner. Excellent fare. We had browned plump pheasant, delicious potatoes, and string beans." She smiled again. "Did you say you had beans and hardtack?"

"Yaz, ma'am."

"Mmm. Sounds good."

"Yess'm," Quincy returned tightly.

She placed her hand over Loyal's, her gaze returning to Creed.

"Mr. Streeter has suggested that in the future we stop and I have dinner with him again. Don't you think that's lovely?"

"Yess'm," Quincy answered. "Dat's real nice of Mr. Streeter."

The muscle in Creed's jaw began to throb and Quincy realized he had to do something.

"Miz Lillie Belle, you bettah be gettin' on back to the hotel, ma'am, we be leavin' real early in the mornin' and you need yore rest."

"Yes, I suppose you're right," she mused aloud thoughtfully.

Hooking her arm through Loyal's, she smiled at Creed. "Sleep well, you two."

On the walk to the hotel Anne-Marie felt troubled. She didn't know why she'd taunted Creed. She didn't want to make him angry; he'd been decent to her, considering all she'd put him through. But a part of her wanted Creed Walker more than anything she had ever wanted in her whole life, and she wanted to see some evidence—be it ever so small—that he wanted her, too. She thought she had her answer.

A small victorious smile played across her lips.

Loyal escorted her to her room, leaving her with the promise that she would have breakfast with him before she continued on to Georgia the next morning. When he placed a benign kiss on her forehead, she felt cold and detached. She tried not to shudder visibly. He was nothing like Creed. Nothing!

Turning the key in the lock, she let herself into her room, relieved that the evening had finally come to an end. Peeling off her hat, she tossed it on the bed. Reaching for the pins in her hair, she glanced up, gasping when she saw Creed sitting in the chair by the window.

Legs propped on the bed, his eyes measured her with practiced ease. "Evenin', Miss Lillie Belle."

"How in the world did you get in here?"

"Through the window. I'm Indian, you know. I know how to get around so no one can see me. I'm sure you've heard the expression 'sneaky as an Indian'?" There was a hint of dry mockery in his voice.

Heaving a defeated sigh, she walked across the room, disappearing behind the Chinese-silk dressing screen.

Reaching behind her, she struggled to undo the long row of buttons fastening the back of her dress. "Where's Quincy?"

"In the barn. He was humming 'Nobody Knows de Trouble I've Seen' when I left him." As Creed heard her frustrated fumblings he got up and walked behind the screen to lend his assistance.

Lifting her hair off her collar, she allowed him to undo her, too tired to put up a fuss. After all, shameful or not, he had seen all there was to see of her, so she guessed it would be senseless to protest now.

"Exactly what was that all about earlier?"

"What?" she asked innocently.

"You and Streeter."

"Oh, that." She exhaled deeply as the middle of her gown gave way. "I wanted to make you jealous."

When the last button was unfastened, he turned her around to face him. His eyes darkened as he viewed the swell of her breasts beneath her chemise. What was it about her that made him want to take her here—now— and to hold her long after his passion had cooled?

Her arms slipped up to encircle his neck, and she knew that she couldn't stay angry at him. Nor could she lie to him. Her love was too deep.

"Did I?"

"Was I jealous?"

She nodded, her breath growing shallow with his nearness.

"What do you think?" He gazed back at her, and she felt a heat settling over her body she now recognized as raw desire.

"I think . . . I don't know," she said primly. She wanted to believe that she had seared his jealousy to the point of madness, but she wasn't certain about anything at the moment.

Trailing a finger along her cheek, he gazed down on her. "You are no longer afraid of me, are you?"

She shook her head, answering truthfully, "No, not anymore."

"Maybe now you should be."

"Why now?"

"Because I want to know you better."

Her eyes lowered momentarily. "In the biblical sense?"

"In your biblical sense, yes."

She sighed as his mouth lowered to take hers. He tasted of sunshine and wind, and she couldn't remember a nicer smell. She knew what she was feeling was wrong—she knew she would never be able to explain her actions to Amelia and Abigail, but she wanted him to make love to her. She wanted him to hold her and touch and caress her until she was powerless to identify right from wrong.

"Are you going to make love to me?" she whispered.

"It is what I want," he whispered against her lips.

"That's what I want also," she admitted.

They kissed, a long hungry kiss that left her weak with desire. She knew that he would be gentle because of her innocence.

Gathering her tightly, he moved sensuously against her, his eyes locked tightly with hers. As she felt the physical proof of his need press against her middle, her eyes widened with wonder.

"Are you frightened now?" he asked.

Gazing back at him, she shook her head. "No." She grinned as he slipped the straps of her chemise over her shoulders, baring her breasts. "Are you?"

"Should I be?"

She nodded, thinking it only fair to warn him. She was no longer a child. She was innocent, but an instinct, ages old and deep within her, knew what would please him, and Mother Superior or not, her own need was crying desperately for fulfillment. Her mind reeled, a part of her knowing what she was about to do was wrong, but she was helpless to stop it.

Lifting her, he carried her to the bed. In moments he

had divested himself of clothing and lay down beside her.

Her hands boldly sought the mystery of his body as his lips hungrily sought hers. There was no stopping now, no turning back.

Whispering her name, he kissed her heated body, moving slowly downward, igniting her body with each sensual flick of his tongue. Every nerve tingled, crying for release, yet she couldn't bear for him to stop.

His body against hers made her dizzy with desire. Boldly her hand closed over the evidence of his pulsating need and she felt gloriously empowered when she heard his groan of approval. His hands gripped her waist tightly as he struggled for control.

"It's all right," she whispered, urgency filling her voice now.

His mouth took hers roughly as desire overcame them. She felt a pain so exquisite it caught her breath as he entered her. At first the anguish was so excruciating she stifled back a cry, and sensing her distress, Creed momentarily stopped, cradling her head to his chest as he told her raggedly, "I don't want to hurt you. I want to go slow, but I'm powerless. . . ."

"No, please, don't stop," she gasped. "It's all right, really it is."

He began slowly, his smooth supple body moving rhythmically with hers. The pain gradually faded, replaced by ecstasy. All Anne-Marie was aware of was his wonderful body moving inside her, taking her to heights she never dreamed were possible. They were one, their bodies joined, hearts beating together, nothing between them but their own fevered flesh.

Great day in the morning!

It was better than Sister Frances's chocolate cake.

Later, as their breathing eased, Creed raised on his elbow to look at her. Suddenly he began to laugh, falling back on the pillow.

Slightly irritated, Anne-Marie sat up, staring at him. "What is so *funny*?" She was getting tired of being the butt of his and Quincy's jokes!

"You." He chuckled.

Anne-Marie jerked her pillow and hit him with it. "I fail to see what I've done that's so darn funny! I *thought* you were enjoying yourself!"

"I was," Creed assured her as his laughter momentarily subsided. "I'm not laughing at anything you did, Anne-Marie. I'm laughing at the way you look."

"What's wrong with the way I look?" she said indignantly. He had a lot of nerve laughing at her when he looked like a . . . like a chimney sweep!

Climbing out of bed, he lifted her and carried her to the mirror, where the small candle still bravely fought to shed its tiny light.

Her mouth dropped open when she saw her reflection.

For a moment she was speechless, and then a ripple of laughter began deep in her throat. She *was* a funny sight! Her face was streaked with soot! Her body, too! Two emerald eyes stared back at her from a charcoal-smeared face.

"Well, I shore does look downright comical, don't I?" she mocked, imitating Tobias's voice.

Chuckling, Creed placed his mouth against hers and whispered. "Why, I would be proud if you were to let me wash you, Miss Lilly Belle. I'd wash real good. I wouldn't miss a speck anywhere.''

"Is that a promise?" Her breath caught as his tongue toyed with her ear.

"Yes, ma'am." His mouth found hers as he carried her back to bed. "That's a promise."

The sun was just topping the roof of the hotel as Loyal Streeter stepped out the next morning, escorting Miss Lillie Belle Willingham. Lillie Belle's two black servants somberly fell into step behind the couple as they crossed the street and walked toward the icehouse.

As the entourage approached, the guards moved to unlock the icehouse door. Once the heavy padlock had been removed, they stepped aside, allowing room for the slaves to enter.

Lillie Belle suddenly reached out, resting her hand on Loyal's arm.

"I wonder if you'd be so kind as to allow me a private moment with my dear sweet departed daddy?"

Patting her hand, Loyal tried to change her mind. "My dear, do you think that's wise? It isn't healthy to put yourself through this agony." He hated to see grief eating away at this lovely creature.

"Please, Mr. Streeter." Her voice dropped persuasively. "I only ask for a few brief moments. There is so little time left that I can look upon my papa's face."

Stepping aside, Loyal relented. He checked his watch. "There isn't much time. The engineer is anxious to be on his way."

In the distance they could already hear the train building up steam.

"I'll only take a moment," she promised, once more lifting her handkerchief to the corners of her eyes.

Malachi started to follow her into the icehouse, but she stopped him. Giving him a pointed look, she said, "Please, Malachi! I want to be alone with Papa."

Malachi looked as if he were about to protest when Tobias quickly intervened. "Miss Lillie Belle, now you don' need to be in there alone," he said. "You all just let Mr. Streeter take you on down to the train. Me and Malachi now, we be right along with yo papa."

She gave him a pointed look, too. "I want to be alone with my father, Tobias."

"Miss Lillie Belle." They had been through all this. Quincy knew that she had been designated to switch the gold, but he still didn't like it, and neither did Creed. But Anne-Marie insisted, saying that it was her plan. She'd caused enough trouble as it was, and she would be responsible for making the switch. At this point Quincy didn't see what he could do to stop her.

"Leave her be," Loyal said sharply as the engineer gave another warning toot on the train's whistle. "We're wasting time. Let her get on with it!"

Nodding sedately, Lillie Belle disappeared into the icehouse, closing the door firmly behind her. Tobias and Malachi faded back, keeping a safe distance from the guards and Streeter.

"We should have insisted that *we* make the switch," Creed muttered.

He did not want her putting herself in this kind of danger. If Streeter caught on to the con, they would all be killed in a matter of minutes.

"We could have insisted all we wanted. Once that

woman has her mind made up, come hell or high water, she's not going to change it," Quincy murmured back.

"If she's caught—"

"We agreed we weren't going to consider that possibility."

The two slaves stood quietly back, hands crossed in front of them, their faces expressionless. As they waited Creed felt sweat trickle down his back. If she didn't come out soon, Streeter was going to get suspicious. Creed could see the man was already pacing back and forth, his eyes trained on the icehouse door.

"Where in the hell is she?" Creed complained.

"Easy, easy now," Quincy soothed. "She hasn't been in there over two or three minutes. It only seems longer."

Creed's eyes fixed on the doorway of the icehouse, willing Anne-Marie to appear. The gold was heavy—would she be able to handle it by herself?

As the moments stretched into long minutes sweat ran in rivulets down the sides of Creed's face. If Streeter looked closely, he would have seen that one of Lillie Belle's slaves was washing out.

Creed's hands closed around the knife strapped to his side beneath his loose-fitting trousers. If Streeter caught on to the con, Creed would take him while Quincy went for the guards. From then on it would be anybody's guess who got out alive.

The whistle blasted again, warning of the train's imminent departure.

Clearly uneasy now, Loyal started for the icehouse door when it suddenly opened and Lillie Belle emerged, wiping her eyes.

"There you are," he said, relieved. "I was just about to come in after you."

"I'm so sorry. I just couldn't bear to part with Papa," Lillie Belle sobbed. She smiled tremulously. "Thank you evah so much for allowing me these last few precious moments alone with him."

"Come along, dear. Come along. The train is eager to leave."

Loyal took her arm and walked her away as Malachi and Tobias quickly disappeared into the icehouse. A moment later they returned, carrying the casket.

The two slaves appeared to have a great deal of difficulty handling Dexter Willingham's remains this morning as they doggedly made their way down the small incline to the railroad tracks.

The conductor and another man were waiting to help the two servants hoist the casket aboard the waiting rail car.

"Must have been a hardy soul," Creed heard the conductor say as he strained to help lift the cumbersome load.

Pulling his handkerchief out of his pocket, the conductor mopped at his forehead.

The engineer tooted the train whistle again, and Lillie Belle turned to Loyal, extending her gloved hand. "You have been evah so kind, Mr. Streeter. I just don't know how I can evah repay your generosity. You've just been such a sweet South'n gentleman!"

Bowing from the waist, Loyal placed a kiss on the back of her hand. "I shall never forget you, Miss Lillie Belle Willingham."

Lillie Belle smiled. "I suspect you won't, Mr. Streeter."

"Now, don't you forget to come on back here once

all the unpleasantness has been attended to," he reminded.

The train began to move as she daintily lifted the hem of her skirt and Loyal helped her aboard. The two slaves, Tobias and Malachi, stood reverently at the head of Dexter Willingham's casket, guarding his remains.

Moving to the back of the car, Lillie Belle stood on the platform waving her hanky at Loyal's disappearing figure.

"Don't you forget, Miss Willingham. You promised to stop off here again and have dinner with me," Loyal called again.

"I shan't, Mr. Streeter. I shan't!" *Be back,* she added beneath her breath. A cheerful Lillie Belle waved and waved until the train finally rounded the bend and was out of sight.

Patting his lapel, Loyal drew a deep breath. Now *that* was a woman!

Turning, he strode quickly back to the icehouse to check on his gold. When he stepped inside, it took a moment for his eyes to adjust to the dim interior. When they did, he blinked, then blinked again, unable to believe what he was seeing.

A skeletal form dressed in monk's clothing sat where the gold bars once rested, grinning wickedly back at him. A note was wedged between a bony thumb and forefinger.

Loyal's face drained of color as he read the terse note. *Fool,* it said.

Two miles down the track, the train once again came to a grinding halt. Passengers groped for support and several were heard loudly grumbling at yet another unexpected delay.

The conductor walked through the cars, soothing their frayed tempers. "Just be a moment, folks, and we'll be on our way again!" he assured them.

Outside, the two slaves quickly loaded the heavy casket onto a waiting buckboard overseen by three Comanche warriors.

Nearby, an Indian chief dressed in a war bonnet sat astride his horse, watching the activities.

Within five minutes the train released its brakes and steam billowed from the smokestack. The conductor blew the whistle again and the cars began to rattle on down the track.

Anne-Marie ran over to stand beside Creed as the unusual assemblage watched the train pick up speed and disappear around the bend.

Slipping his arm around Anne-Marie's waist, Creed smiled down at her.

Returning his smile, Anne-Marie grinned. "Nice job, huh?"

"Nice job," he agreed.

Her best yet.

# Chapter 20

It was as important to Anne-Marie to deliver the gold safely to Commander Lewis as it was to Creed and Quincy. The two men accepted their commander's praise with dignified modesty. Only Anne-Marie knew the real price that had been paid for this victory. With the war over, the money would be used to rebuild the ravaged country.

Tucking her fourth of the gold safely away, she prepared for her return to Mercy Flats.

There was a large celebration in camp that night. The causes of the festivities were twofold. Word had come early that morning, April 9, Palm Sunday, that Robert Edward Lee had surrendered his starving ragged Army of North Virginia to Ulysses Simpson Grant.

The war was finally over.

Anne-Marie watched as grown men wept and others fell to their knees to thank God for their deliverance. Thousands of slain fathers, sons, brothers, and uncles were not here to witness the historic event. The North had won, but any sane man would concede there was no victory in this war. A nation had been split apart, its countrymen left with only a sense of personal valor—a realization that when adversity comes, the most ordinary people can show that they value something more than they value their own lives.

The fighting over, the men were released from duty and told to go home. Many would return to burned-down homes, looted farms, and fields littered with the remains of war. For others, God willing, there would be wives and children waiting for husbands and fathers to return.

Anne-Marie watched as Quincy strapped the last of his belongings into his knapsack and hefted it upon his back. He had a long walk ahead of him, but it didn't matter. He had shoes and a strong back; he was going home.

As Quincy shook Creed's hand his eyes misted. "It's been good working with you, Creed Walker."

Creed's features were solemn as he clasped Quincy's hand tightly, his eyes confirming his deep affection for the black man. Their lives had been on the line many times and they had always been there for each other.

"If you ever get near Coleman Flats, be sure and look me up," Quincy told him. "I'd be real honored to have you meet my Floralee and the children."

"I'll make it a point to ride that way," Creed assured him.

Glancing at Anne-Marie, Quincy cleared his throat.

Smiling, she stepped forward, hugging him around the neck tightly. "I hope the same goes for me," she said.

"Yes, ma'am, especially for you!" He hugged her back, holding her tight for a moment. "When you're back with your sisters, you bring them on over to Coleman Flats.'' He shook his head, grinning at the thought of *three* like her. Lord have mercy.

Shaking hands with Creed one more time, Quincy turned and started through camp, waving to others as they called out to him.

Anne-Marie followed, tears wetting her cheeks as she watched him set off down the road. They had shared a lot in the past few weeks. She'd finally decided her feelings about the war. If she were asked to give her life in order that Quincy's sons would live in freedom, she would gladly do so. She knew now that the color of a man's skin didn't matter.

It was what was in his heart that made the difference.

Then it was time for Anne-Marie and Creed to leave. Anne-Marie prepared for the journey to Mercy Flats with a heavy heart. Two weeks ago she would have anticipated the return with the enthusiasm of a child. Now the realization of what lay at the end of the journey made her sad.

She watched as Creed checked the horses' rigging. Even though she was eager to be reunited with Abigail and Amelia, how would she ever be able to say good-bye to the man with whom she had shared her deepest secrets and thoughts—her very soul?

Turning, Creed caught her watching him. For a moment they gazed at each other, both finding it difficult to speak.

Creed finally broke the silence. ''Commander Lewis has offered us an escort, I told him we wouldn't need one.''

''No,'' she murmured. She wanted their last hours

together to be spent alone. Moving to her horse, she mounted quickly before he saw the tears in her eyes.

Creed swung into his saddle and, with a solemn nod to Commander Lewis, turned his horse.

Anne-Marie brought her animal in behind him and they rode out of camp while the others stood watching.

For the next two days they rode side by side, speaking of nothing more serious than how pleasant the day was and how nice the spring flowers looked blooming along the ditches and ravines.

Creed pointed to a robin pulling fat worms out of the moist ground, and they laughed, savoring the shared intimate moments. Another time he spotted a cotton-wood tree, and they left their horses to peel back the bark of the tree and scrape the spring sap that flowed upward. The jellylike froth was sweet and creamy. They devoured the delicacy like two small children.

Thoughts of the night that lay ahead served to heighten their awareness of each other.

When they camped, Anne-Marie shared his bedroll. Lying under a canopy of stars, they held each other tightly, trying to hold back the sunrise.

"I'll miss you," she confessed.

"I'll miss you, too."

"A lot?"

"More than you'll ever know."

She rolled to her side, and they kissed for a very long time.

"Do you think things might have been different—if the circumstances were changed?" she ventured as their breaths mingled. She longed to know that although he couldn't speak of his feelings, they were as deep and troubling as hers.

Threading his hand through her hair, he held her for a moment, his eyes mirroring her anguish. "Yes, things would be different."

"You would love me?"

His eyes softened. "I could love you no more than at this moment."

A smile lit her features. "Honestly?"

"Honestly."

"Hold me close," she whispered. "Hold me close, and never let me go."

He held her close, knowing that with each dawn she was slipping further and further away.

The closer they drew to Mercy Flats, the more frenzied their lovemaking became. Yet nothing was mentioned about the future.

Even if the subject had been broached, Anne-Marie wasn't sure how she would have responded. She was still uncertain about her feelings. She knew she loved Creed, but she loved her sisters, too. So many thoughts troubled her. Abigail, Amelia. They had made a blood pact as young girls, vowing to stay together forever. How could she break this promise, even though she loved Creed Walker more than she loved her own life? She found herself consumed by guilt. Had she betrayed those she loved by falling in love with Creed?

And there was the matter of Berry Woman.

Her love for Creed had caused her to wish a terrible fate upon another person. If Berry Woman died, Creed would be free.

Did she want that? Would Creed's freedom change anything, or had Anne-Marie McDougal merely been another woman in Creed Walker's life?

So many questions with so few answers.

As the horses topped a rise the final day, Anne-Marie's pulse quickened when she saw the small community of Mercy Flats spread out below her.

For a moment she was filled with homesickness. The old mission looked achingly familiar and comforting. Her life had been simple here, so uncomplicated.

They rested their horses side by side as Anne-Marie gazed down at the tranquil setting below them. Creed watched the emotions play across her face.

"There have been times when I didn't think I'd ever see it or my sisters again," she admitted, fighting the rising lump in her throat.

Creed had thought about that possibility. It was conceivable that Abigail and Amelia's rescuers had not been able to elude the Comanches.

Reaching for her hand, he squeezed it reassuringly.

Smiling back at him, she bit her lower lip to still its trembling. "Will you ride down with me?"

She knew she shouldn't ask. He wasn't hers to invite, but oh, how she needed him to ride the last mile with her.

His eyes filled with love as he gazed back at her. "It is very hard for me to let you go. If I ride the last mile with you, I may find it impossible to turn back."

She summoned up every last ounce of courage she had. "Ride with me anyway, Creed Walker."

Nodding, he released her hand and Anne-Marie allowed her horse to begin to pick its way down the small ravine.

"Creed!" she called over her shoulder.

Creed wouldn't tell her he loved her even if he did. He still felt a responsibility to Bold Eagle, even if Berry Woman died. If a Crow gave his word, he kept it.

"Creed!" she called again.

"Yes?"

"I've been thinking—" She'd have to talk to Abigial and Amelia, but she knew if they loved her as much as she loved them, they'd understand what she was about to do.

"About what?"

"Haven't I heard somewhere that Indians purchase each other with horses and blankets and things like that?"

She didn't know why she hadn't thought of it earlier! She still had money left from the coin—and a fourth of the gold! She was rich! She could buy the finest horses Texas had to offer!

"Some do," he agreed.

"Can, say, someone like me buy, say, an Indian using the same bargaining ploy?"

A slow smile spread at the corners of Creed's mouth. "I suppose it depends on how much the other party needs the horses."

"Well, if anything should happen to Berry Woman— not that I think it will, but if it did—would Bold Eagle take, say, thirty of the finest horses I could possibly buy in exchange for you?"

Creed's features darkened. He had never had a woman offer to buy him. "I am not Cheyenne. Crows barter blankets, robes, and utensils for a hand in marriage— but these are only considered loans."

"Oh." Her face fell. Drat.

"A Crow is permitted more than one wife," he offered. "Sits-Beside-Me-Wife." He paused, then said quietly. "Perhaps we could speak of this."

She paused, turning to look over her shoulder.

"Sits-Beside-Me-Wife is a Crow's first wife—the best in standing," he clarified.

"Is that what Berry Woman will be? Sits-Beside-Me-Wife?"

He gazed back at her somberly, his long hair whipping in the breeze. "If it is your wish, we can speak at greater length about this."

"No, that isn't necessary." Turning back, she guided her horse down the steep ravine. His reluctance to recognize true love when he saw it wasn't going to get her down.

He might be Crow, but he also knew the white man's wisdom when it came to matters of the heart.

She was in love with Creed Walker, and she wasn't about to give up on him.

She'd think of something.

A McDougal always did.

Dear Reader,

I hope you had a good time reading PROMISE ME TOMORROW.

Here's the beginning of PROMISE ME FOREVER, the final book in *The Sisters of Mercy Flats* saga. Look for it in 1994.

Enjoy!

*Lori Copeland*

# Chapter 1

Sister Amelia was a nuisance.

And Morgan Kane couldn't afford a big nuisance right now. After narrowly outrunning the Comanche, he needed to get on with his business.

That delay, though small, had cost him valuable time, and for him time was running out. Now that the imminent danger had passed, his thoughts shifted to the immediate problem—what to do with the sister.

Though the prospect was tempting, he couldn't just leave her by the roadside. It was clear to him that Sister Amelia, whom he had snatched from a jail wagon twelve hours earlier, had a penchant for nature that would result in more delays.

Low-flying birds, blooming flowers, rolling clouds, blinding sunrises, glowing sunsets, and it appeared, life in general, enthralled this woman.

While Morgan could appreciate serendipity, this nun's continual flights of fancy destroyed any semblance of a schedule and played havoc with his system of order. If these postponements continued, he could miss his Galveston contact. He must rid himself of the sister and soon.

Sister Amelia viewed the day's events as unsettling, but far from alarming. At first, she had been perturbed when those awful ole Comanche had swooped down on the jail wagon like a donkey with a pepper up its behind, but when this nice Union officer had ridden to her aid, her fears had flown right out the window.

Two other men had arrived to rescue Abigail and Anne-Marie, so there was nothing to be upset about. The Indians had been outsmarted, and now everything was dandy.

Sighing, Amelia again admired the breadth of the Yankee's shoulders. The way he sat up so tall and straight in his saddle just made her feel all giddy inside. My, he surely was an admirable sight, she thought. Why, he must have at least a hundred women in love with him—that or Texas women were just plain blind.

They had been together for the better part of a day now, and he had seemed so cordial to her and so capable. In fact, he was the most organized, masterful man she'd ever met. He had escaped those wretched Indians with hardly any effort at all.

When this was over, she wanted to introduce this man to Abigail and Anne-Marie. Meeting such a fine, manly specimen might change her sisters' less-than-charitable feelings for the opposite sex. They'd never liked men much.

But they'd like this one. Though the officer had seemed pensive after the ordeal, he had treated her with the utmost respect, seeing to her every need as if she were a welcome guest instead of just some ole bother.

Although they had just recently met, Amelia had a

hunch that this handsome Yankee had taken a fancy to her. Her intuition hadn't been inspired by anything he had said or done: she just saw a glint of interest every time he looked at her with those gorgeous steel gray eyes.

Odd how two people just seemed to gravitate to each other, she mused as she rode in the saddle behind him, admiring a scenic fence post.

Although her knowledge of men could fit in a thimble, she was positive this man thought her attractive. No telling how she knew; she just knew.


"Tomorrow, we'll proceed to the nearest port," the handsome captain told her as they finished their evening meal. The night was clear under a starry sky, but the cold wind had a bite to it. Amelia thought it could snow anytime.

"Where is the nearest port?" she asked as she huddled closer to the fire. She'd never been good at directions. All day long, she hadn't known east from west.

"Galveston." He pitched the remainder of his coffee, watching as steam rose from the frozen ground. "I was on my way to Galveston when I encountered the jail wagon, so you are welcome to accompany me there in the morning."

He would prefer to cover the remaining distance alone, but he could hardly leave the sister without protection, no matter how anxious he was to be on his way. His genteel breeding obligated him to see to her safety.

Amelia gazed up at him warmly, marveling over the way her stomach felt jittery every time he looked at her. Yes, her intuition was right. He did find her attractive, even though he should be ashamed of himself. After all, he believed her to be a woman of the cloth. Still, she smiled, finding pleasure at the thought. "That's very kind of you, but I have no funds—"

"Please, Sister." He lifted his nice, manly hand in protest. "It would be my honor to provide for your meals and safe return to Mercy Flats."

Staring into the fire, Amelia measured his generous offer. Actually, she had little choice in the matter. She was penniless, and the thought of traveling alone frightened her. She felt safe with this man, safe and protected. She couldn't have a more honorable escort, cool in the face of adversity, reserved, competent. And he had been enough of a gentleman not to question her reason for being in the jail wagon.

She let her eyes travel the width of his shoulders beneath his impeccable double-breasted frock coat as she heaved another mental sigh. The North surely must be bursting with pride to have a man like him on its side.

Over the years she'd watched the Union troops going about their business, and she'd developed a certain admiration for them.

To be fair, the Confederacy had its share of notable specimens, but she was drawn to the handsome northerners. Oh, her feelings had little to do with the causes of the war because she had never understood why everyone was so mad. Whatever the reasons, she knew that the quarrel had turned ugly.

No, her fondness for this uniform evolved from her interest in the man wearing it. He was so powerful, so decisive, just like a man ought to be.

Abigail and Anne-Marie would say she was witless for thinking *any* man worthy of second notice, but

Amelia didn't agree. She'd met men who weren't all that disagreeable. And besides, she almost liked men.

Her eyes returned to his tall form as he stood, warming his backside to the fire.

Especially this man.

Since he had seen to her immediate safety, he could simply have gone on with his business. But no, he had offered to let her ride along with him, and that was awfully nice of him, just awfully nice.

So nice, in fact, that her conscience was compelling her to tell him the truth. She knew that he might find her admission shameful, at best somewhat annoying, but considering the pleasant way he was treating her, she couldn't let him go on thinking that she really was a nun. It just wouldn't be right.

"Sir?" She realized she didn't even know his name.

Covering a yawn, Morgan stretched his long torso. Twelve hours in the saddle had taken its toll. "Yes, Sister?"

"There's something I must confess."

From the look on his face, she gathered that the prospect of listening to a long, dreary confession didn't intrigue him.

"Perhaps it could wait until morning, Sister? I am unusually weary tonight."

"No," she replied, her mind firmly made up now. "It's important that I tell you tonight." If she waited until morning, she might have second thoughts. She was bad about that.

"Very well," he conceded.

Rising slowly to her feet, Amelia lifted her hands to her head and peeled off her veil, freeing a mass of luxuriant auburn hair that tumbled over her shoulders.

Afraid to look at him now, she quickly removed her collar and awaited his response. Would he be angry? The last thing she wanted was to make him angry.

As his silence grew more palpable, she mentally braced herself for his reaction, fearing that she had misjudged his character. Was it possible that he would be so furious with her that he would order her to find her way back to Mercy Flats alone?

Oh, he *was* angry, she agonized. She didn't blame him—he *should* be furious with her. He had unselfishly risked his life to rescue her because he'd believed that she was a woman of exemplary virtue. Now he could see that she wasn't righteous, that she'd only been pretending—not that she wasn't righteous, she could be when she wanted to be, but she wasn't nun righteous. None of the McDougal sisters were nun righteous.

Yes, he was livid.

"You're furious," she murmured when she couldn't bear the damnable silence a moment longer.

The captain stared at her.

"Oh, you hate me, don't you?" He should hate her. He really should.

Very little surprised Morgan Kane anymore, but she had. *Why* would a woman parade around the countryside in a nun's habit when she wasn't a nun? That was blasphemous!

"All right." He would handle this calmly. Blowing up would gain him nothing more than another costly delay. "Would you care to explain your disguise?"

"I'm a thief."

His brows knitted in a tight frown. "What?"

"Not a mean thief," she clarified. "But, nevertheless, I am a thief." She felt just awful having to tell

312

him, but if they were going to travel together, he needed to know.

"A thief." He shifted his stance irritably.

"Yes. I thought you should know."

"Thank you."

"You're welcome." A strained smile touched her lips. There, that hadn't been so bad. He had taken it quite well actually.

"So are my sisters. They really are my flesh-and-blood sisters."

"They're thieves."

"Yes." She smiled tightly.

"That's why you were in the jail wagon? Because you're three sister thieves dressed in nuns' clothing?"

"That's right."

He stood for a moment, color building in his face. He had squandered twelve hours and risked his mission for a bunch of thieving women!

"Are you mad again?" At first, he'd seemed to take it well, but now she wasn't so certain. His face was sort of mottled now.

He strode to his horse and jerked open the straps on the saddlebags. After fishing inside, he produced a pair of wrinkled overalls and a plaid shirt.

"What are you doing?"

"Getting a change of clothing," he snapped.

"Why?"

"None of your business."

"Oh," she took a hesitant step toward him, then paused. "You are angry, aren't you?"

"It matters little how I feel, Miss—"

"McDougal. Amelia McDougal," she supplied as she reached out to shake his hand.

For a moment, he stared at her extended hand. Finally, with an impatient sigh, he took her hand and gave it a perfunctory shake.

"Morgan Kane."

"Amelia—McDougal," she shared again. "I'm sorry about the deception."

He didn't say that he'd accept her apology, but he didn't say he wouldn't.

"Is it still all right if I ride to Galveston with you tomorrow?"

Morgan would have liked nothing better than to retract his offer. He should feel no further responsibility for her now that he knew she wasn't a nun, but he did. She was a woman, thief or no thief, and a woman had no business traveling alone.

"To Galveston," he said, turning away, grim resignation in his voice, "and not a mile farther."

"Oh, I won't be a bother," she assured him. "You'll hardly know I'm around."

"Make sure that I don't."

His words stung her. She'd braced herself for a wave of indignation, perhaps fury, but not cold indifference. He'd been so kind to her that she'd expected him to forgive her for the tiny iniquity.

Perplexed, she sank down on her heels. All her life, everyone had forgiven her. When her sisters had grown exasperated with what they called her feather-brained, impulsive nature, they'd railed at her for a few moments and then forgiven her. She'd always been indulged, scolded, and then forgiven.

Cold dismissal was something she hadn't been prepared for, especially from someone she liked so much. She slumped onto a log and let her head drop into her hands. The truth was she hadn't really anticipated his reaction to her impulsive confession. She'd leapt again without looking. She had a bad habit of going on instinct instead of logic, of rushing headlong with a heart full of good intentions only to stumble into a labyrinth of trouble. It had happened again, only this time it was worse.

Morgan Kane didn't know her; worse yet, he didn't want to know her, not anymore. She'd caught the shock in his eyes, watched it turn to disillusionment. Gone from his eyes was the glint of admiration, the glow of respect, the light of infatuation.

If she'd only thought things through, she'd still be basking in his warmth. *When* would she learn, she wondered as she glanced up to see him disappear into the brush.

When he reappeared, he was wearing the wrinkled plaid shirt and the faded overalls he'd dug out of his saddlebag. His military uniform draped over his arm, he brushed past her with only a brief, slanted look.

He no longer looked like her dashing captain. Watching his back as he spread his bedroll, she thought he looked like a poor dirt farmer. But when he rose to his full height and turned to face her, she recognized the pride in his military bearing, the lean muscle beneath the thin fabric.

He was still the captain, but not her captain. The chill in his gaze exposed the degree of his disappointment.

She tried to swallow around the lump in her throat. His icy regard was difficult to endure. His rage she could have handled. She was accustomed to her sisters' bursts of impatience, their stormy retorts, the brief strain of silence, and then the sunshine of their forgiveness.

He tossed a bedroll at her feet. "Turn in. We ride at daybreak."

She had a feeling this was no brief strain . . . that there would be no sunshine of forgiveness. His cool response cut her deeply. A spark of resentment flickered to life. After all, she'd only told him the truth. He could give her credit for that. She could have fooled him for days with her nun's charade. She'd trusted him with the *truth*, and this was the thanks she got.

Her chin lifted, and she brushed the bedroll aside. "You may be accustomed to people jumping when you give orders, but I don't jump—"

"Unless it's from a jail wagon," he muttered as he stretched out.

Her jaw dropped open. "I'll have you know, Captain Kane, that I—"

He rolled over so suddenly that she strangled a cry as his face came perilously close to hers. As his eyes bore into hers, her breath froze in her throat.

"The *rules* have changed, Sister," he said in a low voice.

He was so close she could see the dark flecks in his eyes, feel his warm breath on her face. Her gaze dropped to the firm lips that hovered above hers.

"What?" she whispered as she swayed toward him. She could feel the heat of his anger, but she felt drawn to the flame.

His eyes narrowed ruthlessly. Men facing him in battle would have recognized the danger in his look. An instant later his lips ground down upon hers. Without touching her elsewhere, his mouth ravaged hers. Relentlessly, he plundered, searching, thrusting, driving her backward until she found herself on her back, his body arched above her.

She was sinking into a swirl of needs she'd never known existed. Primitive needs she'd never experienced drummed in her pulse. *What* was he doing to her!

Her head was spinning and her heart pounding in desperation. Nothing her sisters had told her had prepared her for anything like this.

Bells were going off in her head, but she felt powerless to resist. Everything was happening so fast, too fast. The sensations racing through her were too sudden to comprehend.

Terrified, she shoved him back. "Stop!"

He jerked back, his breathing ragged as his mouth left hers.

Wiping her hand across her mouth, she spat on the ground contemptuously. "*Poophhhp!* How dare you!"

With a lunge, he shoved away from her and rolled to his feet. "Little girls who play dangerous games should expect dangerous consequences."

Amelia watched as he stalked off into the thick underbrush. Drawing her knees to her chest, she wrapped her arms around them tightly. Her mind was a haze of confusion. She'd never felt as abandoned as she had when she'd seen the expression of loathing in his eyes.

Rejection and humiliation bloomed on her cheeks. How could she ever look him in the eye again? She couldn't, certainly not tonight. She'd take the coward's way out and feign sleep even though she couldn't possibly sleep. Not now—not after this. Why, he was *dangerous*. Quickly, she spread her bedroll and curled up, her back to the fire, her face hidden under the blanket she drew tightly around herself.

*Why* had he changed his clothes? Just what sort of man was Morgan Kane?

Her body was so tense, she ached. It seemed like hours before she heard him return, his footsteps stealthy. She listened intently as he stretched out beside the fire on his blanket. Hours passed, but she never heard the even breathing of slumber. She wondered if he was a silent sleeper, but she dared not risk a glance. She lay silent and unmoving all night.

She didn't realize she'd fallen asleep until the slanting rays of dawn pierced her eyelids. She rose with a shiver and glanced over her shoulder. The fire was out, and the camp was deserted.

Gone was his bedroll, his coffeepot, his saddle. Her gaze darted to the tree where he'd tethered his horse the night before—no horse. Gone without a trace, without a shred of evidence to prove he'd ever been there except for the army blanket wrapped around her.

Perhaps he'd never existed. Perhaps her entire encounter with him had been only a dream. She touched her fingertips to her lips. They felt puffy, swollen, and tender. That part hadn't been a dream. She couldn't have imagined that kiss.

"Now what?" she moaned. She'd always had someone to fall back on. Here she was in the middle of nowhere with nothing. She sat cross-legged in the middle of the blanket, her mouth agape, her fingertips lightly testing her lips, her thoughts in a blur.

She sat up straighter when she heard muffled hoof beats.

"Time to rise and shine, Sister."

Her head spun around, and she looked up into the blinding rays of the sun. It was only when she raised her hands to shield her eyes that she saw the captain, sitting astride his horse, watching her with a grim expression.

This was no dream. Harsh reality had returned.

He took in the vision of her, sitting on the blanket, her sleep-tossed hair cascading over her shoulders, her fingertips tapping her swollen lips. Something flickered in his gaze before his eyes narrowed and he swung off his horse.

"*Where* have you been?" she blurted.

"Shopping."

"*Shopping?*" If she weren't so relieved to see him she would give him a piece of her mind!

"Better corral that mane of yours under your veil, Sister. It's time to climb aboard your new friend here."

Her eyes followed his gesture to the scrawny mule standing behind his horse. "What's that?"

"Your transportation."

"That ole thing!"

Turning his horse, he mounted and started to ride off. "Take it or leave it."

She'd take it. Scrambling to her feet, she quickly tucked her hair under her veil. "Where did you get him?"

The mule was so skinny that his backbone protruded noticeably under the woven cloth on his back. His coat was long and matted, and beneath his long lashes he seemed to regard her as mournfully as she regarded him.

"You ask too many questions," he said shortly.

Wearing his faded overalls and plaid shirt, Morgan

Kane rode back to give her a leg up. Before she could think of a delay, she felt her backside land on the mule's sharp spine. She was about to voice a protest when she thought better of it. She wouldn't give the captain the satisfaction, nor did she want to face the prospect of being left behind again.

"Here are the ground rules, Sister."

Her eyes widened momentarily as his words from the night before echoed back to her. The rules have changed, he'd said to her before he'd delivered the punishing kiss.

He saw the surprise on her face as his eyes traveled over her kiss-swollen lips. "You will not address me as 'Captain'. In fact, the less you say the better." He raked her with a look of disdain. "Keep your costume in place, and play the role of the good sister."

"Why? Are you trying to hide something?" That must be it. He was doing some sort of undercover work.

Before she could answer back, he turned the animals and moved out in the lead.

A cold wind rolled in off the gulf as the odd couple rode into Galveston late the following day. A wintry sun glittered off the Gulf of Mexico as Morgan and Amelia guided their horses into town. Threading their animals through the crowded streets, their eyes quietly appraised the situation. The town was teaming with Confederate soldiers.

Glancing warily at the captain, Amelia wondered if he was aware that Galveston was a Confederate naval center. Even she knew that, and she didn't know anything.

If Morgan found the atmosphere threatening, he

didn't show it. His features fixed dispassionately as they rode through town.

"For heaven's sake, don't call him *Captain*," Amelia reminded herself under her breath, recalling his earlier warning. It would only set him off again, and he had been sullen ever since she'd told him the truth about her.

The poor dirt farmer and the sister in a threadbare habit casually wove their way past rows of weather-beaten storefronts, trying to blend with the crowd.

The streets were filled with boisterous Confederate naval soldiers. Ship boys and officers alike had set out to get roaring drunk, seeking a few hours reprieve from sea duty with its steamy salt air, heaving decks, and stench of gunpowder.

Amelia's eyes anxiously appraised the troubling situations. Swallowing dryly, her thoughts wandered to Anne-Marie and Abigail, wondering what they were doing now. It hadn't occurred to her to be concerned about the fate of her sisters. Bad things happened to other people, never to the McDougal sisters. Sister Agnes had said that they were all blessed, and Amelia believed her. People were always blessing the McDougal sisters up one side and down the other.

Her eyes darted to the various signs tacked to store-front windows, offering a reward for the notoriously daring "Lannigan," a daring privateer who was barbarously good with a knife. She hoped that she wouldn't meet up with him, but if she did, the captain would protect her.

Spying a vacancy at a nearby hitching post, the farmer and the nun maneuvered their horses toward the rail and dismounted. Securing the reins tightly, they stood for a moment, planning their next move.

Amelia edged closer to the captain and said from the corner of her mouth, "Better watch it. The enemy is everywhere."

Morgan glanced down at her. "What?"

"They're all around us," she repeated, motioning with her eyes to their treacherous surroundings. "The enemy—*everywhere*."

Unbeknownst to her, her voice carried like a feather in a hurricane.

Morgan stiffened.

She stepped closer, working her words through stiff lips. "Did you hear what I said?"

He gave her a glare that would blister paint off a ship.

"What?" she asked, annoyed by his look. She couldn't do *anything* to please him now.

"Lower your voice."

"What?"

"Lower your voice!"

Color suffused her cheeks. Was he saying she talked too loud!

"Lower your voice," he demanded tightly.

"Why? I wasn't talking loud," she argued, appalled that he would accuse her. Wasn't that just like a man? Try to look out for him, and all he can do is criticize. "I was only trying to warn you that you'd better be careful because this town is crawling—"

Her eyes widened as his hand clamped over her mouth.

*"Shut up!"*

*"Shut up?"* she spat in a garbled indignation. Her reaction was starting to draw a crowd.

Well, that did it! Now he had hurt her feelings! He'd been sore since last night when he'd found out she wasn't a nun, and now he'd done it! Never, in her entire life, had anyone but her sisters ever told her to shut up. Tears smarted in her eyes. How *dare* he tell her to *shut up*! Who did he think he was? The president of the United States, Abraham—Abraham whatever-his-name-is!

When Morgan saw her eyes flare with teary anger, he swore under his breath. A crying female—another thing he didn't need.

"Quieten down," he whispered, his tone losing harshness now in an effort to appease her. "Your voice carries. I don't want to be noticed."

"My voice carries?" Her tears grew brighter. "My voice *carries*!"

"Damnit," Morgan snapped, aware that anything he said now would only make matters worse.

"Well, for your information, *Captain Rude,*" she barked, as if they were alone in the New Mexico desert instead of the midst of the Confederate navy, "I was only trying to *help*."

Help . . . help . . . help, her voice echoed.

Turning his back to her, Morgan busied himself adjusting the horse's bit in an effort to divert attention. "I told you not to refer to me as 'Captain'. I know what you're trying to do, but if you want to help, *lower* your voice."

She glared at his back, appalled by the lightning turn of his personality. Where was the formal, courteous Yankee officer that she had found so attractive earlier? Gone, that's where. *Gone.*

"I am aware of the danger," he stated quietly in an effort to calm her, but it wasn't working.

"Well," she concluded, unwilling to overlook his burst of ill temper. Some women might, but not her. And she had certainly misjudged him! "Obviously, since I'm such a loudmouth, you'll want to be rid of me as quickly as possible."

It was a good thing she had discovered what he was really like. To think she'd actually been dreading the moment they would have to part!

Unbuckling the strap on his saddlebag, Morgan removed a roll of currency. He peeled off three bills and handed them to her. "Two blocks down the street is the ship's office. Tell the clerk you want to buy passage on a vessel sailing near the vicinity of Mercy Flats on the morning tide."

"I'm perfectly capable of taking care of myself," she assured him loftily.

His look conveyed that he thought otherwise, but, thank God, she was no longer his problem. "You will do as you're told."

She listened with crossed arms, tapping her foot impatiently as he went on to warn her not to talk to anyone and to keep to herself. He was treating her as if she were an infant in pinnings, and it burned her to the core.

"With any luck," he told her, "you'll be enjoying a hot meal aboard ship within the hour. Are you listening," he demanded when he saw her glaring into space.

"Yes!"

*"Lower your voice!"*

She whirled and marched off. She didn't have to take this. She didn't want his money. He could just take it and stick it up his ole hiney! She would *crawl* to Mercy Flats on her hands and knees before she'd accept any of *his* help.

"Amelia!" All patience left this voice as he watched her trounce off in the opposite direction from the ship's office.

"I can take care of myself, Cap—*Mr.* Rude! You don't bother your head about me one more moment!"

"Amelia," Morgan repeated tightly. "Come back here."

"Go fly a kite."

In a few long strides, Morgan overtook her. Grasping her firmly by the arm, he halted her flight.

"Take your hand off my arm or I'll scream," she threatened.

He had no reason to doubt her. His hand dropped away, his hasty compliance assuring her he wanted to make this friendly.

Allowing her a moment to cool off, he smiled at the small crowd that had started to assemble. Their faces were puzzled as they watched this dispute going on between the farmer and the nun.

"Just a minor disagreement," he assured them in a strained voice, motioning for them to move on.

A young, sturdy-looking chap suddenly stepped forth, doffing his sailor's hat respectfully. "Is this man bothering you, Sister?"

Amelia refused to meet the eyes of her youthful protector, aware that maybe she was causing a scene. "No, he's just trying to buy me off!"

The crowd drew back, stunned.

When Amelia realized what she'd implied, she exhaled a disgusted *ooohft*, spun around, snatched Morgan Kane's money out of his hand, and stalked off.

She'd show him! She didn't need him to get back to Mercy Flats! He could bet his ole stuffy, spit-shined boots he'd seen the last of her!

# PROMISE ME TODAY
## by
# LORI COPELAND

**Lovely and larcenous, the McDougal sisters are experts at swindling men. But has sister Abigail met her match in a devilishly handsome Confederate spy?**